ACCLAIM FOR J.R. RAIN

"Gripping, adventurous, and romantic—J.R. Rain's *The Lost Ark* is a breakneck thriller that traces the thread of history from Biblical stories to current-day headlines. Be prepared to lose sleep!"
—**James Rollins**, international bestselling author of *The Doomsday Key*

"I love this!"
—**Piers Anthony**, bestselling author of *Xanth*

"*Dark Horse* is the best book I've read in a long time!"
—**Gemma Halliday**, bestselling author of *Spying in High Heels*

"*Moon Dance* is absolutely brilliant!"
—**Lisa Tenzin-Dolma**, author of *Understanding the Planetary Myths*

"Powerful stuff!"
—**Aiden James**, bestselling author of *Plague of Coins*

"*Moon Dance* is a must read. If you like Janet Evanovich's Stephanie Plum, bounty hunter, be prepared to love J.R. Rain's Samantha Moon, vampire private investigator."
—**Eve Paludan**, author of *Letters from David*

"Impossible to put down. J.R. Rain's *Moon Dance* is a fabulous urban fantasy replete with multifarious and unusual characters, a perfectly synchronized plot, vibrant dialogue and sterling witticism all wrapped in a voice that is as beautiful as it is rich and vividly intense as it is relaxed."
—**April Vine**, author of *The Midnight Rose*

THE

LOST

ARK

OTHER BOOKS BY JR RAIN

VAMPIRE FOR HIRE
Moon Dance
Vampire Moon
American Vampire
Moon Child
Christmas Moon
Vampire Dawn

THE JIM KNIGHTHORSE SERIES
Dark Horse
The Mummy Case
Hail Mary

THE GRAIL QUEST TRILOGY
Arthur
Merlin (coming soon)

THE ELVIS MYSTERY SERIES
Elvis Has *Not* Left the Building
You Ain't Nothin' But a Hound Dog

The Lost Ark
The Body Departed

WITH SCOTT NICHOLSON
Cursed!
Ghost College
The Vampire Club
Daughters of Eve

WITH PIERS ANTHONY
Aladdin Relighted
Aladdin Sins Bad

*WITH H.T. NIGHT AND
SCOTT NICHOLSON*
Night School

SHORT STORIES
The Bleeder and Other Stories
Teeth and Other Stories
Vampire Nights and Other Stories
Nitemare and Other Stories

THE SPINOZA SERIES
The Vampire With the Dragon Tattoo
The Vampire Who Played Dead

SCREENPLAYS
Judas Silver
Lost Eden

ANTHOLOGIES
Vampires, Zombies and Ghosts, Oh My!
(edited by Eve Paludan)

THE LOST ARK

/ / / /

JR RAIN

Published by
Crop Circle Books
212 Third Crater, Moon

Printed in the United States of America.

ISBN: 978-1-105-84991-6

First Edition

DEDICATION
To my father. Thanks for everything, Pops.

ACKNOWLEDGMENT
Once again, a special thank you to Sandy!

CHAPTER ONE

The dream is always the same.

It's a warm day with the sun hot on the back of my neck as I set up the tripod on the steep mountainside. The sky is clear and Mount Ararat, fabled resting spot of Noah's Ark, sits in silent repose, a dormant volcano that dominates the landscape of Eastern Turkey. A small wind works its way over the rocky surface, bringing with it the scent of wildflowers, ancient dust and something else.

Death.

The great mountain shakes suddenly, violently. I look up, my heart racing. A single word instantly crosses my thoughts: *landslide.* And it's nearby.

Immediately, I snap my head around to where Liz, my fiancé, has disappeared around a bend in the trail to, as she puts it, "go potty." We'd been engaged for the past two years, traveled the world together on assignment with the *National Geographic,* and still she can't pee in front of me. Cute, right? Endearing, right?

Except now I didn't find it so cute and endearing. Now we were separated, and something bad was happening, and it was happening *now.*

And it was happening directly above her.

I'm moving. I snatch my tripod and camera, hastily shoving both into my lightweight field backpack.

The mountain shakes harder.

Angrier.

"Liz!" I shout, but my voice is instantly swallowed by the deep, primeval rumblings of the legendary mountain.

The outcropping of boulders she had chosen to pee behind is fifty yards to my left, along the face of a steep slope. Above, the mountain continues to shake. Dust drifts lazily across the upper slopes. Something is coming, something very bad, and it's coming down on top of her.

I see to my horror that there is no easy trail to the outcropping. Indeed, the path is paved in loose shale, akin to walking on bowling balls. Earlier I had watched as she carefully picked her way over the shifting rock, arms outstretched, balancing herself with amazing cat-like grace, marveling once again at the extremes she was taking for privacy. But, alas, I respected her need for a peaceful pee, although I didn't completely understand it. Indeed, I loved her for all her quirks.

I had never been in love before. Not true love. I was never around long enough for anything to develop, at least anything substantial. I was a photojournalist. The world was my home.

But this was different. Liz was different. We had met in Nepal three years earlier, and the chemistry between us was frightening. She was all I could have imagined—and often more than I dared imagine. Hell, I don't think we left the hotel for a week. It was love and I knew it and I was terrified to leave this one behind, as I had left so many others. So I asked her to join me, to work together as a team. To my utter shock, she had agreed, and now I was traveling the world with the girl of my dreams. Part daredevil and part Mother Teresa, she was unstoppable in her pursuit of justice and equality for those less fortunate. We had been jailed twice for her beliefs, and once sentenced to hang. But that's another story. She was the best photojournalist I knew, stronger than any man and heartier than even me. And, of course, sexy as hell.

Ultimately, she made me happy. Very happy.

* * *

From high above, beyond a rocky cornice to the east, I can see movement. Big movement. Rock and dirt and debris are in motion. Moving slowly at first, but picking up steam, gaining momentum. Massive boulders are soon mixed into the fray.

By my judgment, the landslide is directly over Liz.

And I am moving myself, clawing my way over the loose rocks. Mount Ararat, at least this lower section, is comprised almost entirely of loose shale, which made footing treacherous. At the moment, I could give a damn about my footing. I use my hands to help claw my way forward. I slide and fall often, slashing my knees and palms on the sharp-edged rocks. Whole sections of shale slip out from under me as if they were banana peels. I fall hard, painfully and often, but still I continue.

The mountain shakes harder. From behind me, emerging from his tent, I can hear my Kurdish guide shouting at me, warning me to stay away.

To hell with that. The churning wall of rock has now picked up considerable steam. Anything could have set this rock slide in motion. We are just below the snow line, and so there are some pastures above and around us. A wandering sheep, shepherded by local Turks, could have set off this raging, churning mass of earth. The mountain is called *Angri Dagh* for a reason. The Mountain of Pain.

I continue my mad scrabble forward. My knees are badly cut, pouring blood into my boots. My palms are torn and slick with the stuff.

The outcropping of boulders is just ahead. Thirty feet. I can hear my own breathing rattling in my head and lungs, my desperate gasps mixed with the ominous rumblings around and above me.

Errant loose pebbles shower down on me. I am at the fringes of the coming rockslide. Now larger rocks pelt me, cracking my jaw and skull.

Still, I keep moving forward. Falling, crying out to her.

And there she is. Appearing from around the corner, hastily pulling at her loose drawstrings. She stops and looks up. I do, too. A wall of rock, a tidal wave of earthen fury, rears above her like a living nightmare.

"Sam!" There is fear in her voice. We have traveled through the world's most dangerous places, we have endured tyrants and terrorists, and this is the first time I hear such fear.

And it will be the last.

I move forward, faster, falling hard. A churning cloud of dirt and debris fills the air. Liz lunges forward, moving as fast as she can—

Just as a speeding wall of rocks *slams* into her, hurling her fifty yards into the air. She disappears in a hail of merciless churning debris that continues down the mountainside.

She was there one moment and gone the next. I am left standing in shock, gasping and weeping and bleeding.

It would take me three days to find her mangled body.

And when I do, true to mountain climbing tradition, I bury my sweet girl high on the desolate slopes of Mount Ararat, deep in a secluded mountain cave....

* * *

Now, with the distant rumblings of a thunderstorm approaching, I sit up in bed, gasping, hearing her calling my name over and over again, as if she were just outside my window. The cracking thunder sounds ominously similar—too similar—to the devastating rockslide.

At least, the rockslide in my memory.

Dreams are a funny thing. Often they only give you a *feel* for a memory. Half memories, perhaps. The reality was, Liz had disappeared for many days. She had indeed wandered off to use the bathroom...and that was the last time I had seen her alive. I found her three days later, broken and battered at the bottom of a ravine. She had indeed been a victim of a rock slide. Only, I had not witnessed it. She had died completely alone, and there hadn't been a damn thing I could do about it.

I take a deep breath and my fumbling hand finds my lighter and a pack of cigarettes on the nightstand. I light up and move over to my window, where I sit on the ledge and stare down at the empty street below. The first drops of rain splatter against the glass as I exhale a plume of billowing gray smoke.

* * *

I must have fallen asleep, because Liz is suddenly standing just outside my two-story window, which overlooks a battered industrial street. Liz has no business standing out there in the middle of the night, in the rain. Besides, she has been dead for three years, right?

Another crazy dream.

I dash out my cigarette, mashing it against the window frame. Liz is standing there on the curb in her cargo pants with its too-many pockets, pockets she always stuffed with her essentials. Liz hates purses. Even from here, through the slanting rain and darkness, through the window and my tears, I could see her pant pockets bulging with everything from basic cosmetics to snack food. Once, I had even seen her place an injured lizard into such a pocket.

"Come out of the rain," I say. As I speak, I try desperately to open the bedroom window, but it won't budge. Strange, it has never been stuck before. I frantically work at the lock, growing increasingly desperate and furious. I am nearly ready to drive an elbow through the glass, to get to Liz, when she speaks to me from the street. Her voice rising up through wind and rain and a closed window supernaturally easily.

"It's okay, Sam," she says hauntingly, her voice sweet and raspy. "Leave the window be. I don't mind standing out in the rain. I like the rain, remember?"

"Yes, I remember," I say frantically, thrilled that I am talking to her again, but still frustrated to no end by the stubborn window. "But if I can get this window open you can come inside and stay dry and I can protect you and keep you warm."

"Forget the window, Sam."

I try the lock again.

"I said forget the window. You can be so stubborn. Please, Sam. We need to talk."

At her insistence, I let the window issue drop and settle for pressing my hot forehead against the cold glass.

"Were you just smoking, Sam?"

"Yes."

"When did you start smoking?"

"When you died."

"You've been drinking, too," she says.

"Yes."

"Too much, I think," she says.

"Yes, probably. I miss you. I can't help it. I miss you so much. The drinking...it helps a little. I'm sorry."

She lets the issue go. "So what are you doing with yourself these days, Sam?"

I shrug, suddenly ashamed. "Not much, really. I run a small bar here in town, and lead the occasional expedition. I'm a certified Ararat guide."

The rain continues down. The image of my fiancé wavers briefly behind the glass. Lightning flashes directly overhead, illuminating the street. And when it does, she briefly disappears. But now she is back, to my great relief.

"Why are you still in this godforsaken place, Sam?" she asks.

"Because I don't want to leave you, Liz. Don't you see? I can't leave you. You are buried all alone up on that damn mountain, and I'm the only one who knows where you are buried, and I visit you as often as I can."

"It's been three years, Sam. You can leave me now. It's okay. *I'm* okay. I've moved on. You should, too."

"But you're still here," I say, speaking into the glass at the figure standing on the dark street below. Her pants flutter in the wind, and her raven-colored hair lifts and falls. I could see her eyes sparkling with tears even from here. "I can see you, and you're still here."

"No," she said. "I'm not."

And then my heart breaks all over again, because now I can distinctly see *through* her. Now amorphous, she shimmers like a ghost.

"Please," I say, real desperation in my voice. I press my face hard against the glass, fingernails clawing. "Please don't go. You've only just returned. You're the only girl I've ever loved, the only girl who's ever loved me. I can't live alone, not anymore."

"Go home, Sam. It's time for you to go home."

"I love you," I say.

"I know you do," she says.

And then she disappears, and the wind and rain blows across the now empty street, and I hang my head...and this is the position I find myself in when I awaken in the morning: sitting next to the window, face pressed against the glass, dried tears in the corners of my eyes....

CHAPTER TWO

Dogubayazit, Turkey
Present Day

Faye Roberts was sitting across from me on a rare
blustery day here in Eastern Turkey, telling me that she'd
heard I was the best guide in Dogubayazit.

I tried to look humble.

We were sitting in my upstairs office with the rain
beating down on the big window behind my desk. In the
bar below, rock music thumped up through the
floorboards. American rock music. None of that Turkish
folk crap. Mostly, I was doing my best to forget the
heartbreaking dreams of the night before, but failing
miserably. I was also wondering if it was a coincidence
that an American girl had miraculously appeared in my
bar, seeking my help.

I didn't know, but the word *spooky*, came to mind.

I tried to focus on the girl in front of me. Faye Roberts could not have looked more out of place. In the bar below was a room full of desert nomads and shepherds, smelling of goats and dirt and sweat, and here in my office was this woman who was, well, all woman. And an American woman at that.

"And you say you traveled alone?" I asked again, incredulous.

"You sound incredulous."

"Which is why I asked incredulously."

"Do you always make jokes?" she asked.

"Do you always travel unescorted through potentially volatile Middle Eastern countries?"

"I didn't realize Turkey was volatile."

"Which is why I said potentially."

She looked around my office, then toward my office door. "You own a bar in a middle-eastern country. For a region that shuns alcohol, I can't imagine you have too much business."

"I sell lots of Pepsi," I said. Truth was, I ran a small restaurant, too, and mostly sold alcohol to tourists.

Faye Roberts was a confident woman. Perhaps too confident. She seemed smart and didn't have a problem letting you know it. Perhaps that's how she had survived this far alone, at the far end of a place called nothing. There she sat in a fold-out chair opposite me, looking me square in the eye, daring me to challenge her. She was wearing a USC sweatshirt and blue jeans. Her attire screamed American. Her brown hair was pulled back into a tight ponytail that looked painful, and her opaline green eyes were big and round. She wore little make-up.

"Camilla Constantine suggested that I see you," she said.

Camilla Constantine owned the hotel next to my bar. She was Dogubayazit's wealthiest resident and biggest drunk—and I should know. She was also Greek, and of the Greek Orthodox faith.

"How can I help you, Miss Roberts?"

"Please call me Faye."

"Sure," I said. "How can I help you, Miss Faye."

She wasn't amused. She paused and seemed uncertain how to begin. She tapped her finger on her slender thigh. Her nails were short and unpainted. She sucked in some air and finally said, "I need to get to Mount Ararat."

I sat back. Behind me the rain *pinged* against the glass. Cool air escaped through the shoddy cocking around the window. Laughter suddenly erupted from the bar below. Somewhere nearby a goat bleated. I hated goats.

"Did Camilla mention that the mountain is closed to all visitors?"

"Yes, but I'm willing to pay triple your asking price, including a bonus if we find what I'm looking for."

"I assume you're talking about Noah's Ark," I said.

She shook her head emphatically. "No, Mr. Ward. A month ago my father set out to climb Mount Ararat and he's never returned." She leveled her stare at me. "And I want you to help me find him."

I removed a crumpled packet of cigarettes from my flannel shirt, opened the lid and glanced inside. There were three cigarettes left, and one of them was broken. I put an unbroken one in my mouth, and held the box out to Faye Roberts. She leaned forward and looked inside.

"Do you always offer your clients broken cigarettes?" she asked.

I pulled the last good cigarette out, which had been hiding behind the broken one.

"Not this one," I said. "And you're not my client."

I kept holding the cigarette and she kept looking at it, with the look of a hungry bear eyeing something warm and meaty.

"So, do you want it or not?"

She shook her head after a moment of indecision, eyes lingering on the cigarette.

"I'd better not. I've been clean for two months."

I shrugged and lit a match and touched a yellow flame to the tip of the cigarette.

"I quit fourteen years ago. Luckily, I have a very loose definition of *quit*." I exhaled a steady stream of blue-gray smoke. "So, who's your father?"

She was watching me exhale with obvious interest, green eyes round and envious. "Professor Caesar Roberts."

I knew the name. "Biblical archaeologist from California Christian College. Noted author, and ark researcher. Somewhere in my apartment I have one of his books."

"The one and only," she said, face reddening suddenly. "Don't tell me you actually read that dreadful thing."

I grinned. "Your father's book was quite informative, although I found it a bit too presumptuous. After all, there is no actual proof that the ark exists, and to assume otherwise is just conjecture."

Outside, rain slapped hard against the window. Music pulsed from the jukebox in the bar. I put my feet up on the desk. "What do you know of your father's disappearance?"

"Not much, I'm afraid. A month ago, his research team returned home without him, after their climbing permits had been revoked by the Turkish Department of Interior. Intent on climbing the mountain anyway, my father and one of his graduate students stayed behind and sought the help of a local guide who illegally led them onto the mountain."

I shook my head. "A month is a long time, Faye. A man gets lost on Ararat, he stays lost. Forever."

"If your intent was to cheer me up, you have failed miserably, Mr. Ward."

Her long fingers drummed on the wooden armrest. I could smell her perfume, or at least I thought it was her perfume. It could have been any number of lotions or fragrances that women use to perfume their bodies with. Anyway, it smelled like grapefruit, and I liked it. Through her slightly open mouth, I could see the neat skyline of her tiny bottom teeth. Her tongue slashed back and forth behind her teeth. She was breathing softly. Rain ticked against the window, as it had been all day. Good for the dry land, bad for business.

"You are asking me to break the law," I said shortly.

"I'm asking you to help find my father. If not you, then someone else."

I stood and moved over to the window, my back to Faye. Rainwater slid down the pane, obscuring my reflection into a sort of live-action Dali painting. I knew there were many guides in Dogubayazit. Many good guides, but also many bad guides.

"Why was your father so eager to climb the mountain?" I asked.

"He...he has a map," she said. I could hear the blush in her voice.

"A map? Everyone has a map." I shook my head. "Local shepherds will gladly sell maps to unsuspecting ark researchers. Of course these maps are worthless, and usually lead you in circles."

"Apparently not this one. My father drew it himself, based on his research, if that's what you want to call it." Her mouth twisted in distaste.

In the street below, muddy water, intestinal brown, flowed along broken gutters and over-flowed broken sidewalks. I sighed and rubbed my jaw. I knew I should turn her away and save myself a lot of trouble. Instead, I found myself saying: "I'll make some inquiries, but I can make no promises."

She stood quickly, chair scraping. "That's the best news I've heard in a long time. When can I expect to hear from you again?"

"At dinner tonight, say eight p.m."

"Where?"

"I'll come get you."

I walked her to the door and watched her descend the wooden stairs and go through the quiet barroom below. Most of the male heads turned and watched her leave. I didn't blame them.

CHAPTER THREE

I sat at my desk for another twenty minutes, thinking about the sudden appearance of this feisty American, realizing that she was the first unaccompanied American woman I had seen in three years.

Basically, the first *single* American woman in three years.

I lit a cigarette and thought some more of her and then I thought of Liz and felt guilty, realizing for the first time in a long time that someone had, miraculously, pushed my brooding thoughts of my killed fiancé from my mind for longer than an hour.

With this realization in mind, I stepped out of my bar and into the rain. I turned my collar up and walked north down a tourist street called *Mersin*. Dogubayazit was a town that existed on the tourist dollar, or in this case, the Turkish *Lira*. With Mount Ararat just a short drive away, Noah's Ark themes were predominant. A shopper could choose from Noah's Ark creamers to ark windchimes and bathrobes. I liked the Noah's Ark water fountain. Cute.

I stopped in front of the Hotel *Kiraz*, a brooding, massive eight-story fortress comprised of gray bricks and gray paint. It lacked only a moat and a fair maiden.

I went through the double glass doors into a short entrance hall lined with hanging ferns and multi-colored Persian mohair rugs. I crossed the empty reception room and entered the adjoining restaurant. The restaurant was dark and moody. A fire crackled to my right in a huge stone hearth. The up-turned lights mounted on the walls cast their glow only a few feet, seemingly creating more shadow than light. The bartender was eating a sandwich and reading a newspaper spread out before him.

His name was Crisnik. I think. I could never get it straight. Turkish names are hell on American tongues. He was a weightlifter and liked to show it, rolling up his sleeves to show-off his knotted muscles. He looked up at me and shoved the last of his sandwich in his mouth.

"Did your mother teach you to eat like that?" I asked in Turkish.

"Don't have a mother. You know that," said Crisnik.

"That's right, because you grew up on the streets," I said, reciting Crisnik's life history in a nutshell, "and stole a car before you were nine, and stuck a knife in a guy you caught cheating with your lady. I almost forgot. I mean, I hadn't heard the stabbing story in, what, two weeks? Tell it to me again."

He poured a draft beer and placed it before me.

"Screw you," he said in English. In Turkey, foreigners were welcomed to drink alcohol, but drinking alcohol by Muslims was strictly forbidden.

Crisnik moved over to the kitchen slide and called out my usual order and then went back to reading the paper. He ignored me.

I drank the bitter Turkish beer. The room was empty, mostly. A handful of hotel guests drank and ate and spoke quietly in the back. They looked European. They could have been speaking any number of Germanic languages.

Crisnik turned the page, flattened out the paper.

"Takes you a long time," I said, "to look at the pictures."

Crisnik didn't bother to look up. "I'd better go check on your food," he said. "Because when you're eating, you keep quiet."

He moved off down the bar. Like magic, a hot plate of food appeared in the slide. He scooped it up and set it before me. "Should keep you quiet for a while," he said.

The dish was called *lahmacun pide*. It was a sort of pizza, with ground meat and tomatoes and onions. I ate the first slice and washed it down with the rest of my beer. And as Crisnik poured me another draft, I asked him, "A month ago two Americans were here, one older, one younger."

"You're suppose to be eating, not talking."

"I'm a maverick."

"You're also talking with your mouth full."

"A maverick with bad habits."

Crisnik shook his head. A waitress came by with a drink order. She smiled at me. I swallowed, smiled back. She had big round eyes and rounded everything else. She ordered two whiskeys and sodas. A moment later, Crisnik set two whiskeys and sodas on her tray. She sauntered off, dark pants tight over her posterior. She headed over to the Europeans.

"Healthy kid," I said, watching her.

Crisnik nodded. "Uh huh."

"So, do you remember the Americans?"

"What makes you think they stayed here?"

"Best hotel in town."

"What about Camilla's place?" he asked.

"That's good too, but I happen to know they didn't stay there."

He was quiet, his tan face calm and smooth. He wore his hair long, sometimes in a ponytail, but it wasn't in a ponytail today. Probably because he was tired of me making fun of his ponytail. "Tall kid, if I recall," he said. "But the old man was something else. Frizzy hair and a frizzy beard. He talked fast, even for an American."

"They meet anyone?" I asked.

"Uh huh," said Crisnik.

"Daveed Hammid?" I prodded.

Crisnik looked at me. "If you've got this all figured out, why do you need me?"

I ignored him. "Did you ever see the Americans again?"

His dark eyes were expressionless.

"Never again," he said.

I thought about that while finishing my meal.

CHAPTER FOUR

Daveed Hammid lived on the fourth floor of the Hotel *Kiraz*, in one of those extended stay rooms.

He answered the door wearing only a thin white T-shirt and dark blue boxer shorts. He was a big man with a very small head, completely out of proportion, as if he had fallen victim to a tribe of headhunters in New Guinea. He was also cursed with lots of body hair. Everywhere. Thick eyebrows, thick arm hair and thick mustache. Black lochs even coated the tops of his wide bare feet. In his left hand was a full bottle of beer. Apparently Daveed wasn't a practicing Muslim. His areolas showed darkly through the thin T-shirt. He was a part-time Mount Ararat guide and a full-time smuggler of small arms. A man of little scruples and even less integrity. Although he did love babies and puppies, as rumor had it.

"What the hell do you want?" he said.

"Good to see you, too, Daveed," I said.

"Always a wise guy," he said. "I don't have time for you, *merkep*." *Merkep* means asshole, of course.

He made a move to close the door. I moved too and held the door open with my hand. "You were going to invite me in...."

Turkish hospitality is legendary. Hosts starve to insure guests have an abundance of food. In fact, the amount of one's guests directly relates to one's status within the community: the more guests, the more your status rises.

Perhaps Daveed was unaware of this social custom.

"Go to hell, *erkeklik yala*." Cocksucker.

"We need to talk," I said.

The movement was fast, and suddenly a small handgun appeared in my face. It was a .22 caliber Beretta, with a silencer, the official weapon of the Mossad *katsas*. Daveed was not Mossad. The gun was steady, Daveed's index finger wrapped tightly around the trigger. The knuckles of his index finger were white.

To hesitate would have been a mistake. I pushed the door forward with the palm of my hand. The door smacked Daveed in the forehead. He was thrown backwards, off-balance, recoiling on the balls of his feet. The gun flew up from his swinging arm and clattered across on the floor. I stepped in and punched Daveed in the jaw and he landed hard on his backside.

I picked up the gun and stuck it my waistband behind my back, the metal cold against my flesh. Daveed's beer bottle had tumbled end over end, coming to a stop against a potted fern, foaming profusely. I stood over the bottle and shook my head. Such reckless waste.

Daveed was a small-time hood who considered himself dangerous. He had developed a reputation of being a tough guy. Apparently, he had killed a man in a land far, far away. Convenient. Maybe it had been Darth Vader. Daveed picked himself up and sat heavily in a leather recliner in the living room. The chair creaked and groaned under his considerable weight.

"What the hell do you think you're doing?" he said, holding his jaw in a way that suggested it hurt to speak.

I closed the door behind me, lit another cigarette. The bathroom was to my left. I glanced inside and flicked a lightswitch. End-of-the-world disarray. Towels, pants, shirts, socks and skivvies in every nook, cranny and corner. Some of the smaller clothing were women's. A tiny kitchen was to my right, containing only a stove and refrigerator. The door to the fridge was slightly ajar. Cold frost issued out. A hard-looking roll sat in one corner of the linoleum floor.

I moved down the short hall and entered the living room, which doubled as the bedroom, and saw what I had expected to see. A woman was sitting up in bed, the comforter pulled over her breasts, which appeared ample. Her kinky black hair hung down over the comforter. I didn't know her, nor did I want to. Her face was broad and pale, lips pouty. She didn't appear surprised to see me. Perhaps it was a common occurrence for Daveed to have guests punch him in the face. She busied herself by examining her fingernails, which were long and desert orange. In the process, some of the comforter slipped down, exposing more of her right breast. Ample, indeed. No one bothered to introduce me to the woman, which was just fine

"I didn't know your sister was in town, Daveed," I said. He said nothing, perhaps waiting for the stars inside his head to go away. I knew the feeling well.

"Go to hell," said the woman, speaking Armenian. Folks in this part of the world speak either Turkish, Arabic or Armenian, and most knew at least a smattering of all three. Her voice was high-pitched. Irritatingly so. My ear drums felt assaulted.

"It's better when you keep quiet," I said to her in the same language. One of her bare legs slid off the bed, her painted toes touching the floor. The calf was smooth and strong, and could have supported a horse. It was rare to see so much skin on an Armenian woman. Maybe this was my lucky day.

"And judging by this room," I said to her in the same language, "I may already be in hell."

"Godamn you, *merkep,*" said Daveed, but his voice was unsteady.

I looked at him. "A month ago you illegally led Professor Caesar Roberts and his graduate student, Wally Krispin, onto Mount Ararat. But you made it back and they didn't. So, tell me, what happened to the Americans?"

Daveed suddenly lunged forward, a long steel blade flashing in his hands, concealed within the recliner for just such an occasion. Had I not side-stepped him, he would have happily disemboweled me. I hit him behind his ear and he fell forward and lay on his side, moaning. He landed on his face and broke his nose.

The woman screamed and threw a pillow at me. Luckily I dodged the fluffy projectile. I picked Daveed up by the shoulder and deposited him back in the recliner. Next, I rummaged through his kitchen and returned with a flower print hand towel. He took it from me and held it to his nose, wincing. Blood instantly soaked the dirty towel.

I motioned toward his recliner. "Anything else in that bag of tricks?" I asked.

The woman was still squawking. I told her to be quiet. She didn't listen. I threw the pillow back at her and she looked at me, shocked, but at least she was quiet. I turned my attention back to Daveed. "Tell me about the Americans," I said.

"Screw the Americans."

"That's where you're supposed to turn and spit vehemently."

He blinked at me dumbly.

"Never mind," I said. "What became of the Americans?"

"How am I suppose to know, *merkep*? The old man dismissed me once we arrived at the base of the mountain." He pulled the towel away and looked at it, frowning. His face was pale, probably because most of his blood was in the towel. "I think you broke my nose."

"Yes."

He swallowed. "I never heard from them again. The old man was an accomplished climber. They had adequate mountaineering equipment—a detailed topography map of Ararat, compass, altimeter, etc. And they had enough clothing and food."

I studied him. He disgusted me, and the woman didn't help my feelings of repulsion. "I will hold you personally responsible for their safety, Daveed."

He said nothing. I decided there was nothing else to be gained here, and as I moved toward the front door, the woman hurled an Armenian insult, comparing me to a monkey's ass. It loses some flavor with translation.

Outside, in the rain behind the hotel, I found a foul-smelling dumpster. I removed the gun from my waist and shoved it deep between two white plastic bags.

CHAPTER FIVE

We were seated at the *Sicak Patates*. Hot Potatoes.

The dining room was elegant by Dogubayazit standards, perhaps the nicest in town. Small glass tables. Slender red candles. Menus long and leather-bound. I wore Levis and a plaid flannel. Faye was dressed in black silk pants and a shimmery silver blouse that captured the candlelight and returned it a thousand fold. She seemed well-rested, and in a better disposition, although her lips were still pressed into a thin line, barely displaying the matted mauve lipstick she was wearing. A spot of wine shimmered on her lower lip. Her green eyes were the color of a tropical lagoon. Tonight, her hair was parted to the left, bangs curled just below her eyes. She was the prettiest woman in the room.

I told her of my conversation with Daveed Hammid, leaving out the part about the ample breast. The waiter came by and I ordered sea bass for myself and lamb for her.

When the waiter left, Faye leaned forward on her elbows, and said, "So there's a chance my father may still be on the mountain," she stated firmly. I was noticing that most things about Faye were firm.

"Sure," I said. "But whether or not he's alive is the question."

She sat back, crossed her arms under her chest.

"Ever the optimist," she said.

Although the rain had stopped hours ago, the big window next to us revealed a sodden street and dark skies beyond. I was drinking Turkish beer, and she the house Chablis. We were, I noticed, the only ones drinking alcohol. I lit a cigarette, offering her one. She shook her head, although her conviction was waning.

There were no laws in Turkey about smoking in public places. Turks love to smoke, and they do so everywhere. In fact, a haze of the gray stuff hovered just below the ceiling, roiling in a mini storm cloud.

There was a lull in the conversation. I hate lulls.

"So what is it that you do back home?" I asked, squinting through the smoke, realizing for the first time that this felt like a date.

I swallowed and broke out in a sweat. She didn't notice.

Instead, she picked up her wine glass between her thumb and forefinger and swirled the contents, which came dangerously close to spilling over the edge, but didn't. I studied her as she did so. She sat straight in her chair, chin forward. She looked up at me with clear unblinking eyes.

"I teach archaeology at USC," she said. "Or, more accurately, paleo-linguistics."

"Ah. The study of ancient languages," I said. "Just like your father."

"Very good, Mr. Ward. However, unlike my father, who gave it all up, I'm still doing original research in the field of Mayan cryptology."

I thumbed through my mental image of her father's book. "Your father gave up his tenure at USC to take a position at Southern California Christian to pursue Biblical archaeology, I believe."

"You could say I filled the void left by his vacancy. Father is a foolish man, and a dreamer. He seeks to add validity to his faith, which, I think, is an oxymoron."

When the waiter brought our food, Faye's eyes widened with pleasure. I think she was ravenous. We both were, and ate quickly. The waiter took our plates and we ordered more drinks, another beer for me and a Turkish coffee for her. When he returned with our drinks, Faye picked up the tiny porcelain coffee cup and smiled.

"Positively Lilliputian," she said.

"But with a Brobdingnagian kick," I said.

She nodded her linguistic approval. Somewhere, Jonathan Swift and maybe even Gulliver, were rolling in their graves. Faye tasted the strong coffee, and seemed to like it. The waiter came back and asked me if we would like desert. I said desert was against the young lady's religion. He shrugged and left. Outside, people strolled by the window, watching us drink. I watched them watching us drink. Cars with broken headlights rolled one way. Cars with broken taillights rolled the other.

Faye asked, "So why's the mountain closed?"

I shook my head. "Good question. No one knows for sure, and those who do aren't talking."

"Camilla mentioned something about an Arab prince."

"Emir Omar Ali, a Saudi Arabian prince of tremendous wealth. He's also a well-known adventurer. In fact, the *National Geographic* did an article on his attempt to cross Antarctica. The attempt failed, by the way, with three of his team members forever lost. Now his passion has turned to Noah's Ark. He has ascended the mountain on three separate occasions, myself leading the way on the second attempt. Let me assure you, Miss Faye, he's a royal pain-in-the-ass, although I got along well with his personal bodyguard. Must be the peasant blood in me."

"So what does the Arab prince have to do with the mountain being closed?"

I sipped my beer, placing it directly in the center of the square white napkin. Bullseye.

"That's the rub. While the Turkish military patrols the base of Ararat, the Arab and his men ascend the mountain regularly in helicopters, bringing up a constant stream of supplies from a secured airbase just outside of Dogubayazit. Even the shepherds who live on the mountain with their herds of sheep are forced to stay away. All in all, it's very detrimental to the guiding business."

"Is it common to close the entire mountain?" she asked.

I shrugged. "Depends. Kurdish terrorists often seek refuge on Ararat, or use it as a training ground. The

Turkish military often perform sweeps, clearing the area of all illegal activity. But the military doesn't generally remove the peaceful shepherds who have lived on the mountain for centuries."

"So what do you think is going on?" Faye Roberts asked.

"Some in Dogubayazit speculate that Omar might have found Noah's Ark, and is currently digging it free. Those who prescribe to conspiracy theories think he's a spy or a terrorist. Either way, gossip is alive in well in Dogubayazit."

I signaled the waiter for another beer. Faye declined more coffee with the international shake of her head. I rubbed my full belly, vaguely considering undoing the top button of my jeans.

"Could this Omar Ali have anything to do with my father's disappearance?"

"Anything's possible. But more than likely—"

"More than likely my father's buried under an avalanche. I know," she said bitterly. She had twisted her cloth napkin into a rope. Or noose.

I said, "Let's make one thing perfectly clear, Miss Faye. Mount Ararat is as dangerous as they come. In fact, it can be a deathtrap to those who don't know what the hell they're doing. Your father, according to Daveed, went off on his own. Mount Ararat without a guide is like sailing in rough seas without a rudder."

Her eyes narrowed. She set her coffee cup down. Loudly.

"My father is an experienced climber."

Diners seated around us looked at us curiously. I recognized one, a big man with black hair greased straight back, olive skin shining in the candlelight. He was my banker, which might explain why I couldn't remember his name. I waved; he nodded. He turned back to his slender wife, who completely ignored us.

I was silent, watching Faye. My plan of dissuading her from climbing the mountain was rapidly crumbling to pieces.

"I know the odds are slim of finding him, Sam, but I have to try. He's my father, after all."

I took a big breath. It was time to end this nonsense.

"I may be the only one who tells it to you straight, Faye, as there are others here in Dogubayazit who will surely take advantage of you. What you hope to accomplish is impossible and foolish. You're father is dead, and so is his student. You are wasting your time and money. It would be best if you got on the next bus from Dogubayazit and left. There is much trouble to be had here."

She held my gaze without blinking, lips disappearing into a thin, bloodless line. Cheekbones crimson. It was a full minute later when she finally spoke, and she did so slowly and carefully.

"I am under the impression, perhaps delusion, that it makes sense to look for those who are missing, no matter how improbable the odds." She stood. "I thank you for your frankness, Mr. Ward. After the way you've put it, there's nowhere to go but up."

I did something that surprised even me: I gripped her narrow wrist, and pulled her down to eye level. She made no move to break free.

"You're wrong," I said. "You could die up there."

"I will take my chances, Mr. Ward. I owe my father that much."

She stared at me. I had expected to see tears in her eyes. There were none. Only firm determination. A look like that could conquer nations. Or mountains.

I released my hold. She paused only briefly before leaving the restaurant. I watched her go. So did some of the other men. The waiter came by, glanced briefly at the empty chair. Then handed me the bill.

"Well," I whispered. "That went well."

CHAPTER SIX

I stepped out of the restaurant and into the cool night air. The rain had come and gone, leaving Dogubayazit in muddy ruins. I picked my way carefully over the broken cobblestone sidewalk, slipping once or twice in the slime that had washed up from the street. I was slightly drunk, having celebrated my failure to dissuade her attempt to climb the mountain with a few more beers.

Faye Roberts was headstrong and reckless. And those were two characteristics that can get you killed on Ararat. Her father had probably been the same way.

I turned my collar up and shoved my hands deep into my pockets.

Faye Roberts wasn't my concern. I had done my best to discourage her. And she hadn't listened.

"Stubborn broad," I mumbled.

The shops were closed. The streets empty. The cobblestone sidewalk morphed into a long swath of black mud. My hiking boots made sucking noises with each step. Water drip-dripped everywhere. In the far distance I saw a flash of headlights, heard the grind of a very old motor as the vehicle turned down a side street and disappeared. The air was crisp, and there was the sweet smell of rain on the wind, perhaps the promise of more to come.

Faye Roberts had looked gorgeous tonight. The designer of that silver blouse should receive a fashion award. Or a handshake. It had shimmered in all the right places.

I turned onto a larger street. There were more hotels here, all glowing invitingly at this late hour, foyers brightly lit. Ten minutes later, I stopped in front of my bar with its double doors wide open as dim yellow light issued across the sidewalk. I paused and lit a cigarette. Which turned the pause into something more than a pause.

I leaned against the wooden door frame, smoking contentedly, staring out into the quiet night. Somewhere a dog barked, a deep-throated mean-sounding bark. Another dog responded. This one more of a yipe. This went on for some time until both pooches were suitably caught-up on the night's gossip.

The wooden sign above me creaked in the wind. A dirty spotlight illuminated the sign, revealing three hand-painted English words: The Watering Hole.

I like to keep things simple.

I took one last drag from the cigarette and flicked it away and stepped into the near-empty bar.

* * *

Like the name, the bar itself was simple. There were a half dozen of the requisite neon lights on the stained pine walls. Round tables scarred with cigarette burns, knife blades, fingernails and sharp elbows. Two ancient ceiling fans, powered by exposed leather belts, did little to disperse the pall of white smoke that hung suspended in the air. A typical bar, even in Eastern Turkey.

Five customers remained at this late hour, sitting in wooden chairs of varying degrees of solidity, talking amongst themselves, some louder than others.

Pascal was behind the bar, cleaning glasses with a rag that could have used some cleaning itself. A good kid. Nineteen years old. Whip-thin. Always a smile on his face, which said a lot. Because he didn't have much to smile about. Both his parents were killed by Kurdish guerrillas, a bomb left in a duffel bag on their bus, leaving Pascal to raise a kid sister in a small apartment on the east side of town. During the day he studied accounting, via a correspondence course from the university in Istanbul. The correspondence course had been my idea.

He saw me and smiled from ear to ear. "I was getting worried, Sam *bey*." He used the word *bey* as a sign of respect, or if he wanted to borrow some money.

"Anything exciting happen while I was gone?" I asked.

He pointed to a broken chair in the corner of the room. Two of its legs were gone. "Just one fight, Sam *bey*. Nothing I couldn't handle."

I grinned. Although Pascal was small, he was tough. I motioned with my thumb. "Hit the road, kid."

Pascal pocketed his earnings and untied his apron and hung it on a hook over the sink. He flashed me another grin. "By the way, the American woman came by tonight and asked me to give you this."

Pascal held up two twenty dollar bills attached to a note. The note was short, with big flowing letters: *Sorry for sticking you with the bill. I hope this covers it. The lamb was excellent, by the way.*

Pascal was grinning. "She is very pretty, Sam *bey*."

"I know."

When the kid left, I took up the position of honor behind the counter, staring at the note. I poured myself a splash of brandy. A short while later, I poured another.

"At least she didn't stick me with the bill," I said to the splash of brandy. The brandy didn't respond, of course. But if I had a few more shots, it just might.

Later, an older woman came in through the open double doors. She was three sheets to the wind, weaving this way and that as if she were a detective on a crooked trail. As always, she was beautiful, elegant and stately. She was, of course, Camilla Constantine. My Greek friend.

CHAPTER SEVEN

Camilla was my self-appointed spiritualist and oracle, reading much into my words and actions, coming up with some amazing prognostications. Most were ridiculous. Some were humorous. And a few were deadly accurate. Of course, those were the ones that made me nervous. Then again, even a blind harpoonist can hit the ocean.

"You look good, Camilla," I said. "Drunk, but good."

Camilla sat before me at the bar and shrugged out of a red silk business jacket with ivory buttons. She hung the jacket on the back of the barstool, its black silk inner lining shining under the dusty lightbulbs above.

I placed a glass of *raki*, made from distilled raisins, before her, a favorite of Camilla's. She promptly tilted it back and drained the glass dry and motioned for another.

"Rough day?" I asked, pouring.

"Sometimes I would like to kill all men," she said in English, her voice deep and heavily accented. Sort of sexy. "I would like to kill them all one at a time. And slowly."

I stepped back. She continued. "Men think they can cheat me. But not tonight. I sent two of them on their way. They will never do business with me again, and it is their loss. Men, Sam, are assholes."

"Don't look now, Camilla, but you happened to be seated across from an asshole now."

"None of the above applies to you, Sam." She reached out and patted my cheek with a warm palm. "Though I should grab your ear and shake some sense into you."

"Is that a Greek form of foreplay?"

She shook her head, irritated. When she was drunk, she didn't find me as cute as usual. "I send a beautiful American young woman your way, and you turn her away as if she were diseased."

I raised my forefinger to counter that accusation, but Camilla had moved on. When Camilla speaks, one needs more than a forefinger to break in. "But that's okay, Sam. You had your reasons. Yes, what she asks is stupid and foolish. But she is pretty and nice. I thought you two were right for each other. She was a good omen. After all, you are both Americans."

I shook my head. "There's more to a relationship than nationality, Camilla."

"But I knew you would take care of that girl. I don't trust the other guides." Camilla sighed and took a breath, sitting back in the stool. "However, Faye Roberts is a big girl. Her own iron will got her here. And it is her own iron will that keeps her here now."

"So she didn't leave?" I asked. I tried to sound casual, but the excitement was there in my voice. For now, the Academy Award was safe.

"Of course she didn't leave," said Camilla. "She will not be denied, Sam. I have recommended she speak with Niksar."

"Niksar?" I leaned forward across the counter, frowning.

Camilla shrugged and raised her eyebrows. "At least he will not take advantage of her. He is a decent man."

"But a horrible guide. You'll get her killed. Has she spoken with Niksar yet?"

"She has a meeting with him tomorrow morning at eight."

"What room is she in?"

"Sam," said Camilla. "Don't you dare wake that child now. She has had a long day. If you want to speak with her, you will do so tomorrow morning."

I was breathing hard.

"You seem upset, Sam," said Camilla sweetly.

"You know damn well why I'm upset. And you know what I think of Niksar. Twice he's gotten himself lost on Ararat. The man is a horrible guide, which is probably why you suggested him." I took a breath, seeing red. "I feel as if you've scripted my every move."

She tried to look shocked, but the wicked gleam in her eye gave her away. The woman could damn well make a mouse chase a cat.

"She is a good sign," said Camilla. "It is not often that a beautiful American girl shows up alone looking for your help."

"But she's asking the impossible."

"She's asking for your help to search for her missing father," said Camilla gently. "She needs peace of mind. She needs to know that she had at least tried, Sam. Sometimes, that makes it easier to deal with the loss. I have dealt with such loss. I understand."

In that instant Camilla looked old and tired. Fine vertical lines spread away from her lips, merging with the other lines of her face. Lines women pay thousands of dollars to erase. She had dealt with her own loss, a lifetime of killed husbands and sons. Three sons and two husbands, to be exact, lost through war and disease.

"You are her only hope, Sam."

I said nothing.

"And maybe she's your only hope, too," said Camilla.

"What the devil does that mean?"

"You've been here a long time, Sam. Don't you get homesick?"

"The word implies one has a home and a family. I have neither," I said. "You sound like you're trying to get rid of me."

"You're a gifted photojournalist," she said. "You have much to offer the world, but you can't do so if you waste your life away here, in the back of beyond."

I opened my mouth to speak, but closed it again. At this hour I had little argument left in me, and Camilla was probably right. I lit a cigarette and sat on the corner of the metal sink behind me.

"A vile habit," she said, motioning to the cigarette.

"I agree. Filthy." I shivered to show my revulsion. Then took another drag.

"Then why do you do it?"

"A suicidal desire to know how I'm going to die."

We were quiet. Steely Dan played from the chrome and glass jukebox on the opposite wall. The jukebox was shipped over from the United States. What's a bar without a jukebox? When she finished her *raki*, I helped her into her coat, even buttoning it up for her. Together, we exited the bar and stepped out into the cool night air.

"Help her, Sam."

I stood there in the cold night air, shivering. I could have used a jacket myself.

"You're a good man, but you do not belong here. Dogubayazit is not your home. You need to move on." And with that she left. I watched her go, swaying into the night, disappearing into the brightly lit foyer of the hotel next door, where she lived in a spacious suite on the fourth floor.

I lit another cigarette and stepped back into the bar, closing the doors behind me.

CHAPTER EIGHT

At 7:34 a.m., we were seated at a counter in the *Gule Gule's* cafe.

I had ordered *bork* for us, a fine Turkish pastry. I was sipping grapefruit juice and Faye Roberts was staring into a small cup of Turkish coffee. She was dressed in black jeans and a red long-sleeved shirt, cowboy-like. Her hair was up in a ball, held in place by a few strategically placed hairpins. She didn't appear to be wearing make-up, but I could have been wrong. Anyway, she didn't need any.

"You look like hell," she told me.

"Thanks," I said, yawning on cue. "It's still the middle of the night for me."

"Have some coffee," she said.

"I can't."

She looked at me over her tiny coffee mug. "Can't or won't?"

I nodded. "I have an aversion to coffee that tastes like mud."

"Then this must be pretty important."

The blond pine walls were bare, save for the occasional early Impressionistic painting. Reprint, of course. The café was half full. Ever the optimist. We were alone at the counter, although I could hear the cook whistling in the kitchen. Another morning person. One of them.

"I want you to know," I said, "that Camilla has been strumming us like a six string."

Her eyes narrowed behind the tiny coffee cup. "What do you mean?"

"She's playing matchmaker, thinks she knows what's best for me. For us."

"And she thinks I'm what's best for you?" Faye laughed pleasantly. "And that you're what's best for me?"

"You just happen to be the first American woman to come this way. Perhaps ever. And I just happen to be the best guide in Dogubayazit."

"Or so rumor has it," she said. "So what makes you so good?"

I sipped the bittersweet juice, and tried not to make a grapefruit face. "It's my guarantee."

"Guarantee?" She sounded dubious.

"Uh huh. If you don't think I've done one helluva job, then you get your money back."

"That's good to know. So how many times have you ascended Mount Ararat?"

I did the math. We were quiet a while. "Over fifty," I said eventually.

She sipped her coffee, and seemed to enjoy it, which was beyond my comprehension. "So you know the mountain well?"

"I wouldn't call us sweethearts, but mutually respectful friends, surely."

The cook ruthlessly banged pots, whistled more happy tunes. An older man sat down next to me. He smiled, and I grinned back, until I realized he was smiling at Faye Roberts. Faye smiled back politely.

"Pretty women get all the smiles," I muttered.

"You think I'm pretty?" she asked, grinning.

"Never mind."

She stared at me. "So why did you ask to see me, Sam?"

"Because Camilla knows what she's doing."

"What does that mean?"

"She purposefully suggested an alternate guide for you to use, one for whom I have a low opinion."

Faye Roberts made sipping noises around the coffee mug. She waited.

"So I'm here to rectify the situation," I said.

"Really?" she said, raising her eyebrow. "Or do you just like to say *rectify*? Never mind, I don't want to know. Niksar will be here in ten minutes, I believe."

I shook my head. "I took care of that. Niksar is aware that plans have changed."

Our food came, served by an older woman in a hair net. Faye ignored the food. Instead, she stared at me with increasingly narrowing eyes until she looked like a hatless cowboy riding into the sunset. "Couldn't you have just recommended a different guide, one for whom you have a higher opinion?"

I shrugged. "To be honest, I had hoped you would go away. But, seeing that you're determined to climb the mountain, I won't trust your safety to anyone else. So now I'm forced to keep you out of trouble."

"Keep me out of trouble? Sam Ward, I don't need your charity work."

"Yes you do."

She thought about that, then nodded. "Then I insist on paying you triple your asking price," she said two bites later.

"And I insist on accepting your payment."

"When do we leave?"

"I'll need at least a day to prepare." I said.

"What do I need to bring?"

"Four or five days worth of undergarments. I'll bring everything else. Of course, you will carry your fair share."

Faye grinned. "Of course. I've backpacked numerous times."

"Numerous is good," I said.

"Is there going to be much rock climbing?"

I shook my head. "Most of Ararat can be ascended on foot, following well-worn sheep and goat trails, without the use of carabiners and rope ladders. However, we will be roped together for safety's sake when we reach the glaciers."

The old man continued to smile at Faye. She ignored him. I finished the *bork* and wiped my mouth on a paper napkin. Instead of finishing hers, Faye placed some

Turkish currency on the counter, enough to pay for her own breakfast.

"Tomorrow then?" she said, standing.

"Before first light," I said.

When she left, I promptly speared her *bork* over to my plate.

CHAPTER NINE

Later that morning, working in the small, hot storage room next to my upstairs office, I selected pairs of long underwear, wind- and rain-resistant nylon/polyurethane jackets, a dozen or so pairs of synthetic socks, insulated wool caps, insulated wool/polyester pants, gaiters, compass, altimeter, isobutane fuel stove, flashlights, plastic topographic map of Ararat, sunglasses, first-aid supplies, aluminum pots, pocketknives, matches, ice axes, crampons, carabiners, snow shovels, and kernmantle ropes. And more. All of which I packed into two internal frame backpacks. Lastly, I selected two four-season expedition tents. One tent might have been presumptuous.

Downstairs, I opened a bottle of beer, dipping into my stock again. I lose more money that way. As I leaned against the counter, contemplating the many mysteries of life, and whether or not I should have a second beer, the bar's front doors opened.

The mid-day sun illuminated the scarred floor at the entrance. Two silhouetted figures stood in the doorway. One figure was abnormally tall, head rising above the door frame. The other was tall, as well, but not abnormally so. The smaller of the two appeared to be wearing a headcloth, which was not uncommon in these parts.

"I'll be open in an hour," I said in Turkish. "Although the big fellow can do whatever the hell he wants."

"I'm not here for drinks, my friend, although that wouldn't be such a bad idea." The voice was filled with pride and arrogance. And a touch of humor. The humor always made him sound sadistic. I knew the voice well.

Emir Omar Ali stepped into the bar, and his massive bodyguard, Farid Bastian, followed silently, ducking under the door frame. He closed the door gently behind him and stood quietly off to the side, shoulders hunched forward as if his arms were too heavy to support.

"May we come in, Mr. Ward?" asked Omar Ali.

"How much more in do you want to be, emir?" I said.

Omar shook his head. "I can always count on you, Mr. Ward, to put me in my place. There are those who would fear for their lives if they spoke to me in such a manner."

"I think I just piddled myself."

He shook his head. "You are a typical American, Mr. Ward. Insulting and discourteous."

"A nation of assholes."

Omar Ali stepped from the shadows and into the dim light of the bar, and I saw him clearly for the first time. I stared, shocked. Since our expedition two years ago, he had lost much weight, enough to reveal the dark hollows of his cheeks and temples. As always, his thick mustache was immaculately trimmed, flecked with gray. His deep-set eyes studied me from under a heavy brow. There was something different about his eyes, something that wasn't there two years ago. Desperation, perhaps. Fatigue. Or both.

"You're dying," I said suddenly.

He inhaled loudly, the air rattling in his throat. Omar closed his eyes and crossed his arms over his sunken chest. His stomach seemed inverted. I could see his ribs through the fabric of his robe. "Yes, Mr. Ward. In fact, I should be dead now. I was given six months to live. That was three years ago. My strength is gone, and so is my fight. I have, since last we met, rapidly deteriorated." His rheumy eyes studied me dispassionately. "As you know, Mr. Ward, I'm engaged in a highly classified operation upon Ararat."

"I just love secrets."

He continued as if I had not spoken. "I am here for two reasons. First, I've come to ask you a question." From his robe, the emir removed a thick envelope and set it on the counter before me. I glanced inside. Lots of hard currency.

"You didn't have to rob a bank just for me, emir."

"Your expertise could prove invaluable."

I motioned toward one of the round tables. "I can hardly wait to see what I know."

Using a silent command, perhaps a dog whistle, his bodyguard moved forward from the shadows and pulled a wooden chair from the table. The emir sat slowly and (like any good date) the bodyguard pushed him back in. I sat opposite the emir. Farid moved back into the shadows.

"What do you know of Jans Struys?" asked Omar.

I drank my beer, and wiped my mouth on the back of my hand. A baboonish gesture. The emir watched me curiously as if I were an exhibit at the zoo. Finally, I said, "Struys was a Seventeenth Century adventurer and soldier and part-time surgeon. He would have disappeared into obscurity if not for his association with Noah's ark." I paused, getting my facts straight. And for dramatic reasons, of course. "Struys claimed to have seen *and touched* Noah's ark."

The emir shrugged. "There are many such eyewitnesses."

"True. However, most eyewitnesses put the ark within a glacier or perched somewhere within an ice cliff. Jans Struys, however, has a different story."

Emir Omar sat forward and put his weight on his elbows. Obviously, he was unable to contain his excitement. "Please continue, Mr. Ward."

"After Struys cured an Armenian shepherd of what must have been a world-class hernia, the thankful shepherd, who lived on Mount Ararat, showed Struys a secret route to Noah's ark. The route involved a series of tunnels within the mountain. According to legend, the tunnels lead to a massive cavern of ice, and within the cavern is the ark." I grinned and drank some warm beer. "That's Struys's story. Even in ark lore, it's pretty wild."

"Has anyone ever come across these tunnels?" asked Omar.

I shook my head. "Many have looked. Although Ararat is riddled with caves and tunnels, no one has ever found an extensive network of them. Which is why Struys's story is considered nothing more than fantasy."

The emir studied his thick, perfectly manicured fingernails. Perhaps the only thick and healthy thing on his body. He rubbed his mustache with his thumb and forefinger, hand shaking terribly. "Did Struys mention something that would indicate the secret tunnel? A marker perhaps?"

I nodded. "The marker is a narrow protrusion of rock which Struys describes as an arthritic finger, gnarled at the joints. The marker would indicate the secret tunnel." I paused and looked Omar in the eye. "When did you discover the marker, emir?"

He was quiet, then shrugged as if he had nothing to lose. "Perhaps a month ago, or more. But the tunnel is blocked by a cave-in. We have men clearing it now, but there is little headway due to the extent of the cave-in. Your comments have satisfied my curiosity, Mr. Ward, for I have been relying on the questionable advice of others."

"Is that what this is all about?" I asked, exasperated. "Is that why the whole mountain is closed? Because of the goddamn marker, which in fact could be a fluke?"

Omar's skull grinned. "No, Mr. Ward. There is much more going on here than a marker, more than you may ever know. The secret tunnel just happens to be a bonus, more for my archaeologist than me, of course, as I care little for what he may or may not find in the tunnel."

"What do you want then, emir? Why are you here?"

He seemed about to speak, but then paused. Farid, the stone-faced bodyguard, appeared suddenly interested in the conversation, but then that could have been just gas. Omar looked at me, "I'm here for revenge, Sam."

"What does that mean?"

He simply sighed and shook his head. He was done talking.

As he stood, I continued pushing, "Last month, two American scientists disappeared on Ararat, about the same time you found your marker." I let my words hang in the air for a moment. "This would be a coincidence, correct?"

Omar turned, his smile revealing his sharp canine teeth, a wolfish smile. "I can hardly be responsible for the safety of two men foolish enough to trespass upon Mount Ararat."

I drained the last of the beer, considering the significance of his words. "And how did you know, emir, that both American scientists were men? Was it just a Freudian slip, cultural bias or just male arrogance?" I paused, swirling the contents of my near-empty beer bottle. "Or do you know something about their disappearance?"

Instead of answering, he inhaled deeply, ribs pushing out against the material of his robe, forehead dotted with perspiration. He looked directly into my eyes and held my gaze. "The second reason I'm here, Mr. Ward, is to give you fair warning. My sources tell me that there is an American woman in town, a young college professor. She has come to Ararat to search for her missing father. She will be seeking a guide. Being a fellow American you are a likely candidate." Omar paused. "She wishes to illegally obtain access to the mountain, *my mountain*. This is not wise, my friend. Consider the money as an incentive to stay away. Good day, Mr. Ward."

With that, the emir left. And as Farid Bastian followed, he caught my eye. He nodded simply. The heavy door clicked softly shut behind them.

When they were gone I opened another beer. To hell with inventory.

CHAPTER TEN

At 4:53 a.m., I was leaning against the fender of my Range Rover in front of my bar, smoking a cigarette and watching a potato chip bag scuttle across the dirt road, sunrise still an hour away. The air was cold and damp, and a faint mist crept along Dogubayazit's empty dirt streets. The air smelled clean, but also like more rain, too.

At 4:57 a.m., Faye Roberts emerged from within the *Gule Gule*. Bright-eyed and bushy-tailed. She moved quickly and confidently. Long, even strides. Probably an athlete in college. Volleyball? Swim team? Full contact bingo? She wore loose-fitting blue jeans and a green windbreaker with a wide white stripe across her chest. Her tan hiking boots were brand spanking new. I shook my head and exhaled a long stream of smoke and silently predicted she would get blisters within an hour of climbing. Her brown hair was pulled back through the rear opening of an L.A. Dodgers baseball cap. She was holding a small, colorful knapsack, pulled tight with a drawstring.

"Go Dodger blue," I said when she was close enough to hear.

"Dodger who?"

"Never mind," I said. "You sleep well?"

She shook her head. "Too nervous and too excited."

"Both of which can be detrimental to sleep."

She nodded and shoved her hands deep in her pockets, keeping her arms close to her body for warmth. A single horse-drawn cart slowly emerged from the mist. Wearing only a thin white robe, the solitary rider seemed inadequately dressed for the cool morning. As the cart approached, I saw that the driver was an old man, a farmer, with a long gray beard that threatened to swallow his face. Two brown geldings shouldered the load of figs and olives to be sold in Dogubayazit's open market. I waved to the farmer. He waved back, eyes lingering on Faye. He grinned toothily, and I figured the old man could probably count on one hand the number of American women he had seen. And with Faye Roberts looking fresh and pretty and alert, his perception of American women would be slightly skewed.

"Are we ready?" asked Faye, rubbing her hands together.

"Packed and ready," I said. I opened the rear door and placed her knapsack with the backpacks, then opened the front passenger door for her. Which apparently was a mistake.

"Please, Sam, if I need help, I'll ask for it. I'm here to find my father, not to make friends or to propagate the myth that women are inferior to men." She took a deep breath and I gulped and tried to shrink away. "I would like to warn you, Sam Ward, that I have taken many self-defense classes and can take care of myself. I don't want any problems on this trip."

"Are you finished making me feel like a sexist pig?"

Apparently not. "Although Camilla assures me that you are completely trustworthy, spending time alone with a stranger is a frightening prospect. I want your word that you will not try any funny business."

I held up my right hand and put my left on an invisible Bible. "I do solemnly swear that I will not engage in any funny business or any gestures of random kindness."

She eyed me carefully. I gave her my most serious look. She finally relaxed, exhaling a long stream of frosted air. She stepped into the passenger seat and closed the door firmly. I let myself in through the driver's door and started the engine, which sputtered and coughed. Then roared to life. I shifted gears and headed north into town.

I maneuvered around the old farmer, who waved again, leaning forward to get a look at Faye. On the corner of Mersin and Alanya, I waited patiently for a young shepherd to regain control of his unruly sheep. He was running this way and that, having a horrible time of it. I turned the Rover off and stepped out into the cool morning.

"Wait here," I said.

"Where are you going?"

"Just sit back and enjoy. This should be entertaining."

Soon I was chasing sheep up cobbled sidewalks and down flooded gutters. I darted and slashed and would have made Barry Sanders proud. I slipped in mud and sheep gifts, and a short while later, with the woolly beasts under some semblance of control, I returned to the truck, out of breath. Faye's cheeks, as if pinched by a loving grandmother, were brightly pink.

"That *was* entertaining," she agreed. "Now let's get the hell out of here."

I moved the Rover forward, and a minute later glanced her way. She was still smiling. A minor victory in trust through humiliation. After all, anyone who would *run with the sheep* must not be all that bad, right?

* * *

I stopped the Rover in the middle of Dogubayazit's massive outdoor market, which covered many dozens of square acres. Although some of the booths were still setting up for the day, others already displayed fruits and vegetables and baked goods, meats, dairy products, grains, pickles, nuts, peaches, grapes, tomatoes, lemons, watermelons, onions, eggplants, potatoes and peppers. Also, fine mohair rugs, pots, clothing and cheap jewelry. One booth sold perfume. That booth always gave me a headache.

"Want some breakfast?" I asked. "It's part of the package."

"In that case, sure."

Faye Roberts attracted most of the attention. Shopkeepers and store owners called out to her, beseeching her to consider their goods. She ignored them all like a pro. At one such stall I selected two loaves of bread; at another a quarter pound of goat cheese.

Twenty minutes later, we were headed east along the *Trabzon-Erzurum-Teheran* international transit highway, an unusually excellent asphalt road for this part of the country. Already the highway hummed with traffic. We silently ate our cheese and bread as the motor chugged comfortingly and the eastern sky turned from purple to violet.

CHAPTER ELEVEN

The *Bayazit* plain spread to either side of the road in swatches of browns and tans, the colors of coffee-stained teeth, without the bad breath. The plain was sprinkled sparingly with firs, cedars and alders, and liberally with tall grasses and massive sun-bleached boulders. The sky had become pinkish and bright, although actual sunrise was still a few minutes away.

Hunched forward over the wheel, I was studying the side of the road, headlights on high. Thick foliage lined the road, a product of nearby swampy lands.

Suddenly I turned the wheel hard, and we went down a dirt embankment and Faye Roberts screamed and dropped her loaf of bread. I plowed through a crop of rhododendrons and fir saplings and waist-high reeds, branches slapping the windshield, doing a number on my paint job. The Rover bounced like a happy hooker, and I fought the wheel bravely and soon we came to a slight clearing.

I looked at Faye. Face ashen, her right hand clutched the roll bar with the sort of grip that could pinch a cobra's head off. "Almost missed the turn-off," I said sheepishly. "As you can see, it's not the easiest road to spot."

She leaned forward, peering out the windshield. We were surrounded by lush plant life, some of which rested on the hood of the Rover. Somewhere a bird chirped.

"You call this a road?" she asked incredulously.

"As the saying goes: Once a road, always a road."

She shook her head dubiously. Apparently she wasn't familiar with that saying.

With the naked eye, the road was difficult to discern, and admittedly there was very little that was road-like about it. Especially considering there was a massive boulder sitting directly in front of us. However, on my office wall is an aerial photograph of the region, and from above, the road is surely there.

I picked my way around the boulder and through stunted firs and thorny bushes, destroying crocuses and snowdrops and orchids. The Rover had no problem bounding over the uneven ground and smaller rocks.

But the bigger boulders posed a problem. Some sat within the road like trolls guarding bridges. Eastern Turkey is a rocky land, the result of millenniums of volcanic activity and grinding glaciers. I was forced to find a clearing around the massive formations, usually angling off the path over smaller shrubs, and in one instance scattering a small herd of ibex feeding on the arid grass.

A short while later, Faye asked, "Is this the route my father took?"

"It's possible, though I don't detect any recent passage." I swerved to avoid a cedar which had materialized out of the mist. "Access to the mountain from the north and east would have been too time consuming. More than likely, Daveed led your father this way, coming up from the south. Then again, I could be wrong. After all, Ararat has a base of twenty-five square miles. That's a lot of mountain to cover."

Once on a smooth stretch of bronze-colored earth dotted with clumps of ankle-high grass, I reached into the back seat and grabbed two bottled waters. "Thirsty?" I asked.

She shook her head. "I think I'm getting car sick."

"Is it my driving?" I asked.

"Yes," she said.

"It's always my driving," I said.

I stopped the Rover and left the engine running and lit a cigarette. The morning was quiet, with little animal activity, although a red squirrel did appear around the thick bole of a cedar. The little booger watched us nervously, then scurried back behind the safety of the tree. It was about as cute as cute can be.

Before us, filling the entire windshield, was Mount Ararat. Its continuously snow-capped peak was hidden behind thick cumulus clouds, and from here, the mountain appeared unimaginably massive. Ararat is, in fact, a perfect conical volcano. Detached from any mountainous chains, it's a free-standing entity reminiscent of Japan's Mount Fuji, with canyons and lakes and glaciers. And its own weather systems.

And, some claim, a very old ship.

We were still seven miles from its base. Faye stared up at the mountain, mouth slightly open. Leaning forward in her seat, she looked up through the windshield as if she were watching the departure of the latest space shuttle.

"How big is it?" she asked finally.

"Seventeen thousand, give or take a few hundred feet."

"And just how dangerous?" Her words sounded distant and strained, as if Faye were talking behind a wall. Ararat has that effect on people.

"Supremely."

"And you're not just saying that to make me feel better?"

"We can still turn back," I said. "I'll give you a full refund and even pay for your plane ticket home."

She shook her head and set her jaw. Her lips were a thin pencil line. "That's very generous, Sam. But I'm too close to back away now. Not with my father still up there. So why is the mountain so dangerous?"

"All mountains are inherently dangerous. But particular to Ararat would be wolves, wild dogs, poisonous snakes, scorpions, brown bears, etc."

"Bears?"

"They're mostly harmless if you keep your distance. Higher up you have avalanches, gale-force winds, blizzards, electrical storms and hidden crevasses. Those are some of the reasons why the Turkish Department of Interior requires all climbers to use the local guides."

She was quiet. I ground the last of the cigarette in the over-flowing ashtray. "Feeling okay?" I asked.

She nodded and I pressed the gas and we moved forward again.

Almost immediately, we were forced around a stretch of soft sand that would have mired the Rover. As I struggled with the truck, the sun appeared above the distant foothills, burning away the last of the mist that had been clinging tenaciously to the earth. But with the appearance of the sun, something flashed in the distance. I stopped the Rover.

"What is it?" Faye asked.

"Trouble."

CHAPTER TWELVE

I removed a pair of binoculars from the console between us, bringing the object into focus. "It's a military truck," I reported. "And a small camp. Maybe three or four soldiers. Sitting around a stove, drinking coffee. Unfortunately, they are guarding this very road."

Faye shook her head. I think she still wasn't convinced that this was a road. "Have they seen us?"

"Doesn't appear so. And if they have, they plan on finishing their coffee before doing anything about it."

"So what do we do?"

I scanned the surrounding brush with the field glasses. There. Two or three miles to the east, was another military Jeep, moving slowly over the uneven ground. And near the base of the mountain was yet another vehicle, discernible only by the trailing dirt cloud kicked up by the tires.

I lowered the binoculars. "It doesn't look good for the home team, but I'm not without a back-up plan." I pointed thirty feet ahead of us to where the land seemed to disappear below the horizon and start-up again a few dozen feet away. "It's an arroyo, a dried riverbed, a one-time tributary from Ararat's glacial run-off. In hotter summers, with severe glacial melt, the arroyo will transform into a raging river. But now it's dry and should afford some cover. We should be well hidden."

I moved the Rover forward, and out into the open. I knew we were exposed for the time being. But I was willing to gamble that the soldier boys were too sleepy to bother looking up from their coffee mugs. And just as I reached the arroyo, a small round bullet hole appeared in the Rover's left front fender. I briefly wondered if my insurance would cover that when the report of a rifle echoed down along the arroyo.

Fifty feet away, hidden in the shadows and leaves of a copse of birches, was another Jeep with two camouflaged soldiers inside. One was leveling a semiautomatic weapon at us, grinning like a villain. We were his early morning target practice. After all, he could always tell his superiors we had resisted arrest.

He fired again and the weapon bucked in his arms like a hiccuping baby.

* * *

"Down!" I yelled, mashing the gas pedal to the floor. I heard the *thud-thud-thud* of bullets impacting the Rover's side panels.

The tires spun, spewing dirt like a geyser. But we didn't move, sinking deeper in the sand. Dust surrounded us, blown by the wind. The side window exploded. Glass washed over the dashboard. A bullet lodged into the air conditioning.

More thuds. White steam hissed from the engine.

Across the arroyo, the military Jeep roared to life. A ferocious sound.

And then the Rover's tires found purchase, and we shot forward like a rocket. Over the edge of the arroyo, and down into empty space.

* * *

We landed hard. The Rover bounced on rubber tires and squeaky shocks. My chest slammed into the steering wheel as air exploded from my lungs. Uncontrollably, the Rover slid sideways through the loose dirt. A vertical dirt wall appeared through the missing driver's side window, approaching rapidly. I fought for breath even as I struggled with the unresponsive steering wheel.

The wall rapidly filled the entire window. "Hang on!"

The Rover side-swiped the dirt embankment and Faye was thrown against me. There's something to be said for wearing seat belts. Rocks and dirt spilled over the hood and over my lap. I wrenched the wheel with all my strength, and we finally shot away from the wall and out into the open arroyo, over a smattering of loose rocks.

I looked in the rearview mirror. Behind, the Jeep bounded over the rocks, big tires clawing like an angry animal. I stepped on the pedal, and we tore down the middle of the arroyo, fish-tailing slightly.

Thick trees with Spanish moss hung over the embankments. A red cloud of crimson-winged finches erupted from one of the branches, startled by our sudden appearance. Together, as if controlled by one mind, the finches darted this way and that, and disappeared out of sight. Ararat rose directly before us, indifferent to our plight.

As I swerved around the bigger boulders, I kept an eye on the rearview mirror. The soldiers drove recklessly, sometimes on two wheels, heedless of their own safety, like two drunken teens out for a weekend joy ride.

The shooter stood in the passenger seat, gripping the roll bar, hips shifting left and right like a Hula dancer. He rattled off a few wild shots. Some shots were wilder than others as dirt exploded to my left and sparks chipped off distant boulders to my right.

"We need to lose these assholes," I said, and reached under my seat, removing a black 9mm Smith & Wesson. "Grab the wheel, Faye."

I kept my foot on the accelerator while Faye fought to keep us on a straight path, and leaned out the window. Dirt embankments blurred passed, just a dozen feet away. I held the 9mm in my right hand, and sighted my target carefully—

And pulled the trigger.

* * *

The report from my 9mm was deafening. Faye jumped, jerking the wheel. The truck swerved violently. I grabbed the door, and just managed to stay inside the vehicle.

But the shot had missed. The soldier ducked, dropping below the windshield. He gesticulated wildly to his partner. I positioned myself again, and pulled the trigger. And promptly put a nice hole in the radiator. But I wasn't aiming for the radiator.

The Jeep slewed to the right.

I fired again. And again. Small dirt clouds exploded near the left front tire. Next to me, I heard Faye grunt as she struggled with the steering wheel.

"How many shots do you have left?" she asked.

"Two," I said.

Soldier boy leveled the weapon again and loosened a rapid series of shots. I ducked inside the truck. The back window disappeared. One shot went through the rear window and out the windshield, instantly spreading a series of web-like cracks.

When the soldier paused, I fired again. And blew out their left headlight.

"Last one."

I squinted carefully down the sites. Sucked in air. And fired.

The tire exploded into black strips of steel-belted bacon. The Jeep swerved violently. The shooter was thrown from the vehicle, tumbling in the dirt. The driver fought the wheel bravely, but the Jeep hit the embankment hard, and spun like a top, coming to rest in the center of the arroyo, steaming.

* * *

Ten minutes later I drove up and out of the arroyo and cut across an empty stretch of land and over hard-packed earth that would leave little in the way of tire tracks. Then I pointed the vehicle through a strand of fir trees, and, to avoid leaving an obvious trail of trampled brush, I used the least-dense route.

Soon, a wide stream opened before us. The clean water moved quickly over smooth flat stones. Not very deep, but that was okay. After all, I wanted to hide our tracks in the water, not drown the vehicle. I drove the Rover into the stream.

CHAPTER THIRTEEN

I drove steadily but cautiously down the center of the stream. Ararat rose slowly before us like a Japanese monster emerging from the depths of the ocean. Faye drank from her bottle, perhaps influenced by the noisy water sounds the tires made. The water reminded me of another bodily function, but I felt it best that we press forward and not stop. As we worked our way upstream, there were no other signs of military patrol.

"Camilla mentioned we may come across thieves or terrorists," said Faye, keeping her voice even, although I detected a slight undercurrent of concern.

I turned the wheel sharply, avoiding a dark pool I suspected was deeper water. "To insure that Omar Ali and his men would be safe, the Turkish military swept the mountain clean of all Kurdish guerrilla activity, which in turn rid the mountain of thieves and terrorists, as well."

A dry, hot wind rippled the water; the ripples, in turn, glimmered in the sun like golden coins. The wind poured through the many shattered windows in the Rover, courtesy of the Turkish military.

Always my eyes scanned the surrounding shrubbery, alert for military patrols. And just before noon, as the Rover plunged through slightly deeper water, Faye said, "Thank you, Sam."

"For what?"

"Giving me the opportunity to look for my father."

"And opportunity is all it may be," I said. "He's been missing for a long time."

"You would fail miserably at writing greeting cards."

Minutes later, I stopped the Rover. About a hundred yards upstream, the mud banks merged into steep granite cliffs, and the stream grew in size into something more than a stream. I only hoped that I had put enough distance between us and the Turks.

I turned out of the stream and spent the next five minutes fighting the loose mud. Two feet forward, one back. White steam issued from the engine. The Rover was losing water. The coolant system was probably shot-up.

Once on dry land, we moved quickly through reeds and grasses and the occasional mean-looking thorny bush that might have been cultivated in Hell's half acre. The shrubs gave way to larger boulders, and soon we were driving up through a massive limestone canyon, carved by eons of flood waters and glacial melt. A pair of Egyptian vultures rose and fell with the turbulent updrafts created within the canyon. Waiting for something to die. Or for some privacy.

When the canyon became too steep and dangerous, I parked the vehicle deep within the shadows of the canyon wall between two huge boulders. A hell of a parallel parking job, I might add. I threw a canvas cover over the vehicle. The Rover now looked remarkably boulder-like. It should escape detection at first or even second glance.

"What about the alarm?" Faye asked, shielding her eyes like a saluting soldier from the glare of the noon sun. There was something akin to a smirk on her face, but with Faye it was hard to be sure.

"A shepherd boy wouldn't know what to do with the Rover," I said, scanning the horizon with the field glasses. The land was a living green and bronze blanket. I stood within the shadows to eliminate the possibility of a telltale gleam from the lens of the binoculars.

I spotted a quick-moving jackal, its sand-colored coat wet with dew. Nose to the ground. Tracking rabbits or pheasants. Or even young ibex or chamois. There was no other movement. The land was empty and majestic, harsh and wild. Just the way I liked it. I exhaled. My breath fogged before me.

"I think we're safe," I said, letting the heavy field glasses hang from the strap around my neck. We stood shoulder to shoulder, her shoulder just below my shoulder. Faye's eyes were slits against the morning sun.

Perhaps a mile away something flashed under the sun. I raised the binoculars. A camouflaged military truck was moving languidly along a well-worn trail along the river.

Was this a routine patrol? Or had something alerted them? That something being us.

"What is it?" Faye asked.

"Military truck."

"Are they on to us?"

"I don't think so, Dick Tracy."

The truck moved on without incident, disappearing within the deeper foliage along the stream's bank. Just a routine patrol, I hoped.

With the toe of her hiking boot, Faye kicked a loose pebble into another such pebble in a pre-historic game of marbles. "So this is the infamous Mount Ararat."

I shook my head. "Hardly. The true Ararat is high above, and a lot closer to heaven than you or I."

"You sound like a song."

"You wouldn't say that if you heard me sing."

Later, we dressed in long underwear, polypropylene socks, nylon pants and windbreakers. The nylon outer shell would keep the wind and rain out; the long underwear to keep the warmth in. A good recipe for mountain climbing. To complete the look, I handed her a wool cap and a pair of ski glasses. Now she looked ready to conquer a mountain, or hold up a liquor store in Aspen, Colorado.

A dry wind swept along the canyon. I lit a cigarette. The vultures were gone, probably gorging on the carcass of some poor creature who had propagated the myth that women were inferior to men.

"Are we ready?" she asked, voice tight, managing to sound excited and impatient all at the same time.

"Almost," I said.

I helped Faye into her backpack and slipped into mine. Both packs jangled with crampons and carabiners. I slipped a hundred foot kernmantle rope—coiled in a classic mountaineer coil—over my backpack.

"Now, we're ready."

The sky was clear, although thunderheads lay on the distant horizon, waiting like an invading Medieval army for the command to storm the castle. The wind was crisp but manageable. It was good hiking weather. I crushed the cigarette under my boot, leaving my mark on the holy mountain. I led the way forward, and upward.

CHAPTER FOURTEEN

The ankle-high grass gave way to loose volcanic rock, which was akin to walking across a field of bowling balls. A cold wind swept down through the canyon, funneled between the massive rock walls, whistling over the many rock protrusions. The cliffs were layered with basalt, limestone, quartz, sandstone and dolomite in a sort of geologic rainbow.

An hour into the climb I stopped in the shade of a rock buttress. Faye was breathing steadily, a film of sweat on her upper lip. She wiped the sweat away with the back of her hand.

"Why are we stopping?" she asked impatiently.

"Water," I said. "If that's okay with you."

She nodded her consent. "A little water does sound good."

"I'm glad you approve."

When I had finished drinking, Faye was still guzzling away. Precious liquid trickled down her chin and neck.

"You might want to conserve some of that," I said.

Reluctantly, she pulled away from the bottle like a baby from a teat. She stared in shocked silence at the half-empty contents. "I hadn't realized I was so thirsty," she said. "Where do we get more?"

"Reconstituted urine. I have special baggies and distillers in my backpack. When done properly, the water doesn't taste bad. Sort of coppery."

"That's not funny, Sam."

"Of course not." I grinned and pointed farther up the canyon. "We'll be passing a stream about an hour's climb from here. And higher up, we'll use melted ice and snow."

"No yellow snow."

"No yellow snow," I agreed.

The wind blasted over the rock buttress, moaning like the dead. Now all we needed were flapping shutters. Preferably broken. Higher up, between the canyon walls, the narrow strip of sky revealed storm clouds approaching from the east, dark and gray, as if composed of a million lost souls. On Ararat, storms hit quickly, and hard. From blizzards to hailstorms to surreal electrical storms.

Faye slipped out of her backpack and sat on a stool-sized rock, which wobbled slightly. I glanced down to see if anything slithered from underneath. Nothing slithered. There was a smudge of dirt on Faye's right cheekbone. A slow-moving rivulet of sweat passed over the smudge. She undid the laces of her boots and slid two slender fingers down into the sock, and winced.

"Blisters?" I asked.

"I think so."

I found another pair of old polyurethane socks deep within my backpack, and handed them to Faye. "The blisters are unavoidable but you can impede their advance with these."

"Thank you, General Schwartzcoff."

A half hour later, we stopped before a tunnel carved naturally within the canyon wall. The arched opening was veiled by gently swaying cobwebs. "Shortcut," I said, grinning.

Faye shook her head. "Men and their shortcuts."

I removed a small flashlight from my backpack and pushed aside the thick cobwebs and ducked into the tunnel. The passage was narrow and continued as far as the light would reach. Dust motes swirled in the air. A tiny creature with bright red eyes stared at me before scuttling off along the floor, its tiny little claws clicking on the stone.

We moved deeper into the tunnel. Once or twice I ducked to avoid the low ceiling. Once or twice I didn't duck soon enough. Our boots echoed off the surrounding walls, and sometimes we came across soft pockets of sand, which muffled our footfalls.

Just ahead, obscured by the gently swaying ectoplasm-like cobwebs, was a faint glow that marked the tunnel's end. And as we moved closer, the glow became a bright archway of yellow sunlight, washing over the smooth stone floor.

"How do you fare with heights?" I asked.

"I'm good with heights. Why do you ask?"

I was the first to exit the tunnel, stepping out onto a narrow ledge. Below was a thousand foot drop into a massive canyon, reminding me of a scaled-down version of the Grand Canyon, with its multi-colored layers, sheer walls and levels upon levels. Two golden eagles circled far below, wings outstretched, looking for trouble.

Faye stepped out behind me. She immediately gasped, grabbing my bicep. Her talon-like grip would have impressed any golden eagle. I pried her fingers free and looked over my shoulder. "That good, huh."

She took a moment to collect herself and eased out onto the ledge like a scared puppy sampling rain for the first time. "I'm OK with heights, Sam. I just wasn't prepared to be slapped in the face with it. How did we get so high?"

"Ararat sits on a three thousand foot plateau, not to mention we've been climbing for the past two hours."

The raptors circled below, their auburn feathers ruffling in the updraft. Somewhere a rabbit didn't stand a chance.

I led the way along the narrow ledge.

CHAPTER FIFTEEN

Long ago, I had grown accustomed to the weight of my pack on my shoulders. It had become an extension of me, like a big deformed hump, attractive only to gypsy women in bell towers. As we moved along the ledge, my legs felt strong, although they burned with the effort of carrying forty pounds up a sharp incline. After all, I was out of shape, as it had been a slow summer, thanks to Emir Omar Ali. Faye didn't show any signs of tiring, keeping pace with me stride for stride. I was impressed.

As the sky began to darken, the wind brought with it the sweet smell of rain, and later, when the ledge merged into a steep grassy slope, the rains finally came. Attached to our windbreakers were hoods, which we immediately utilized. Still, the drops were like ice on my face and neck, until my skin grew completely numb and lost all feeling.

I led the way across the field, trampling through the tall grass. The patter of rain was somehow comforting against the nylon hood. Next, a low fog moved in. There's something to be said about a swirling mist clinging to the side of a mountain, as if we had stepped into a fantasy land created by Tolkien. My tongue felt fat and sticky—the brutal reality of this world. I stopped in the middle of the grassy field and removed my backpack. Faye did the same and we both drank eagerly.

As we did so, a distant figure emerged from the fog. Seconds later, the figure proved to be a man. He stumbled once, but held himself up with a long wooden staff. He was dressed in a tattered robe. I could see blood on the cleaner parts of his robe.

Faye pressed against me; the feeling of closeness was not unpleasant, and her need for comfort was surprisingly appealing to me. "He's a shepherd," I said. "And, like us, he's trespassing."

The shepherd paused, swayed on his feet, and then fell forward.

* * *

He lay face-down, torn robe spread around him like broken angel wings. I carefully rolled him over. Faye gasped. His nose was broken and swollen and split from side to side. Blood poured from his nostrils and into his gray beard. His equally gray hair was caked with blood. He could have been seventy years old, and in those seventy years he surely had seen better days.

"What happened?" Faye asked, dropping to her knees.

I shook my head. "Could have taken a fall, or been caught in a rock slide. A few years back, an American astronaut was struck by such a falling rock. When they found him, he looked similar to this."

Faye reached under his head and lifted it and poured water over his puffed and cracked lips, washing away some of the blood and exposing more deep wounds around his mouth. The old man opened his brown eyes for the first time and tried to sit up but Faye held him down.

He drank more water, then spoke for the first time, a rambling stream of nomadic Kurdish. When finished, I responded in the same language.

"What did he say?" said Faye eagerly. "What did *you* say?"

"His name is Makmur, and he knows of me. *The great white guide*, as I'm known to his people. I said I knew of him as well, a dedicated shepherd and respected patriarch."

"Is that true?"

"The great white guide business?" I shrugged modestly.

"No, Sam Ward. Have you heard of him?"

"Of course not. I was being courteous. It was expected of me."

Makmur's eyes flicked to Faye, and the old man spoke again: "He says you must be an angel, because surely he has died and gone to Heaven."

Faye Roberts blushed. I didn't know she had it in her. "Spunky little devil," she said. "Tell him that's the oldest line in the book."

I did. "He also says you would make a fine shepherd's wife, and he has a grandson available."

"Remind him that he's too injured to play matchmaker."

Sheet lightning flashed, illuminating the dark underbelly of the storm clouds. The old man spoke in a long rambling stream and I translated between his many pauses: "He says he has a right to live and work and eat off the mountain just as his father did before him, and his father's father before him, etc., etc. He was beaten as a warning for others to stay away."

"Who beat him?"

"Soldiers."

We were silent. Makmur's breathing became increasingly labored. Blood bubbled from his lips, mixed with saliva. The rain came down steadily. The rain somehow made the setting even more forlorn.

Faye asked, "Has he seen my father?"

I repeated her question and the old man responded: "There were two men, foreigners, above the Gorge. That was a month or two ago. But he does not know who they were or why they were here."

Faye closed her eyes and seemed to pray a silent prayer. Meanwhile, I opened Makmur's robe. There was a pool of blood spreading like a disease under the paper-thin skin of his abdomen. Internal bleeding. His ribs were broken, and maybe also a punctured lung, judging by his ragged breathing. Faye held his head in her lap as the wind and rain swept over us. We bundled the old man back up and sat with him until he died. His last breath was extraordinarily long, and his chest seemed to shrink down into the rocky soil. I shut his eyes.

Five minutes later, Faye was still holding his head. I reached over and touched her shoulder. She looked at me, eyes troubled and wet. "Why did they kill him, Sam?"

Thunder rumbled overhead. Water dripped steadily from the end of my nose. I looked at the beaten body. "My guess is that Emir Omar Ali has something to hide. Perhaps something very important."

We stared down at the sodden, broken body. The rain washed the blood away from his face. Faye finally said, "Won't the wild animals get him?"

"Probably."

"Well, I won't have that."

Faye shucked her backpack, scavenged the area for the dark volcanic rocks and began placing them around the body. I slipped out of my own pack and helped, taking us the better part of an hour to completely cover Makmur's small body. Finally, I broke his gnarled staff a third of the way down and secured it with twine from my backpack and shoved the makeshift cross between the stones over his head.

CHAPTER SIXTEEN

The rain turned into a freezing drizzle. We had been
hiking for the better part of six hours. During that time I
thought of Makmur. He was murdered, that much was
true. A powerful man like Omar Ali, acting within Turkish
authority, could do just about anything. And trespassers
were fair game. A simple beating of an old shepherd would
go unnoticed, even if it resulted in death.

The temperature continued to drop; our breaths fogged
before us. Later, the drizzle stopped and there was a break
in the clouds and the sun shone brightly down as if making
up for lost time. A pair of white snowfinches streaked
overhead, followed by an alpine chough that turned its
head and watched us, then disappeared up through the
clouds.

The grassy slope was mostly barren, with the occasional outcropping of igneous rock. Later, we stopped beside a crystal clear stream, which wound down from above, bubbling over smooth stones. I handed out dried fruit and almonds. Almost too exciting for words. After eating, we sat back in the lush grass. Faye laced her fingers behind her head and stared up at the overcast sky. "Let's be reasonable, Sam. There is no ark."

"Not according to Mrs. Dartmouth," I said.

"Who's Mrs. Dartmouth?" she asked.

"My Sunday school teacher."

"Of course."

The water made relaxing bubbling noises, the sort that's recorded and sold in alternate health stores everywhere. I pulled out a shoot of grass and stuck it between my teeth. It tasted just like grass.

I said, "I've heard all the arguments before. The arguments bore me. It's a moot point. A classic example of science versus faith. I don't know much science, and I don't have much faith."

"That's taking the easy way out, Sam," Faye said. "Other than some unusual animal deposits that may be the results of a massive *local* floods, there's just no evidence of a world-wide flood."

"They say God works in mysterious ways."

"But where did the water come from, Sam? And I don't buy into the Canopy Theory. There's little if any evidence supporting that Earth was covered in a layer of water vapor which contributed to the flood. Even so, where did all the water go? How did all the animals fit into one ark? How did the animals come to be on the ark?"

"Refer to my prior comment."

I closed my eyes. My stomach made some digesting noises. Something rustled in the grass maybe twenty feet away. Probably a field mouse.

"To be fair," she added, "there's substantial evidence of a massive flood occurring in the Black Sea basin about seventy-five hundred years ago. Two colleagues of mine, both noted oceanographers, have proven this event to be the largest in recent history, geologically speaking. Many lives were lost, including whole communities. The evidence even suggests that this disaster helped spread farming into central Europe, and could be the basis of the Noah's ark story, along with the Babylonian epic of Gilgamesh."

"Should I make copious notes for the quiz later?"

"Are you ever serious, Sam?"

"Look," I said. "You scientists have all the proof you need to denounce it, the believers have all the faith they need to believe, so who the hell cares what I think?"

"But you make a living endorsing that myth."

"Correction, I make a living safely guiding people onto a very dangerous mountain. What they do on the mountain is their business."

"Have you ever seen any evidence of the ark?"

"No."

She sat back, satisfied. "As I said, it's a myth. Bedtime stories. A classic hero tale, one man conquering nature and all that."

"Now that you've got it all figured out," I said. "Perhaps we should get going."

And that's when Faye screamed, and not because of a field mouse.

* * *

The creature was long and beautiful and as deadly as they come. Relative to the North American cottonmouth, the puff adder, with its patch-work pattern, was perfectly camouflaged for its surroundings. It moved languidly through the dry grass a foot away from Faye's out-stretched leg.

"Sam!"

Puff adders were deaf; or, more accurately, *lacked* hearing. Good thing.

"Christ, Sam, do something!"

"Just be still."

Its forked tongue, covered in sense organs, flicked in and out, testing its surroundings. The adder was long, perhaps the longest I've seen on the mountain. And it was shedding. Seen in a different light, the snake could look ghastly, which was probably the light in which Faye was seeing it.

"I'm going to faint, Sam."

"Not a good idea," I said.

"I-I can't breathe."

I moved forward, crouched low to the ground. The adder paid little attention to me, or even to Faye, for that matter. It seemed intent on the bubbling stream, and suddenly made a turn for the worse...slithering over Faye's ankle.

"Sam!"

"Sit still."

"I can't breathe."

The snake's tongue flicked out rapidly, wiggling like a worm on a hook. Faye's eyes suddenly rolled up into her head and her elbows slipped from under her. She fell silently back into the soft grass. It was just as well, and a whole lot quieter.

I grabbed the snake's tail and pulled it away from Faye. True to its name, the creature puffed out extraordinarily and swung its jaws, bubbling with venom, at me, but they fell just short. Thirty feet away, I set the creature free in the wet grass.

CHAPTER SEVENTEEN

We followed a series of sheep trails along a rocky slope as the wind hit us first from one direction, then another. Sparring like a boxer. The effect was complete instability.

I checked on Faye. She appeared to be doing fine. Her face was set in grim determination. Grim determination was an asset on this mountain. We stopped under a rock overhang and drank from our water bottles. I watched a dust devil move up the slope, then lose its steam and dissipate into nothing. Faye said, "I've never fainted before."

"It's nothing to be ashamed of," I said.

"But nothing to be proud of either."

"Then I promise not to tell," I said, "no matter how much the tabloids offer."

The wind tousled her hair. Her hair looked good tousled. She removed her sunglasses and looked at me.

"You can be very sweet behind the jokes and tough-guy attitude."

"Sweet, tough and funny," I said. "A hell of a combination."

"Notice I didn't say modest?"

"I noticed."

Her eyes followed the slope all the way to the snow-capped peak thousands of feet above. "Do you think we're wasting our time?" she asked.

I shrugged. "Maybe not. Maybe Emir Omar Ali has some answers to your father's disappearance."

"Why do you say that?"

I said, "The shepherd established that your father and his student were above the Ahora Gorge, which may be near Omar's camp. If your father did come across Omar, he would have stumbled upon a whole hornet's nest of trouble—just look at what happened to the shepherd."

"Do you think Omar killed them?"

I shrugged.

"So what do we do?" she asked.

"Maybe we should have a look at Omar's camp," I said.

Faye chewed her lower lip, alternately moistening it with the tip of her pink tongue. I didn't chew my lip; instead, I watched her. Same effect, less chewing. "But how do we get in?" she asked finally.

"We'll cross that ice bridge when we get there," I said.

"I suppose we can't just say we were in the neighborhood," Faye said.

"No," I said.

"And selling Girl Scout cookies is out of the question."

"That was funny."

"Maybe you're rubbing off on me."

"Just take a hot shower and you'll be fine."

She laughed. The wind abruptly died down, and all was silent. Not even the chattering chirp of a krupers nuthatch. She suddenly turned to me, eyes flashing. "If Omar had anything to do with my father's disappearance, I'll want justice."

I detected something hard in her voice. "Justice, or revenge?"

She set her jaw. "Both."

"On Ararat, there is no justice. And revenge will cost you extra."

* * *

We followed a shallow gully, its rock-strewn floor uneven and difficult to traverse. Like witch's hair, patches of dry grass grew futilely among the rocks. The sun continued to set, slowly disappearing behind the distant foothills, casting the sky into a brilliant orange glow. A male caspian snowcock, its little white chest puffed out, watched us from the branch of a scraggly bush.

From the gully we followed a winding sheep trail until we reached a jagged ridge. Here, the wind hammered us like batting practice. My chapped lips hummed with pain. Rarely was there a time when my lips weren't chapped. Faye's dark hair blew behind her like a tattered battlefield flag. She held onto the sleeve of my jacket. Unfortunately, there was nothing for me to hold onto. We had a perfect view of the *Bayazit* plain below which shimmered in patches of browns and tans and greens. I could see the town of Dogubayazit on the western horizon as a finger of black smoke rose from it. I hoped Pascal hadn't burned down my bar. Again.

We continued along the crest of the ridge. Almost immediately I spotted a lithe creature darting expertly from rock to rock, pausing every few feet to test the air. Suddenly it stopped, ears twitching. It must have caught wind of us. The white ghost, as the local shepherds call him. The snow leopard turned slowly and displayed its long white teeth and black gums, and in a blink of an eye the big cat was gone, disappearing among the huge granite boulders.

We moved forward into the sunset, the horizon a fiery canvass, painted orange and red and violet with the rays of the setting sun. And as we wound our way up a narrow path, sprinkled liberally with loose rock, Faye Roberts cried out behind me.

CHAPTER EIGHTEEN

I turned in time to see Faye crumple to the ground in a heap. I dashed to her side, sliding down the loose rock. I saw that her right leg was sticking out at an awkward angle.

"Can you stand?" I asked.

"I don't think so."

"Is it your knee?" If it was her knee, we were heading down the next morning.

She shook her head. "Ankle."

I helped her into a sitting position. She unlaced her right boot and massaged her ankle, wincing. "I don't think it's bad. I've twisted it before in racquetball. Just give me a minute."

"You need ice," I said.

She looked around the rocky slope. "If you see some, tell me."

"The streams here are at near freezing temperatures," I said.

"So what are you saying?"

"I'm going to carry you to the nearest stream."

"No thank you. I'd prefer to wait."

"No waiting. As it is, we have precious little light to negotiate the trail."

She continued to protest even as I lifted her into my arms. I moved forward, carrying two backpacks and a full grown woman. Once, my own foot rolled over a loose rock, but I managed to keep my balance. My legs burned and my arms shook and I did my best not to pass out from exhaustion.

Not soon enough, the rocky trail gave way to plush grass. Here, a trickling stream cut through the plateau. Near the stream's grassy bank, I set her down. She removed her boot and sock and put her foot in the water and promptly yelped.

"Jesus, it's cold."

I grinned and stretched my aching back. "It's glacial run-off. With any luck, it should stop the swelling."

"And with any luck I'll feel my toes again."

* * *

I staked our tents side by side. As I worked, Faye watched me from her perch near the brook. "That was a very nice thing you did, Sam."

I shrugged. "It's all part of the service. You know, helping damsels in distress and all that. How's the ankle?"

She pulled her foot out of the water. Her foot glowed palely under the moonlight. In a dazzling feat of dexterity, she pulled her ankle to approximately three inches from her face, and examined it up close and personal. Then she put her foot back in the water. The water rippled and glistened like black lava under the moon.

"It'll turn purple, but the swelling appears to have stopped."

"Good."

I dug a fire pit within the rocks, and fueled it with dry grass and a match. The sky above shone with a million and one stars. The pot of tea came to a boil over the small butane stove, and I poured a cup for each, and handed out beef jerky and trail mix. The trail mix was tilted more toward dried cranberries than anything else, which was fine by me. Faye drank and ate alone by the brook's edge. When I finished the trail mix, I sat next to her and sipped my tea.

"Feeling sociable?" she said.

"You looked lonesome."

"Can I take my foot out now?" she asked.

"Not yet."

"Who died and made you Dr. Quincy?" she said.

"Dr. Quincy?"

"It's the first doctor that came to mind," she said sheepishly.

"But he was a medical examiner," I said. "You know, autopsies."

"He probably knew a thing or two about swollen ankles."

"Then again he was a fictional character. The extent of Jack Klugman's medical knowledge is in the script."

"But he played the part well."

"Yes, he did."

"So can I take my foot out?"

"If you promise to leave Dr. Quincy out of any future arguments."

"Agreed."

"Fine," I said, and handed her a hand towel with the embroidered symbol of the *Gule Gule*.

Faye wiped her foot and examined the towel. "Does Camilla know you have this?"

I grabbed the towel from her. "No. And neither does she know of the others." I rummaged through my backpack and produced two crumpled cigarettes that had seen better days. I lit both and handed her one. I lay back in the dry grass and watched the clouds congeal into something much larger.

Faye exhaled a steady stream of blue-gray smoke. "You're a bad influence on me, Sam Ward."

"I've been known to have that effect."

"But it *is* relaxing," she said. "And if ever there was a day that I needed a cigarette, it's today."

"When you're quitting, every day is that day."

The wind picked up, forcing Faye to wipe her long hair away from her forehead. As she inhaled, the tip of the cigarette flared brightly. "Have you ever been married, Sam?"

"No."

"Have you ever been close to marriage?"

"Yes."

She looked at me, letting her unvoiced question hang in the air. So did I. The tents made flapping noises. More clouds accumulated above. "Let's take another route," she said, rolling to her side, eyes both mischievous and curious. "How does an American end up living in Eastern Turkey?"

I flicked my unfinished cigarette in the fire. I needed something stronger. I produced a metal flask from the backpack. I undid the cap, and took a drink. "Single malt Turkish whiskey. Not the best stuff in the world, but good enough." I held the bottle out to Faye, but she declined.

"Three years ago," I said, "my fiancé was killed on this mountain."

Faye brought the cigarette to her lips and inhaled slowly, blowing the smoke out through her nostrils. "Father always said I was too nosy."

A snowflake touched her lower lip and melted. I could smell Faye's shampooed hair, a mixture of berries and roses. I shook my head in wonder: *we elude the Turkish military and spend a day climbing and she still comes up smelling like roses.* Women are amazing.

"She was killed in a rockslide," I said. "I found her face-down in a ravine, the back of her head smashed in, partially covered in loose rocks."

"Ah, shit."

"I buried her in a cave above the Abich Glacier." We were silent. I had brought the morale down a notch or two. "And I'm the only one who knows where she's buried."

"Which is why you're still here in Eastern Turkey," she said with surprising insight.

I nodded. "If I leave, she will be forgotten. Who else will visit her grave?"

The snow continued to fall, and shortly we retired to our separate tents. I left the fire smoldering in the pit.

CHAPTER NINETEEN

The next morning we were sipping coffee in front of the campfire. The snow had stopped during the night, leaving behind a thin blanket of ice over everything. I held the warm coffee mug in my cold hands, which made for a good combination.

Faye's hair was in a ponytail, held in place by a blue rubberband. She was dressed in dark blue insulated wool pants, wind- and rain-proof synthetic parka and a thick sweater. The rubber soles of her hiking boots were crusted with pale brown dirt. I was dressed similarly, save my parka was red and the soles of my boots were permanently encrusted with dirt. And no blue rubberband.

A flock of alpine swifts, white shadows against the dark morning sky, swept silently overhead. When we had finished our coffee, I helped Faye into her backpack and noticed she was putting more weight on her left foot.

"How's the ankle?" I asked.

"Serviceable."

"That doesn't sound encouraging."

"It will have to do."

I led the way up the snow-covered slope, which was bordered by short cliffs layered with quartz and calcite. The faint skyline of distant rolling foothills came gradually into view as the sun made its morning appearance. We passed a large sandstone boulder. A small monitor lizard, its green spiny back dotted with yellow specks, was perched on top, thermo-regulating. It never even moved.

At noon, we paused next to another stream and filled our bottles and watched a red squirrel work precariously among the roots and weeds jutting from the cliff face. It paused just long enough to look at us sideways.

"Busy little fellow," Faye said.

"Hunger does that to you."

As we drank, water ran down Faye's slender neck. Actually, most ran down her neck. "It's heavenly," she said when she had pulled away from the bottle.

I said, "Could be a slogan for a water bottling company."

"We could make a lot of money," she said.

"We? It was my idea," I said.

"But my slogan," she said.

"Noah's Water?" I suggested.

She made a face. "It's gotta sound clean, Sam. A nine hundred and fifty year old prophet who spent the better part of his time with a boatload of dirty animals doesn't sound clean. How about Ararat Glacial?"

I said, "Ararat *Agua*?"

"Maybe it's not such a good idea."

We moved on, making good progress. And as evening came, the sun a massive ball of orange fire sitting on the western horizon, we had climbed a total of four thousand feet. Together, we stood on a rocky cornice overlooking a vast and empty Bayazit plain. The wind blew with gale-like force, carrying with it the sweet scent of wild poppies and cloves.

"It's breathtaking," she said.

I agreed in silence and closed my eyes and felt the sun on my skin, the wind in my hair. The hood of my parka flapped on my shoulders like something trapped. My hair, cut militarily short, didn't do much flapping. Faye held onto my sleeve.

"There's nothing for me to hold onto," I said.

"Quit complaining and hold onto me."

I grinned. And did. We stood like that for some time. I think I could have stood like that for quite a long time.

"When will we reach Omar's camp?"

"Two days."

She nodded. We stood quietly. The wind tugged at us like a child looking for attention. "Have you ever been afraid of heights, Sam?"

"I used to be."

"Not anymore?"

"Rarely. Why?"

"Because I think I'm getting sick."

"That's our cue," I said, and led the way down from the cornice.

CHAPTER TWENTY

We were in a favorite cave of mine eating dehydrated vegetable soup, which I had expertly hydrated with boiling water. Afterward, we sipped tea and watched the snow blow across the cave's entrance. It could have been static on a TV set.

"How did you know about this cave?" Faye asked.

"It's a sort of home away from home for me."

"It's cozy, but needs some cleaning." Faye kicked at a mound of dirt covering the floor.

We both saw it. Faye's boot uncovered a small wooden pencil buried in the dirt. The sort of pencil found in libraries everywhere. I plucked it out of the dirt and studied it. The graphite point was worn to a nub, teeth marks on one end. Probably tasted horrible.

Faye reached out with a shaking hand, and I passed it over. She studied the pencil until her eyes moistened, gleaming in the firelight. "It's my father's," she said. "I'm sure of it. And he's always losing them, too."

"And apparently taking them from libraries as well," I said.

With a flashlight, I moved carefully around the cave. More footprints. All relatively fresh. I pointed to the larger of the two prints. Maybe a size fifteen. "Bigfoot lives," I said.

Faye said, "Wally Krispin. He's a smart kid who's afraid of his own shadow. How father ever convinced him to climb this mountain is any one's guess."

"Big kid," I said, running the flashlight along the length of the print. And it took a while to do so.

"Big and awkward, all knees and elbows," said Faye.

"And feet."

We were quiet, ingesting the new information. Outside, the snow streaked horizontally across the opening. A full-fledged blizzard. The wind made high pitch noises. The high-pitched noises failed to bring images of warmth and security.

"I would hate to be out in this weather," said Faye.

"Even Frosty would agree with you."

"Frosty?"

I shrugged apologetically. "It's late. My humor's on cruise control."

We watched the storm in silence. Faye held the pencil tightly. She sat straighter and with a noticeable spark in her eye. The spark of hope. She waved the pencil in front of me as if it were a magic wand and she could make her father appear. "This is a good sign, Sam Ward."

"True, but not an answer to your father's disappearance."

She lay back in her sleeping bag, clutching the pencil to her chest. She positioned her other hand behind her head in a fleshy pillow. "Answers can come later, Sam. For now, I will take what I can get."

I lay back, too, and closed my eyes and listened to the shrieking wind and knew there was no argument for hope.

* * *

It was much later when I awoke to complete silence and darkness. The storm had moved on and the fire had died. Silver moonlight poured through the cave's small opening, blanketing the dirt floor. There was enough light to see that Faye's sleeping bag was empty and that I was quite alone.

An inexplicable dread came over me, constricting my chest, tightening my stomach.

I pulled on my boots and coat, and moved over to the cave's opening. Faye's small tracks led down the slope, disappearing. She was probably on a potty break. I moved back into the cave and rummaged through my backpack and pulled on a full mountain climbing body harness and attached a coil of rope to my hip. If she needed help, I intended to be prepared. And if she didn't need help, I intended to be prepared.

I stepped out of the cave and into the cold and followed her small footprints. I moved carefully over the fresh snow. My breath fogged before me. The snow made crunching noises with each step.

I had one fundamental rule: *no one leaves on their own, not even me.* Faye had broken that rule, even for a potty break.

The wind was cold enough to hurt the bones in my cheeks. I was sweating inside my clothing. Far below, a river rushed over submerged rocks, frothing whitecaps glowing in the moonlight.

Faye's tracks continued down the slope until they moved parallel along a wide rock shelf. To my right, the mountain rose majestically in a sweep of glowing white ice. To the left, was a three hundred foot drop to the river far below. Faye's tracks continued as far as the moonlight would reach.

Fifteen minutes later I rounded a slight bend and found her sitting on a rock, crying silently. Between her fingers was the little yellow pencil. I moved towards her, boots crunching. She looked up, startled, and wiped the tears from her eyes.

"Sam?"

"Faye...." I inhaled deeply, my heart pounding in my chest. When I found my voice, I said, "We need to get back to camp. It's not safe here."

"I needed to be alone with my thoughts...I'm sorry." She paused and touched my arm. "Sam, you're shaking."

"The last time I went looking for a woman I cared about, I found her dead."

She stared up at me. Suddenly she lunged forward, throwing her arms around my waist, squeezing. A burst of air escaped from my lips. I moved my hands down her slender waist to the small of her back. When she spoke, her breath was warm on my neck, lips brushing my skin.

"I didn't mean to worry you, Sam." She looked up, her wet eyes searching my face. "You care about me? But I thought you hated me."

"Why would I hate you?"

"For dragging you out here on this wild goose chase, for breaking the law—and because I can be a pain in the —"

"You didn't exactly put a gun to my head."

"But you would rather be anywhere but here, I just know it."

"Right here is pretty good."

"Yes, it is." Faye squeezed me tighter. Suddenly, she cocked her head like a puppy, listening. "What's that?"

I heard it too. A distant rumbling, like a runaway freight train. Gradually, the sound increased and became more distinct. Smaller rocks along the ledge bounced and rattled, and snow from above sifted down. Faye looked up into my face. "Sam, what is it?"

I set my jaw. "Avalanche."

* * *

It was still too dark to see much of anything, but the avalanche was coming, as surely as if we were standing in the path of stampeding buffaloes. And it would only be gaining momentum, accumulating more and more followers like a Satanic cult.

We were completely exposed in either direction along the featureless rock shelf. *Nowhere to run to, baby.* With sickening dread, I realized there was only one option.

Faye suddenly pointed up, mouth widening in a silent scream. I turned and saw it. A billowing cloud of ice bearing down on us, moving impossibly fast. We were, of course, directly in its path.

I faced the river fifty feet below. Five stories, roughly. Could we survive such a fall into water? I didn't know. The current foamed and churned like molten silver. I kissed Faye hard. Her blazing eyes told me she knew what we had to do. And as the thunder filled my head and the ground began to crumble away, we jumped out into the night air.

* * *

We fell at a terrifying rate, the walls of the canyon flashing by in a blur. I heard myself screaming, but never once did I lose my grip on Faye. Wind blasted over my ears. My jacket flapped like a failed parachute. Below, the river continued to widen rapidly until we hit the surface hard, feet first. Surrounded by tiny white bubbles, we plunged straight down to the sandy bottom, where Faye finally broke loose from my grip. We tumbled over and over like rag dolls, and as the powerful current swept us away, I glimpsed briefly a mountain of ice filling the river behind us like a frozen dam.

I pushed off the river bottom and streaked through the water, air bubbles escaping from my nostrils. A large chunk of ice flashed by like an albino meteoroid. I broke the surface, gasping. Fighting to keep my head above the frothing waves. I scanned the churning surface for Faye, calling out her name. The water was freezing and choppy. I gulped large amounts as I shouted her name.

To either side of the river, the water line was lowering, revealing glistening mud banks. A white chalky line indicated where the river had once been at its most abundant. Lowering rapidly, the source of the river dammed, the water was already a dozen feet below the chalky indicator.

Then I saw her, bobbing up and down in the currents, coughing. I kicked in her direction, dodging a frozen cannonball hurtling through the currents. She saw me, shouted my name, then promptly disappeared below the black surface. I dove in and swam blindly until my groping hands found her narrow waist. I pulled her into me, and we broke the surface, gasping like newborns. She clawed at me as if I were a human buoy.

"Easy now," I said.

I did my best to keep both our heads above the water. Mostly, I was successful. The shore was still thirty feet away, which was discouraging at best. But the river was rapidly diminishing with the accumulation of ice. I decided to hold our ground, so to speak, and tread water until the river ran itself out. Shortly we began to eddy, swirling in a sort of watery waltz. Then I felt bottom, or more accurately, a moss-covered boulder, and in another moment I was able to stand. As the river continued to lower, we ended up sitting together on the moss-covered boulder. Faye promptly vomited water, her body spasming with the effort. When she was done, she rested her head on my shoulder.

"Not my finest hour," she said, wiping her mouth.

"Reminds me of prom night," I said.

The night was silent, although the mountain still made grumbling noises. High above dark clouds swept across a star-filled sky.

"I feel like we're on a tiny island in the middle of the river," said Faye.

"Except there's not much of a river now."

Faye coughed up more water, finally emptying her lungs. She rubbed her chest. "God that burns." Then she glared at me. "What took you so long, Sam Ward? I could have drowned out there."

"A hero's job is to save in the nick of time," I said.

The river was nothing more than a trickling stream wending its way through the narrow canyon. My eyes followed it back to the ice wall. Water sloshed over the frozen fortification. The whole thing seemed unsteady at best. "C'mon," I said. "We need to get out of here."

We slid off the boulder and sludged through the muck. Snails crunched underfoot. Creatures, glistening in the moonlight, flopped frantically. Because we were soaked to the bone, the wind appeared colder than it was. I wondered if heroes shivered. I knew that the river, which wound through the bottom of the limestone canyon, was often banked by steep, towering walls. It was no different here. Finding a way out of the river might prove to be a problem, especially if we needed to do so quickly, which was beginning to be the case.

As we moved forward, I looked back over my shoulder. Water poured over the dam as it rapidly melted and crumbled away. The dam pulsated like a giant frozen heart.

I grabbed Faye's hand. "C'mon!" We moved rapidly, slipping, looking for an opening within the bank. Long, wiry grasses clung to our ankles.

Suddenly, behind us, came the sound of a thunderclap, as if lightning had struck directly overhead. Or the boom of an ocean wave pounding the surf. The sound reverberated violently down the canyon's steep walls. The ice dam had been compromised. Despite ourselves we stopped and looked back.

Water gushed through the ice with supernatural malignancy, the watery stampede spreading from bank to bank. Like a desert flashflood, it would obliterate anything in its path. I yanked on Faye's hand, and we ran before the floodwaters.

There, to our right, the mud bank dropped to about fifteen feet. A tangle of roots grew out from the bank to dip down into the river. I grabbed a slimy root and stepped up onto the mud. Faye did the same, until she lost her footing and fell backwards into the muck. I looked behind us. Water ripped through the canyon like hounds on the hunt.

I jumped down and helped Faye back onto the mud wall, lifting first her hips, then her posterior until she had pulled herself to safety. Next, I jumped up onto the wall and grabbed a root and pulled. My boots dug into the mud bank. I could *feel* the water coming, sensed it breathing down my neck like something feral and hungry, feel the spray of water on my face and hands—

I ducked my head and closed my eyes and held onto a thick elderberry root as a tremendous force slammed into me—

Water filled my mouth and nostrils.

Instinctively, I reached up with one hand, searching blindly for the next root. But something hit my shoulder—perhaps ice—and almost tore me loose. I held on by one hand. I couldn't breathe.

Maybe I should let go, I thought, *and take my chances*.

But to let go was to drown or bash my skull against one of the many rocks strewn along the riverbed. My hand searched for the next root. Found it, pulled. My next grab was not a root, but cold flesh. It was Faye, and with her help, I lifted my head out of the currents and flopped over onto the mud bank, gasping. There, I turned my head and vomited the water that filled my lungs.

"You're right," I gasped, rubbing my burning chest. "It burns like hell."

I closed my eyes, exhausted, and wanted to sleep forever.

CHAPTER TWENTY-ONE

Hours later, with the morning sun strong on our backs, we sat together and watched the river. We were both in our long underwear, which wasn't as exciting as it sounds. Our jackets lay open next to us, drying, as were our boots and socks. Faye's head was resting against my shoulder and I was chewing on a blade of grass, idly wondering how many bugs, sheep and goats had chewed on this same blade of grass.

"You okay?" I asked Faye for the tenth time.

"Yes," she answered. "For the hundredth time."

Apparently, Faye Roberts was prone to exaggeration. Three hundred yards upriver, snow and ice continued to sift down over the ledge in a fine spray of sugar. These were the stragglers, trailing behind the avalanche. Some of the ice floated past us like miniature icebergs.

"Doesn't look so scary when you see it one piece at a time," I said.

Faye was silent. "Why did the avalanche strike, Sam?"

"Most avalanches strike either during or just after a storm, especially storms that dump a lot of snow. Add to the mix a slope with more than a twenty-five degree angle and high winds, and you have a very typical recipe for an avalanche. All of which were in place last night. We were in the wrong place at the right time."

"I'm so sorry."

I shrugged. "Ice under the bridge."

She snuggled a little closer to me. "Where does this river lead?" she asked.

"The Ahora Gorge," I said.

"How often have you traversed this river?" she asked.

"Rarely," I said.

"Why?" she asked.

"It's called Bear River for a reason."

"What a mess," she said, running a hand through her sun dried hair. "And it's all my fault." "So, Miss Roberts, what did we learn from this lesson?"

She stood and held her hand over her heart as if she were giving the Pledge of Allegiance. "No one goes out on their own, not even the great Sam Ward."

"You college professors learn quick."

She ignored me, concern suddenly crossing her face. "What about our gear?"

I shook my head. "We leave it. It would be another day and half to climb out of this canyon even with adequate climbing gear, which I lost in the dip in the river. No, we'll follow the river to the Ahora Gorge."

"But what do we eat?"

"Anything we can find."

Faye made a face. "What about water?"

I undid a leather pouch attached to my belt, and laid out in the grass my pocketknife, a small first-aid kit, and a plastic hermetically sealed container with small pellets. I pointed to the pellets. "Emergency iodine pellets," I said. "To purify drinking water. All good guides should have them handy."

"Luckily, you just happen to be a good guide."

"Luckily."

* * *

With our jackets and boots dry, we followed an animal trail which ran parallel to the riverbank. Thick foliage lined the shore: rushes, reeds, tamarisks and even buttercups. The canyon walls, disappearing up into the sunlight, were salmon-colored and reflected the noon sun like a giant mirror. A narrow strip of sky shimmered between the towering cliffs, like a blue sky river.

The path was heavily overgrown, and almost immediately I was forced to stop before a particularly dense section of reeds and rushes. A machete would have been nice. I suggested that we backtrack and search for a more accessible route. She said fine, you're the guide. Faye's hair was plastered to her sweaty red face. I concluded that a lack of food and water, and a general sense of hopelessness had gotten her in a foul mood.

The sun glinted off the churning water. Sunglasses would have been nice, too, but they were back in the cave, like everything else. We made good progress, despite frequent back-tracking. I used my forearms as a machete, parting long branches and thick reeds. Occasionally, when the foliage became too dense and the backtracking method failed to turn up an accessible route, we were forced into the river, wading with boots in hand.

With increasing regularity I was noticing how Faye's blue polyurethane mountain climbing pants hugged her hips and buttocks. The muscles in her calves and hamstrings bulged through the material. I never realized how interesting mountain climbing apparel could look.

The river made pleasant gurgling noises, and the hum of insects filled the air. I continued to part the reeds and grasses with my forearm until finally we stepped out into an open field of dry grass. But we were not alone. I stopped, and Faye bumped into me from behind. "Hey, why are we stopping?"

I held up my hand. But it was too late. An adult female brown bear turned her massive head to stare at us from the shallows of the river. A partially masticated trout hung from her jaws. She was a huge creature, thick fur hanging down around her belly, dripping water. The trout dropped from her jaws and was swept away on the current.

That wasn't good, because she was giving up one source of food for another.

Her head dipped down and swayed from side to side, as if looking at us with alternate eyes. And then she roared, a deep-throated sound that echoed off the canyon wall behind us. I grabbed Faye's hand. "C'mon!" And we turned and ran back the way we'd come.

* * *

Faye stumbled and fell, reaching for her previously injured ankle. Behind, I could hear the bear crashing through the underbrush. I picked Faye up in my arms and moved as quickly as possible. We broke through the shrubs, and the ground became rocky, angling up toward the great limestone cliff.

My arms shook and my feet felt leaden. I could hear the rapid *click-click* of the bear's claws over the rocky earth. I didn't have to look over my shoulder to know the bear was gaining on us. I made for a cluster of boulders at the base of the pink-stoned cliff.

I helped/threw Faye onto the boulder, and as I pulled myself up, swinging my right leg onto the rock, a powerful force knocked my left leg out into space. I dropped to my elbows, clawing at the surface of the boulder. The bear snorted below.

"Sam!" Faye shrieked, gripping my forearms, giving me the leverage I needed. With her help, I flopped over onto the sun-baked rock, safe.

CHAPTER TWENTY-TWO

The bear paced before us, snorting and growling.

Faye and I huddled together as far away from the female bear as possible, our backs pressed up against the hot surface of the smooth canyon wall. When she got tired of pacing, or realized that we were not just going to sacrifice ourselves to her, she lay down in the sun, pink tongue flopping out like a big happy man-eating dog. The bear lifted her massive head to the sun, and seemed to lose interest in us.

"Treed," I said. "Metaphorically speaking."

"What now?" Faye asked.

"We wait."

Waves of heat shimmered off the granite boulder. Faye examined my left calf. The bear had ripped the material down to my skin, opening a minor wound. Blood ran steadily into my sock.

"It's going to get infected," she said. "Who knows where those claws have been."

"I'll clean it later."

There was no wind. I felt as if I were sitting in a frying pan. The bear didn't move; a frozen, hulking statue.

"Doesn't it have something better to do," said Faye, exasperated.

"This is probably the better thing to do."

"Doesn't it realize I have a father to find?"

I was pretty sure it was a rhetorical question. A small wind moved over us. Somehow it made the heat even worse.

"Is this your first bear encounter?" Faye asked.

"Third. I've discovered that bears have real issues with folks getting between them and their young. Or standing next to one of their buried meals."

Faye shuddered. "I think I'll have nightmares about bears and avalanches for the rest of my life," she said.

"Join the club," I said.

"I'd rather not. Think she might go to sleep?"

"Maybe, although bears are diurnal," I said.

"As opposed to nocturnal," she said.

"You must be a college graduate."

My pant-leg was now air-conditioned. Our shoulders were touching. I saw that Faye's hands were shaking in her lap. I reached out and gently took one and held it in my own. We said nothing for a long time.

"She's watching us," said Faye. "Do you think she's noticed that you're holding my hand?"

"She's probably waiting to see what happens next."

A steady wind swept over us. A gift from God. I half-closed my eyes and felt the wind on my skin. The half-open part watched the bear. The coming and going of adrenaline had left me exhausted.

As the sun continued to sink, and as the shadows deepened within the river canyon, my eyes threatened to close for the evening. The bear turned in a small circle and found a better position among the low grass and reeds. The reeds waved gently in the breeze.

"Looks like a big cute dog," I said. "In a man-eating sort of way."

"She's too close to be cute," Faye said.

A gray-necked bunting swooped down low and hopped across the bare rocks looking for whatever gray-necked buntings look for. It pecked into a fissure and came away with a small white seed. Satisfied, the bunting flew over the low shrubs and down to the river. If only life could be so simple.

Faye rested her head on my shoulder. I continued to watch the bear as the sun descended slowly and the night insects came out in full force and deep shadows formed within the limestone canyon. The night insects seemed to out-number the day insects.

CHAPTER TWENTY-THREE

The sun had set long ago. The night insects were busy. A pleasant breeze touched our skin and did its best to cool the warm rock beneath us.

Faye slept soundly, breathing lightly, while I drifted in and out of sleep. The bear, however, never strayed far, and each time I opened my eyes, she was there, waiting. Sometimes she would switch positions, lying on her side or back.

Once I had opened my eyes to discover she was staring up at me just a few feet from the boulder. I sat up, startled, my heart pounding. Next to me Faye stirred and made a cute sleeping noise. Wafting up from the bear was the stink of putrid fish. The stink was anything but cute.

"You need a bath," I said to her.

The bear didn't move, although her ears might have twitched. After a staring contest (in which I won), she lumbered back to the clearing and plunked back down with a groan.

Finally, after dozing for an unknown amount of time, I opened my eyes to discover the bear was gone. I touched Faye's shoulder. She awakened instantly.

"Are you ready?" I asked.

"The bear...?"

"Gone."

She sat up. "I'm ready."

* * *

We moved north along the base of the limestone cliff, away from the river and away from the bear. Pools of moonlight guided our way. I could still hear the sound of the river in the background: insistent, clean, powerful. The hum of insects filled the night air—and even my hair.

"Thirsty?" I asked after awhile.

"Very."

I changed course and headed for the river. There, frothing whitecaps gleamed under the faint moonlight, churning over unseen rocks. Most important, the river was bear-free. At the water's edge, the buzz of insects reached such a frenzied crescendo, that I just wanted to yell: *"Quiet!"*

Faye slapped her neck, looked at her hand, then wiped the bug guts in the grass. "Please tell me malaria isn't alive and well in Turkey."

"You've had your shots, right?"

"Yes."

"Good," I said. "Now think unappetizing thoughts."

To contain the water, a tortoise shell, sea shell, or a hollowed rock would have worked nicely. With none around, I improvised. I removed my jacket and unbuttoned my hood, dipping the water-resistant nylon into the fast-moving current and coming up with a hood-full of water. I added an iodine pill, waited for it to dissolve, then cinched the hood with the drawstring and swirled the contents. A moment later, I took a drink. The water had a slightly chemical taste, like drinking pool water. But most important it was quenching, and safe. I drank about half and handed the rest to Faye. She was careful not to spill.

"So what happens when you drink unpurified water?" she asked, handing back the empty hood, which I reapplied to my jacket.

I said, "In your immediate future would be cholera, typhoid and flukes, which bore into your bloodstream and live as parasites and cause diseases. Not good. Luckily, iodine tablets take care of all that."

She sighed. "So what do we do for food, sir?"

I thought about that, then removed my boots and socks and waded out into the cold river, moving slowly along the shallows.

"What are you doing?" she asked.

"Hunting," I said. "Men do these sorts of things."

A rock shifted under my bare foot. I reached into the water and felt around under the rock. Nothing but muck. I moved farther upriver. Faye kept pace along the riverbank.

"Whatever you hope to find under those rocks can just stay there. I've lost my appetite."

"I think you'll change your mind when you get hungry enough."

Another rock shifted. I stopped and pried it up and something scurried over my boot. I plunged both hands into the water, coming up with a writhing crayfish. I held it up proudly.

"Yummy," said Faye.

I ignored her and continued upriver until I found another such creature under another such rock. Back on the riverbank, I used a flat, sharp-edged volcanic rock to dig a pit. I surrounded the pit with medium-sized rocks, large enough to deflect some of the wind, but not large enough to deflect all the wind. I collected some dry grass, twigs and reeds for fuel; and finally used two smaller branches to spear the crayfish.

Now came the hard part. With my pocketknife, I struck down on a medium-sized rock, but failed to produce a spark. I struck again and again, the steel blade clashing off the rock.

"I think you killed it, Sam," said Faye. "What can I do to help?"

"Pray," I said.

She must have prayed hard, because my next swipe produced a white hot spark that caught in the dry grass. Blowing gently, the spark blossomed into a burning flower. I turned the grass over until the entire bundle was ablaze. I added the thicker reeds for kindling, and shortly we had a campfire. Ten minutes later, stomach gnawing at me like a caged rat, I set the cooked shellfish on two lotus leaves.

"They're hot," I said.

She dove in immediately. "Ouch!"

I smiled and blew on mine, then split the shell and removed the white meat. Soon, the caged rat was happy.

Faye followed my lead and took a small bite, although *bite* might have been too strong of a word. She chewed it like a mouse nibbling on cheese. Her next bite was much bigger. I think she approved. For dessert, I ate the lotus plant itself, which tasted like seaweed. Faye declined hers.

"Full?" I asked.

"Full enough not to eat my plate," she said. "How are we going to sleep?"

"We'll be fine next to the fire."

"What about bears?" she asked.

"We'll take it one bear at a time."

CHAPTER TWENTY-FOUR

There were no bears that night, and when I awoke in the morning, Faye was using my arm as a pillow, brown hair completely covering her face. I hoped she could breathe through all that. I moved her head gently as she made tiny mewing noises like a stretching cat.

Although the morning was still dark, the sky was beginning to brighten. My breath frosted before me as I added more fuel to the fire, which blazed up nicely. As Faye slept, I whittled a portion of the crayfish shell into a sharp point, then carved a small elderberry branch to the size I wanted, then wove the fibers of fresh reeds into something resembling twine, then used the twine to attach the sharpened shell to the branch. When finished, I held the contraption up for inspection.

"Cute," said Faye from behind me, voice groggy. "But what the hell is it?"

I looked over my shoulder. There was a leaf in her hair, and crease lines from my coat on her cheeks. "It's a fishing hook."

She yawned. "Of course. How silly of me to ask."

I spent the next few minutes undoing our shoelaces and then tying them together into a sixteen foot line. During that time Faye left for some privacy, returning shortly and sitting next to me. "It's beautiful up here," she said.

"No one's ever accused Mount Ararat of not being beautiful," I said.

"It would be more beautiful if we had some coffee."

"If we find some dandelions, I'll grind the roots for coffee."

Faye shook her head. "Where did you learn all this stuff?"

"On assignment with *The National Geographic*, you pick up a thing or two."

At the river's edge, the sky was now pale blue, although the sun was still hidden behind the limestone cliffs. Clear water swept quickly over smooth rocks, gurgling pleasantly. I baited the hook with crayfish entrails and tossed it near a cluster of water mint, and waited. The smell of mud and mildew was strong in the air. There were other smells, too, but I couldn't place them, try as I might. Faye stayed near the fire, watching me with her head cradled in her hands.

Twenty minutes elapsed. I shifted positions on the rock. A bright green oval leaf floated past on the current. I decided to count all the oval leaves on the current, but after ten minutes, there were no more leaves. Slow day for oval leaves.

I pulled in the hook, checked the bait, then tossed it near a small island of rocks near shore. Fifteen minutes later, something hit hard, the line zigzagging crazily. I hauled the laces in hand over hand until a silver, whiskered snout broke the surface near shore. The catfish flopped about madly, splashing like a child on vacation. With a smooth riverock and a well-delivered blow between its bulging eyes, its fighting came to an abrupt end.

Faye said, "Poor thing."

I gutted the poor thing and removed two huge filets and cooked them over the fire and we had a hell of a breakfast.

"Ideally, we smoke the rest of the fish, but we don't have the time. If the weather were cool enough the meat would last another day. But this canyon is too warm, and the meat would spoil within hours."

"So we leave it?" she said.

I took a last bite, making sure my belly was full. "Yes, we leave it." I said.

And we did.

* * *

With little excitement, we followed the river until noon, although we did come across a jackrabbit that would have made for a good lunch. I made a sort of half-hearted effort for it, knowing that rabbits generally need to be trapped. As it hopped happily away, I noticed Faye using tiny hand movements to urge it on.

"I see you were rooting for the rabbit," I said.

"It was so cute."

"When you're hungry enough," I said, "*cute* will be the last thing on your mind."

We stopped near a bend in the river. Here I found more lotus plants. Faye could barely contain her excitement. I pointed out that the rabbit would have tasted better. She ignored me. We sat in the shade of a boulder and drank the purified water from the nylon hood, and ate the lotus plants.

"How many tablets do we have left?" Faye asked.

"There's still a few," I said.

The river bubbled serenely over submerged rocks. The wind made swishing sounds through the reeds. I said, "Higher up, the snow is safe to eat, so we won't need the tablets."

"The same way rainwater is safe to drink."

I nodded. "Ideally we melt the snow, as it takes our bodies less energy to process warm water than cold water, but either way it should be safe to drink."

We moved upriver until I found a switchback trail that led up the steep canyon wall. "This is our stop," I said.

The path was no wider than a bookshelf. To make matters worse, loose rock littered the way, just in case we started getting too comfortable. Brown hawks circled above, taking the easy way.

We climbed the narrow trail steadily for a half hour. Below, the river looked thread-like. At this height, the river was too narrow and shallow to protect us should we fall.

Faye suddenly grabbed my arm and leaned back against the warm rock, breathing quickly. "I can't make it, Sam." There was panic and exhaustion in her voice.

"Sure you can," I said.

She took a few breaths. "Is that your idea of a pep-talk?"

The wind slammed us hard. I gripped her hand. The sun shone straight down onto her up-turned face, which glowed almost angelically. Then again, I could be biased. The hawk screeched, perhaps encouraging Faye onward. The wind made moaning noises not of this earth.

I waited, feeling the warmth of the wall against my back, the wind in my hair. The hawk banked to port and grew steadily smaller. It looked like a kite.

"Take as long as you need," I said.

Faye squeezed my hand, eyes closed tight. Finally, as if tapping into some inner strength, she said she was okay. I asked if she was sure and she nodded, and we moved forward again.

A short while later, the ledge opened onto a grassy plateau, and Faye sank to her knees and thanked all the gods and saints and lesser deities she had ever known or heard of.

Here, the temperature was near freezing, but we were dressed warmly. The grass was sweet on the wind, as if it had been freshly cut. Or freshly chewed. Faye looked at me, face ashen. "That was scary, Sam."

"It was," I said. "But you did a good job, Faye Roberts."

And when she had collected herself, we continued across the grassy plateau for the remainder of the afternoon.

* * *

The plateau ended in a sharp cliff, and we looked down into the massive Ahora Gorge as a mighty river surged far, far below. The cliffs were staggered and multi-colored, and seemed to have been carved by the hand of a master sculptor.

Faye held her hand to her chest. "It's beautiful."

We followed a path along the cliff's edge that afforded a perfect view into the gorge. Here, the wind was fierce and the sun was only an illusion.

And as patches of snow accumulated into larger clumps, we reached the terminus, or snout, of the Abich I glacier.

CHAPTER TWENTY-FIVE

As we lacked the crampons and climbing gear necessary to scale the twenty foot snout, we searched instead for an alternate route onto the glacier. As we walked, I explained that a snout is the forward most extension of the glacier, the same way a snout is the forward most protuberance of an animal.

"Thank you for the lecture, Sam, but I happen to know a thing or two about glaciology."

"Really? Cryptology and glaciology. That's a hell of a resume."

We came across a jumbled pile of boulders. The boulders were evidence of the glacier's immense strength, pushing the huge rocks around like toys. The boulders, however, were a perfect platform onto the glacier. We hopped from boulder to boulder until I stopped next to a young puff adder thermo-regulating in the sun. The snake was oblivious to us, soaking in as much of the sun as possible.

I pinned the adder to the rock and promptly removed its head with my pocketknife, careful of the fangs, as the teeth could still emit poison even in death. I let the blood drain steadily for a minute or two (although the blood would have been nice, too). I coiled the carcass and carried it in my hand. Here, the cold weather would preserve it nicely.

The wind blowing off the ice was cooler by at least thirty degrees. We pulled on our hoods and tied them tight and walked silently side by side. The sun cast our shadows across the smooth ice and within minutes we were surrounded by a desolate sea of white emptiness as the glacier spread before us as far as the eye could see.

Faye broke the oppressive silence. "How thick is this glacier?"

"Here, it's only a few dozen feet deep," I said, raising my voice above the wind. "But higher up, it can be as much as fifty. The peak itself, which is covered in ice year round, is two hundred feet thick."

I zipped my jacket up to my neck, and shoved my hands deep in my pockets. I let the snake hang over a shoulder. Faye shuddered at the sight. The glacier was painfully white, reflecting the sun up into our sore eyes. Sunglasses would have taken care of most of that soreness. Sunglasses were now a distant luxury.

The ice spread away from us in all directions, smooth and without much formation. The wind blew steadily, kicking up powdery snow. I shielded my eyes with my forearm.

Ahead, the glacier seemed to dip down in a slight depression, and within minutes, we stopped at the edge of a deep crevasse. The inner walls glowed wetly, reflecting the sun.

"And I assume you know all about crevasses?" I asked.

"Crevasses are rips, or tears, within the ice. As glaciers move up and down mountains, the ice separates and forms crevasses. The fissures are deep—and deadly—if one is not alert." She paused and gave me a rather flirtatious look that seemed entirely out of place but still took my breath away. "The running water you hear is due to meltwater rushing below the glacier, which forms rivers such as Bear River, which, in turn, are the headwaters to the Tigris and Euphrates Rivers."

I raised my eyebrows, impressed. "Very good, Professor Roberts. Will this be on the quiz?"

She smiled. I smiled. I took some air, filling my lungs. She had a hell of a smile.

Later, as the sun continued to set, a pea-soup fog rolled in, completely engulfing us. Without an altimeter and compass to guide the way, we had little choice but to sit it out, which we did in the middle of the ice. Faye held my hand and rested her head against my shoulder. Our polyurethane pants kept the cold and wet out. The wind blew over us with gale-like force, just in case we weren't truly miserable. My clothing flapped like a sail. The wind thundered in my ears. I tightened my hood and ducked my head and closed my eyes and listened to the fury of the wind. We were just two forlorn figures in the middle of nowhere. It was surreal and breath-taking and a little nightmarish. When the wind had finally died, I lifted my head. Thankfully, the fog was gone as well. And as the setting sun angled directly into our faces, as a mild wind scattered loose snow over the glacier as if pushed by an invisible broom, I helped Faye to her feet and started forward.

Almost immediately, we saw the tents for the first time.

* * *

The tents formed a large camp, set within a horseshoe of granite boulders, shielded from the wind and spread over perhaps five acres. To the right of camp were rows of barrack-like pup tents, room enough to house two or three men. To the left was a much larger tent that I knew to be Omar's personal and rather extravagant tent, as big as a double wide mobile home. However, it was the center tent that aroused my curiosity. Like something from Barnum and Bailey, minus the red stripes, the tent was big enough to host the Super Bowl. All activity seemed centered around this tent, as men and supplies came and went through the main entrance on the south side.

We moved from the open glacier to the relative safety of the ring of boulders. It appeared we had gone unseen.

"What now?" asked Faye.

"We wait until dark."

"Then what?"

"Then I'll tell you what's next."

As night fell, and the shadows emerged from the rocks like phantoms escaping into the night, the tents cast dark silhouettes against the clear night sky. Powerful floodlights clicked on, illuminating the entire perimeter of the camp.

While we waited, I gathered some dry grass that had withered among the boulders, then used my pocket knife to cut a notch on one end of an elderberry branch. Like a lumberjack, I sawed the notch with a similar branch until the heat ignited the surrounding tinder. The fire, soon crackling, was built low into the boulders, which diffused the rising smoke. With luck, it should go without detection.

I held the snake over the small blaze; it crackled and popped in my hands. It smelled like used oil, but that didn't stop my stomach from growling.

"Smells awful," said Faye, shoving her nose in the crook of her arm.

I cut off a large chunk for her. Inside, the meat was snow white. She stared at it with open revulsion. Grinning, I took a bite or two. "Tastes like chicken."

She held the chunk of snake meat with her thumb and forefinger, examined it up close. "What about the skin?" she asked.

"Don't eat the skin."

"Then why did you leave the skin on?" Her face was white, pale in the moonlight.

"The skin locks in the juice."

"Oh, God."

She nibbled at the rubbery meat. Juice oozed down her chin. She ate perhaps one mouse-sized bite in all.

"How is it?" I asked.

Before I could get the words out, vomit launched from her mouth and immediately extinguished the fire. We were thrown into complete darkness.

"That good, huh?"

* * *

The moon shone down like a pale cycloptic eye, its silver light touching down on everything, although we were safely hidden within the shadows of the boulders. Faye was breathing hard in the thin mountain air. So was I. After all, we were nearly twelve thousand feet above sea level and oxygen was sparse at best. The wind picked up and whistled through the small openings in the rock, and brought with it the inviting smell of a fire from somewhere within camp. On the distant horizon, a lumbering cloud slowly approached on the wind, spilling across the sky like an oil slick.

The main tent rose like a Celtic monolith from the center of camp, and glowed in the artificial lights. The lights were powered by generators I could neither see nor hear. The tent's fabric flapped wildly in the increasingly cold wind, which numbed my own lungs with each breath. I would kill for a hot cup of joe. I would kill for *hot* anything. The smaller tents all flapped in unison with each gust of wind.

"I'm hungry," said Faye.

"There's more snake. We didn't touch the tail."

"That's not funny, Sam Ward."

"But I thought archaeology professors will eat just about anything."

"You're thinking of Indiana Jones, Sam. And if I have to keep Dr. Quincy out of any arguments, then you have to leave him out, too."

I grinned. It was probably too dark for her to see me grin, but I did so anyway.

"So what do we do next?" she asked.

"We need to find some answers."

We heard it coming from the west, a distant pulsing thunder that rolled across the open ice plateau. Approaching rapidly was a low-flying helicopter, bearing down on us like an owl hunting field mice. However, it turned to port and moved up the mountain. A typical military-issued helicopter, it was an Italian-built Ab-212 ASW, designed for submarine hunting and electronic warfare. It was out of place here on Ararat.

And Noah's ark, as far as I knew, wasn't a submarine.

The chopper settled carefully within Omar's camp, causing tents to flap crazily. The wide cabin door opened and a handful of men emerged from within the craft. First was the massive form of Farid Bastian, Omar's personal bodyguard, followed by Omar Ali, resplendent in a pure white robe that blended with the surrounding ice. A second, larger version of Omar appeared, followed by a handful of soldiers. The prince led his small entourage back to his tent.

CHAPTER TWENTY-SIX

"I would guess the thin guy with the mustache is Omar Ali," said Faye, sitting back and crossing her arms over her chest.

"The one and only."

"So what do we do now?"

"We wait for things to quiet down."

"Then what?"

"Then I'm going to find some answers, while you wait here."

"No way, Sam—" She raised her voice and made as if to stand up.

I pulled her back down. I put my finger to her lips and shook my head. The whites of her eyes glowed brightly.

"But, Sam…"

"No buts."

She made a pouty noise. It was too dark to tell, but she was probably sticking out her lower lip. "I can't just sit here."

"Yes you can," I said.

I watched the camp. All was quiet. The arrival of His Holiness seemed to be the last of the day's excitement. The temperature continued to drop. I felt as if I were inhaling tiny bits of freezing glass. I scanned the camp, looking for the person I knew had to exist.

And then I saw him.

* * *

He was dressed in white, camouflaged with his surroundings, although his dark mustache stood out like a pimple on a supermodel's nose. Strapped to his back was a menacing-looking semiautomatic weapon. He was moving slowly through the north end of camp, working his way south, down between the rows of pup tents, pausing occasionally to rub his gloved hands. From the south, he strolled west towards us. I heard Faye's breath catch in her throat, but I was confident we were still well-enough hidden. When the soldier neared the western perimeter, he stopped and rubbed his jaw—and looked directly at me.

Something must have tipped him off. A reflection of starlight on white teeth. The flash of a white palm. Our misting breaths. I reached down and eased my pocketknife from my belt. It felt horribly inadequate, but it was all I had.

He swung his weapon around and moved out into the darkness. Faye choked on her last breath and gripped my upper arm down to the bone, and whispered: *"He sees us, Sam."* Her breath was hot in my ear, and a little exciting.

"Just sit tight."

The soldier stopped and rubbed his eyes, frowning. I tried my best to blend into my surroundings, thinking rock-like thoughts. Faye's grip was becoming increasing tighter on my arm.

The guard pulled his hood away from his head and scratched his thick mane of black hair. Finally, he re-shouldered his weapon and turned away, moving back through camp at the same leisurely pace.

I let out a long sigh of relief. I hadn't realized I was holding my breath.

"That was close," I said.

Faye didn't say anything, but mercifully relaxed her hold on my upper arm. Then she leaned into me and whispered in my ear: "Why is there only one guard?"

My heart was still hammering like the king's blacksmith with a deadline. "The camp probably doesn't need more than one," I said, "Which means that whatever they're guarding doesn't affect Turkish national security."

"So it's probably not military," concluded Faye.

I shrugged. "Probably not."

"Then why is the military here?"

"The Turkish government will do that, to protect important dignitaries visiting from other countries."

I continued to watch the guard for some time, trying to discern his pattern. After forty-five minutes, I realized he had no pattern. He moved slowly one way, and then slowly another, meandering in and out of the rows of tents, pausing often to blow on his hands or light a cigarette. His heart just didn't seem to be into it. He stopped near one such tent and reached inside the flap and removed a packet of cigarettes.

I told her to sit tight. And, while she protested, I worked my way down the rocks.

CHAPTER TWENTY-SEVEN

I slipped from the shadows and crossed the open ice field, feeling naked and exposed. The twin spotlights cast my shadow in two different directions. My boots crunched loudly over the ice. An eternity later, although it had only been twenty seconds, I reached camp. I moved as stealthily as a grizzly intoxicated on fermented berries.

Once in camp, I moved low to the ground, stepping quickly from tent to tent. From within most tents came a cacophony of snores and mumbles and wheezes. Sleeping on ice is hell on the sinuses. Shortly, I was crouched before the desired tent. So far, I had gone unnoticed. I took a deep breath and eased the zipper down, and waited. Nothing stirred. No alarms. I slipped inside, leaving the flap partly open to allow for some light.

I scanned the tent quickly. Two bunks. The left contained a figure of unknown size, age or sex. Beneath the bunk was the gleaming barrel of a sub-machine gun. By the looks of it, a Russian AK-47. The right bunk was empty. A quarter would have bounced nicely on the smartly-tucked blanket.

I moved forward in a crab-like crawl, my boots brushing silently over the nylon floor. Without warning, my head banged into an unseen lantern. The loud clang of metal and glass could have woken the dead. However, the figure on the bed barely stirred, simply mumbling: "Idiot, the open flap is letting in the cold."

"The flap has let in more than that, my friend," I said.

He sat up suddenly, eyes wide in the half-light. He made a futile effort for the weapon under his cot until I pressed the blade of my pocketknife into his throat. "Do not make a sound!"

He bit my hand, tearing the skin. I shoved my fist into his mouth. He looked like a stuffed pig at a Hawaiian luau.

"I will remove my fist," I said in Arabic. "If you promise not to yell. Do you promise?"

He nodded; my fist nodded with him.

I pressed my knife blade into his throat, drawing blood. "But if you do decide to yell I will cut your throat. Then you will be dead and I will simply get what I need from someone else. Do you understand?"

He nodded.

I removed my fist. He sucked in air like a newborn. He was a young, good-looking kid.

"Very good. What's your name?"

"Hayik."

"You are a soldier?"

"Yes."

"Do you know who I am?"

He paused, turning his head slightly, scanning my face. A curious grin touched his lips. "You own the bar in Dogubayazit," he said.

"I am a long way from my bar, Hayik. I have come for answers, and I will get them from you." There was a long pause. He stared at me. I shifted my weight and got my shoulder into a better position across his chest. He wasn't going anywhere.

He shook his head. "I will give you no answers."

I respected his resolve, but there was no time for it. "You will, or you die. And you will not be dying for your honorable country. You will dying for the Arab's greed."

His eyes wavered. A few seconds later, he said, "I will not die for him." He swallowed. "Can you remove the knife?"

I adjusted the point, but kept the blade firmly against his throat. "What do you know of the American professor and his student?" I asked.

He nodded and said, "Ah."

"Speak quickly," I said, emphasizing my urgency by pressing the knife deeper into his skin. "Are they alive?"

When he spoke, he did so carefully, not wishing to make any sudden movements. "They are alive, as far as I know."

I eased the pressure. "Where are they?"

"There is a cave above camp, perhaps an hour's climb. They are there."

Hayik gave me the directions. I knew the cave all too well. "Why are they there?"

"They work for the emir as slaves, removing the rocks that block the tunnel."

"Are there guards?"

"Two."

In a quick movement I discarded the knife and slipped my arm behind his neck, pressing my hand into his right temple. I twisted his head and held him like that for many seconds. He kicked once and then lay still. A classic sleeper hold. He should be out for a few minutes. Next, I found some rags and tied his hands and feet together. I shoved another rag in his mouth, and (ever the soft-hearted fool) checked his breathing. He seemed to be doing okay.

I grabbed the AK-47 and the bottle of vodka and slipped out into the night.

CHAPTER TWENTY-EIGHT

We peered down onto a small tunnel opening from a rocky escarpment thirty feet away. Snow fell sporadically around us, fluttering like tiny white butterflies. Two guards were posted just inside the tunnel's entrance. A small fire illuminated the opening, highlighting the dark granite walls. The guards sat on folding chairs. Between them was a rickety table. They were playing cards and smoking and totally oblivious to us.

Near the entrance, off to the side, was a narrow finger of rock jutting up through the ice. The rock appeared to have been recently excavated from a drift of snow. Indeed, it looked more like an arthritic finger pointing accusingly into the sky.

Son of a bitch, I thought. *The marker.*

Faye grabbed my arm and pointed to the stone marker. "That's the marker, Sam. The finger of rock. It must have been hidden in ice all this time. This is the cave. My father is here. I know it."

As I studied the entrance, I saw myself holding my dead fiancé, the side of her head cracked open and bleeding. I saw myself burying her with my own hands. In a cave. In *this* cave.

Faye asked, "Sam, are you okay?"

I took a deep shuddering breath, and when I spoke again my voice didn't sound my own. It sounded like someone much older and far too tired. "No, I'm not okay."

"What's wrong?"

"I know this cave," I said.

Although I wasn't looking at Faye, I could feel her eyes on me. She had heard the pain in my voice and asked softly, "How do you know this cave, Sam?"

"Because it doubles as a tomb," I said. "I buried my fiancé here."

* * *

We were quiet. I studied the soldiers and the cave opening. I was pretty sure I could make out their semi-automatics leaning against the cave walls, along with other supplies, such as backpacks and flashlights. I gripped my own AK-47. One guard suddenly threw his head back and guffawed, slapping his knee. The other tossed his handful of cards disgustedly onto the table and lit another cigarette, the flare briefly illuminating his sharp chin and nose and cupped hand.

I said to Faye, "We don't have much time."

I wanted a cigarette. I wanted Liz. I wanted Faye. I took a deep shuddering breath and rolled over onto my back and felt the ice crunch between my shoulders. I looked up into the night and watched the snow blow across my face. I closed my eyes and felt each freezing fleck on my skin. "This is going to be a long night," I whispered.

* * *

I stepped out of the shadows and into the ring of firelight. I held the AK-47 loosely at my side. The two guards didn't see me at first. The glow from their fire cast my shadow behind me as I stood there. The warmth was nice on my face and hands. The soldiers were young, although one was clearly older than the other. A cigarette hung from the older one's lower lip. Both wore military green jackets with hoods on, their weapons too far away to do them any good. I cleared my throat.

They jumped comically, cards flying from their hands. Instinctively, they reached for their weapons. In Arabic, I told them that wasn't a good idea. The young one didn't listen and continued to move toward his AK-47, fingers out-stretched. I threw back the bolt of my weapon, the metallic sound echoing in the tunnel. The soldier froze. Slowly, both sets of dark eyes turned toward me. I nodded to them, ever the kind stranger.

"Good evening, gentleman," I said.

They said nothing, perhaps too shocked for words. Two of their playing cards ended up in the fire. They turned black and curled into nothing.

"Sorry about the intrusion," I said in Arabic. "But I believe you have something I want."

The oldest was in his early twenties. Thick beard. Crooked nose. He regained some of his composure and eyed me coolly. "What would that be?"

"You're going to lead me to the old man and his student."

And then I told them to put their hands behind their heads and turn around, in that order. The youngest did as he was told, but the older continued to stare at me, perhaps considering testing me. My finger tightened on the trigger. Finally he turned.

"A wise decision," I said. I called Faye over and she trotted boldly from the shadows. She had a look of expectation on her face, for she knew her father may be just around the corner. I gave the order, and the four us promptly marched into the tunnel.

CHAPTER TWENTY-NINE

As we made our way around a slight bend in the tunnel, and as the light from the fire slowly faded into the background, we were forced to use the soldiers' flashlights. The tunnel was high enough to walk through without ducking. The jagged granite walls were coated with lichen, which grew in clumps and seemed to emit a soft green light, although that could have been my imagination. The tunnel angled to the right and up. Sand muffled the sounds of our boots. The ceiling was cloaked in stygian darkness, and as we moved deeper within the tunnel, the temperature began to rise.

"It's getting warm," said Faye, loosening her collar.

"As a rule of thumb," I said, "the temperature rises five degrees for every one hundred yards in most subterranean tunnels."

Suddenly, the older sentry dropped a hand to his waist and removed an object from his hip, and started to turn, all in a blink of eye. But I was waiting for this one to try something, and so I moved quickly, smashing the stock of the rifle between his shoulder blades, knocking him forward into the sand. He got up slowly and turned, gasping for breath. I leveled the weapon at his chest.

I had knocked the wind *and* snot out of him, judging by the gleaming spittle on his thick beard. Glinting dully near his feet was a small knife. I stepped over and kicked it away, and the black-handled blade scuttled over the sand and hit the far wall with a clang.

I turned to the younger one. His hands shook over his head. "Is your friend always this stupid?" I asked, but the kid didn't answer. Asking the kid's name, rank and serial number would have gotten the same results: *nothing*.

I turned back to the older soldier. "Raise your hands up high. Good boy."

Then I stepped over and punched him solid in the face, and his head snapped back and he stumbled against the granite wall. It had been a good punch, splitting his cheek and hurting my hand. He wanted to fall, or at least slide down to his rear end, but pure hatred and stubbornness kept him on his feet. He would be a good soldier. "You challenge me again, and you die," I said. "Do you understand?"

Slowly, probably when the stars stopped flashing in his head, he nodded.

"Good," I said. "Now get moving."

I gave him a moment to find his feet, and then he stumbled forward, hands still in the air. I told the younger soldier to walk next to me. He was crying silently, tears glistening in the dark corners of his eyes.

"What's your name?" I asked.

"Harim."

"How old are you, Harim?"

"Fifteen."

"Why are you not in school?" I asked.

He stared at the weapon in my hand, then finally looked up at me. "I have never gone to school," he said.

I nodded. In Turkey, boys and girls in most rural villages did not to attend school; instead, they worked at home with their families. "Which village are you from, Harim?" I asked.

"Arsuz," he said. And amazingly, he mustered enough courage to say it proudly.

I knew of the village. It was on the southern coast of Turkey and even doubled as a minor resort area for the wealthy. Most citizens of Arsuz, and other such cities along the southern coast, were either dirt poor or in employment to the wealthy.

"Beautiful place," I said.

He nodded eagerly.

"Do you miss your home?" I asked, correctly reading the longing in his eyes.

He shrugged nonchalantly, some of the soldier still in him. "I guess."

"You are not a soldier, Harim" I stated. "So why did you become one?"

If he took any offense to my hasty conclusion, he didn't show it. "My brother is a soldier. Father is very proud of him."

I nodded, understanding. "A father's approval means much, perhaps too much," I said. "You do not belong here."

I told him to put his arms down. I slipped back and walked next to Faye as the tunnel turned sharply and we suddenly stepped into a dimly lit cave. The remains of a fire smoldered in the center of the cave. Around the fire were two sleeping forms, covered in blankets, their features indistinguishable from this distance. Farther back was a massive wall of rocks, blocking further access into the cave, the result of a previous cave-in. To the right was a small mound of dirt that marked Liz's grave. To my great relief, the mound was undisturbed. To the left was a moderate pile of scattered rocks that had been removed from the lower section of the wall of rocks.

"What are they doing here?" I asked Harim.

"They remove the rocks, to clear a way through the wall."

I nodded, then raised my voice: "Rise and shine, sleepy-heads."

From the center of the camp, two heads rose from the dirt floor. Both men had been sleeping on their arms, in rather crude fashion. One of them was an older man with a thin face and frazzled gray hair. Faye shrieked with joy and sprinted across the cave.

CHAPTER THIRTY

Her father was about what I had expected. A man in his late fifties. Gray hair worn long over his collar, parted down the middle and slightly mussed from sleep. He looked like Einstein, if Einstein had bothered to use a comb. He was dressed in dirty jeans and a dirty flannel shirt, and smelled like a stray dog. But that didn't stop Faye from wrapping her arms around the startled man, who was fumbling around with one hand near his blanket until he found a pair of wire-rim glasses, cracked in one corner. He hastily put them on, completing the look of the eccentric professor.

Wally Krispin was sitting cross-legged, knees as sharp as arrows, next to the glowing bed of coals. The student's narrow face was criss-crossed with red lines, the result of sleeping on the sleeve of his jacket. His thick brown hair was wildly disheveled, and he appeared malnutritioned—in fact both of them did. And depending on how long they had been held in captivity, that just might be a possibility. I could see that both Caesar's and Wally's fingertips were cracked with scabs. Neither seemed concerned that I was holding a very deadly weapon at the ready.

"My darling Faye," said professor Caesar Roberts, wrapping both arms around his daughter. His voice was groggy and frog-like, a combination of sleep and cold-like symptoms.

Faye said nothing. She held on tight and I could see that she was crying pretty hard. I kept quiet, although I was feeling the strong urge to get everyone moving, as our time was quickly running out. Harim seemed to be watching with interest, perhaps visualizing his own homecoming.

Wally was saying over and over that he could not believe Faye was here. But no one seemed to be listening to Wally accept me. The kid's voice was surprisingly soft-spoken. He was either shy or polite. I couldn't decide which.

Faye pulled away and nodded toward me. "Father, this is Sam Ward. He helped me find you."

Caesar Roberts looked at me, confused eyes flicking to the weapon. He turned back to his daughter. "Find me?" he asked, perplexed. "Whatever do you mean?"

Faye blinked, then looked at me for support. I shrugged in a supportive way. She said, "Yes, father, *find* you. You've been missing for a month."

He shook his head. A jolly grin spread across his face. It was hard not to like the old guy. "I haven't been missing," he said, laughing. "I've been right here."

I said, "Technically, the man has a point."

"You're not helping, Sam Ward," she said, ice in her voice. She looked at her father. "You're being held prisoner, dad. Forced to work like slaves."

"No, my dear. This is a partnership, of sorts. The emir and myself are helping one another. He provides food and supplies and Wally and I provide the labor. This is *the* cave, Faye. This is the cave on the map!" He clapped his hands excitedly.

"Father, this is crazy. There are guards outside the cave. You are not permitted to leave—ever!"

Caesar shook his head. "The guards are to keep people *out*, my dear. This is a very important operation. Much is at stake."

As he spoke, I looked at Wally Krispin. He was frowning and playing with something in his hand, turning it over and over. It was something small and plastic-like. On closer inspection, I could see that it was a baseball card, sheathed protectively in hard plastic, held together by copper screws on each corner. The player on the card could have been a young Mickey Mantle, a baseball bat resting on one shoulder. Wally held the card tight, rubbing a thumb over the plastic as if it were a talisman. Although the kid wasn't voicing his opinion, he did not appear agreeable to his professor's position.

"Valuable card," I said, stepping closer to have a look.

He looked up at me. Dirt was in his hair, in the corners of his eyes. "I collect them," he said. "But this is my favorite. 1951 Mickey Mantle rookie card. My good luck charm. It's kept me alive so far."

I looked at my watch for no real reason. It seemed the thing to do. "Kids," I said. "We should be leaving very soon."

"Father, the Arab and his men will be here at any moment. We must leave now."

"I have no intention of leaving, my dear. We are close, so very close to the ark."

Faye's jaw dropped. I looked at Harim. He was watching with wide eyes and a grin on his face. I was pretty sure he didn't understand a single word. The older one shuffled his feet impatiently, keeping his hands high in the air like a good little soldier.

I spoke up, as this was getting out of hand. "Your daughter speaks the truth, Professor Roberts. Emir Omar Ali is a killer. When he's done using you, I predict you will meet an unfortunate end on the wrong side of a cliff."

Caesar was shaking his head. "But he and the little Arabic professor has been so kind to let us—"

Wally cut him off. Although the kid's voice was soft, it was full of emotion. As he spoke, Wally avoided his professor's eyes. It was obvious Wally was unaccustomed to speaking out against the older man. "You're wrong, professor. He has *not* been kind, and he forces us to work like slaves. And he *is* going to kill us. I've heard the soldiers speaking among themselves."

"Then why haven't you said something," said Caesar.

"I *have* professor, but you choose not to listen. And what good was it anyway? There was no hope for escape. Until now. The ark is your dream, professor, not mine. I only came for extra credit." Wally stood. The kid was tall. I almost asked him how the weather was up there. "Please take me with you," he said to me. "I miss my family."

I nodded, and looked at Caesar. His confused face was an intricate display of light and shadow.

Suddenly, from behind us, came a tired but familiar voice: "Your student speaks the truth, professor. You would have done well to listen to him. You're old and foolish, and now useless. And Mr. Ward, will you please toss aside the weapon and raise both your hands over your head."

CHAPTER THIRTY-ONE

In a small tent back in Omar's camp, Faye and I sat opposite each other with our hands cuffed behind our backs. A young Kurdish soldier sat near the tent's opening, glowering, armed to the teeth. He was doing a helluva good job at looking mean and inhospitable. Just a kid with an automatic rifle and a bad case of acne. The weapon was tucked under his armpit, his index finger resting on the trigger guard. In that position, he could fire almost instantly. I advised Faye not to make any sudden movements.

"So what do you think Omar will do to us?" Faye asked.

"Do you want the sugar-coated version?" I said.

"You mean the one where you blow sunshine up my ass?"

"Yeah, that one."

She said, "Give it to me straight, Sam."

"He's going to kill us."

She inhaled deeply, chest moving forward and upward, pushing out on her jacket. I tried not to be obvious in my observational skills. She was silent, biting her lower lip. Her cheeks were sunburned to a rosy hue. A single dusty lantern hung from a hook between us, casting the shadow of her nose sharply across her face. She sighed and sat back, closing her eyes. "I think I would have preferred a little sunshine up my ass." She nodded toward the guard. "Can he understand us?"

I shrugged. "Say nothing incriminating, and try not to comment on his acne."

"I'll try to refrain from the obvious," she said. "Sam, what is Omar doing here?"

"It's difficult to say offhand. A year ago, I led him and his team onto Mount Ararat. In the evenings, after a full day of searching for the ark, we would drink together in his massive tent, which he made clear was my privilege. One evening, he confided in me that he had an overwhelming desire to make his mark in the world and to distinguish himself from his royal family."

"What do you mean?" Faye asked.

"An hereditary title proves little of a man's accomplishments," I said.

"But there are other ways to prove your worth to mankind," said Faye, perplexed. "He could have been a doctor or work with the homeless—"

"Hardly an avocation of a crown prince, don't you think? No, he chose to follow in the footsteps of the great explorers and adventures. For instance, three years ago, he attempted to circumnavigate the globe in a hot air balloon, but failed miserably when he crashed into the Pacific Ocean."

"But that's been done," said Faye.

"Exactly. So two years ago, he sought to find Noah's ark. But that expedition proved fruitless. Last year he hired me, which proved equally fruitless. But now, he is here, a third time, and apparently he means business, arranging for the entire mountain to be closed exclusively for him. Wealth has its privileges."

Voices came from outside, speaking rapidly in Arabic. Farid Bastian stepped inside the tent, which didn't leave much room for anything else. Farid dismissed the guard, who left with nary a glance back, taking with him his bad attitude and acne.

"Farid, my friend," I said. "You've come to see us off."

Snow had settled on his wide shoulders like dandruff. The man hadn't bothered to wear gloves. He reached out and touched my arm in a surprisingly gentle way. "The emir wishes to speak with you and the lady." He paused and looked at his hands. "It does not look good for you, my friend. The emir is not himself. He is irrational, and quick to make bad decisions."

"What are you saying?" I asked. This was the most talkative I had ever heard Farid, who normally stood quietly off to the side, looking big and forbidding, which he did quite well.

"You are a threat to his operation."

"Then we do not wish to stand in his way," I said. "We came for the professor and student. Give them to us and we will be gone, and Omar can play his games."

"It is not that simple," said Farid quietly, shaking his massive head. He always spoke quietly, but carried a big stick. Hell, he *was* the big stick. "The game is more complicated than you think, my friend."

"Who's the big guy with the emir?" I asked.

Farid's lips curled in distaste. "He is the Emir Kazeem Ali of Riyadh."

"Omar's brother?" I asked.

Farid shrugged. "Kazeem was sired from one of the king's many wives. I have lost track which. But, yes, his half brother."

"You don't seem particularly fond of him," I said.

Farid shrugged, and that was all I would get out of him. "We've had our differences in the past."

I changed the subject. "Why are we being held prisoners?"

Farid shook his head. He looked like a big sad elephant. "I'm just the hired help, remember? Come, the emir will show you himself."

CHAPTER THIRTY-TWO

Emir Omar Ali sat behind a long oak desk. The desk, bare, save for a laptop computer and a battery-powered desklamp with a pliable neck, seemed entirely out of place on the glaciers of Ararat. Faye and I stood before the emir, Farid guarding the exit, a pistol jutting from the bodyguard's hip. I was confident Farid could draw and shoot before I took two steps. An Arab gunslinger.

The emir was typing slowly on the laptop, hunting and pecking. The monitor glowed in eyes that seemed listless and dull. Omar wore a plain white robe, open at the neck, revealing a dark nest of curling chest hair. His mustache, as always, was immaculate. Omar had not yet bothered to acknowledge us.

Leaning casually against the tent's center pole was a larger version of Omar, and dressed similarly. Emir

Kazeem Ali. The young prince watched us contemptuously, lips turned down. His dark eyes flashed from under an equally thick brow. His eyes moved casually over myself, lingering longer on Faye. His lips curled up, and he inhaled deeply, massive chest filling out like a dirigible. Obviously, he had seen something he liked.

Kazeem pushed himself away from the pole, and stepped lightly before us, casting me the merest of glances. I could have been nothing more than a road sign to nowhere. He eyed Faye slowly, molesting her with his eyes. Then he admired the view from behind.

The big son-of-a-bitch reached out and stroked Faye's auburn hair, and she cringed and leaned into me. I sensed a tiger stalking his prey, and I moved to knock his goddamn block off when one of the guards shoved the barrel of his weapon into my neck.

Suddenly a large hand fell across Kazeem's bare forearm, followed by Farid's deep voice: "You will not touch her, emir Kazeem."

Slowly, deliberately, Kazeem allowed Faye's hair to slip between his fingers. He turned calmly and faced Farid. The two massive men could have been professional wrestlers. "You dare threaten me, nomad?"

"You will not touch her," repeated Farid, "by orders of Emir Omar Ali, your brother."

Kazeem's chest rose and fell rapidly, perhaps as adrenaline filled his bloodstream. "You were plucked from the desert, where you washed your hair with camel urine, to do our bidding, which does not include carrying out orders against me."

Farid, to his credit did not let go of the arm.

Omar snapped shut his laptop and leaned back in his swivel chair, crossing his arms over his shrunken chest—a chest that had once been strapped with muscle. "Enough you two. Farid, unhand my brother. You know better than that."

Farid did as he was told.

"And, Sam, you would do well to remember that Kazeem is hot-tempered and prone to violence, and I can control him only so far." Omar chuckled. "Kazeem is threatened by Farid. You see, Farid may be the only man in my country who does not fear Kazeem. Someday, I will let them go at it, and see who's left standing."

Kazeem grunted and stepped away, knocking Farid with his shoulder. The young prince disappeared through the tent opening. Omar turned his attention to me. "You're supposed to be dead, Sam Ward," he said evenly. "Or so I was told. Killed in an avalanche."

"Courtesy of your men, I presume."

"You presume correctly. The avalanche was not an accident or coincidence, and would have been a fitting end for a man such as yourself." He shook his head sadly with great regret.

"It's the thought that counts," I said. "We were followed?"

"We knew you were coming the moment Miss Roberts arrived in town. It was just a matter of time."

I leveled my stare at the Arab prince. "You have no reason to imprison us, emir."

"Regrettably, I cannot permit you to leave, Sam."

Faye stepped forward, balling her fists, but Farid calmly reached out and restrained her. She tried to shrug loose from his grip, failed. She had guts. "Not only have you kidnapped us, but you've murdered a defenseless shepherd. Are the Turkish authorities aware of the atrocities being committed on their mountain?"

Omar's lips tightened. I think most of us were holding our collective breaths, except Faye, who was breathing through her nose like a raging bull through the streets of Pamplona. "I *am* the authority on this mountain, Miss Roberts. When you speak to me, you speak to judge, jury and executioner. You would do well to remember that. And the shepherd was not meant to die. He was to serve as a lesson for the others to keep away." Omar suddenly stood. "Come. You will follow me."

* * *

The eastern sky was brightening from a midnight black to a midnight purple. Snow continued to drift across camp in a satiny veil with irregularity and little enthusiasm. We were led from Omar's private tent to the massive tent that dominated the center of camp, rising before us like a skyscraper of white nylon. The whole thing was anchored in place by stakes so massive that the Titanic would have been kept at bay. The flapping of hundreds of square yards of white nylon fabric was thunderous—the sound of ocean waves crashing against a rocky shore.

At the entrance stood a handful of soldiers, submachine guns strapped to their backs like arrows in a quiver. Omar and his Merry Men.

The wind pressed the emir's robe against his frail body, revealing his narrow, emaciated frame, as his headcloth flapped behind him like a cape. Omar was inconspicuously hanging on to the arm of his bodyguard, should the emir be blown away on the wind. Farid was carrying an odd sort of metal suitcase that appeared quite heavy, even for him. There was another man I noticed for the first time. He was small, with round features. His glasses had ice on them, which he rubbed with a gloved finger. He looked nervous and anxious.

Faye's hand found mine, and squeezed. I squeezed back. Her fingers were frighteningly cold. I lifted her hand up to my mouth and let out a steady stream of hot air from deep within my lungs to warm her fingers.

As Omar spoke, there was a brief flicker of his old self: slick, cool, and ready to conquer the world. He grinned wickedly, looking remarkably like a ringmaster at a circus, about to introduce the next freakish display of human deformity. All he needed was a top hat and a whip. Omar motioned with his hand and Farid pushed aside the tent opening.

Omar said, "This way, if you please."

CHAPTER THIRTY-THREE

Powered by humming generators, a dozen or so spotlights dazzled my eyes upon entering the massive tent. I blinked back the tiny black spots that swirled across my vision, like flies over a picnic lunch. In the center of the tent there appeared to be a tangle of black metal. At first it was impossible to discern what the hell it could be, especially with the shadows created by the powerful floodlights. But then recognition set in. Faye must have come to the same conclusion at roughly the same time because she squeezed the hell out of my hand. A knuckle or two popped, both mine.

Before us was a blast from the past. It was a reusable mobile MAZ-543 transporter-erector-launcher, or TEL. I knew it well. Straight from the Persian Gulf War. In the war, I had flown my share of sorties: the endless search for

Iraq's ballistic missiles. The infamous Scuds. Nowadays, Scuds fly further and more accurate. And can carry increasingly more dangerous payloads.

The black metal of the static launcher gleamed dully as workers swarmed over the aperture, like termites over a mound. Although such launchers were mobile, and could often be pulled behind a truck, it took a lot of planning to haul one up twelve thousand feet, while not alerting the Turks themselves.

"I assume the launcher was assembled piece by piece over a matter of months," I said.

"You assume correctly, Mr. Ward. Let me assure you, the Turks are unaware that a launcher has been erected in their backyard. Ironic that their soldiers protect my privacy, even as I plan their destruction"

"But why here on Ararat?" I asked.

"The perfect cover. The local Kurdish freedom fighters have a huge base here on Ararat, even *within* Ararat in some locations, well hidden from the Turks. These rebels provided the launcher and missile—and I provided the final ingredient."

I looked again at the gleaming metal case in Farid's hand. The case was heavy even for him. I nodded as realization dawned on me. "You're not planning to launch a conventional warhead."

Omar's eyes blazed. He looked truly insane. "No, Sam."

Faye turned to me. "What do you mean?"

"The emir's gotten his hands on a weapon of mass destruction. Possibly nuclear. Russian-built, no doubt.

Auctioned to the highest bidder and all that. Nothing that a lot of money can't buy."

Faye stared at the metal. "Can it be that small?" she asked. "My God, it's no bigger than a school backpack."

Omar grinned. "To create the high temperature required to start the fusion reaction within a thermonuclear bomb, my dear, one needs a space no larger than a coffee thermos." Omar turned to me. "However, Mr. Ward, this is *not* a nuclear warhead."

"What is it then? Chemical? Biological?"

"The scientific term for it is *bacillus anthracis*."

"Anthrax," I breathed.

"Yes, Sam. Anthrax. Only the United States and Russia have successfully converted this biological toxin into a weapon of mass destruction. Others have tried. Iraq has made a laughable attempt at it, but they have failed to succeed in distilling the anthrax into powder form. Russia, in particular, has perfected the process of converting the toxin into powder form, which makes it easily inhaled. On a good day, with the wind in my favor, the toxin spores could kill hundreds of thousands of people." Omar paused. His face was flushed, burning with intensity. "And shortly, once my ballistics technician arrives, the anthrax warhead will be fitted and armed." He grinned. "The final peace of the puzzle."

"For a night launch, I assume," I said. A night launch could go undetected, with little chance of noticeable emissions.

"In fact, I'd hoped for tonight, but I've been informed that my ballistics expert is late. I'd do the job myself if I could. Unfortunately, I'm no expert in biological warfare."

"Unfortunately," I said.

At the rear of the tent, a sort of golf cart wobbled in, driven by a shivering Kurdistan worker. He was pulling a rattling flatbed. On the platform, covered in a blue plastic tarp, was a cylindrical object four feet in length and as wide as a man's body. It was the Scud missile. Although not the most flattering name it is the missile of choice in the Middle East. North Korea and Russia make them dirt cheap, cranking them out the way Nike cranks out Air Jordans.

"So who's getting the bomb?" I asked.

Omar was silent. Behind me the cart containing the Scud missile came to a screeching halt. Sub-zero temperatures are also hell on brake pads.

"Istanbul."

* * *

"I assume you have good reason for obliterating one of the world's oldest and most significant cities," I said.

Omar shook his head, staring off into the middle distance. "I do not need to justify myself to a prisoner." He paused. "But I will tell you a little story. Forty-five years ago, the Turks, in their vehemence to eradicate the troublesome Kurds, destroyed a simple village in Eastern Turkey. There were few survivors. One was a small boy who found his home in burning ruins. There he saw the burned corpses of his brothers and sisters. His mother, still alive, writhed as the skin pealed from her face. She died in agony.

"Later, in an orphanage, the boy would meet a very generous woman. In fact, she was a Saudi princess, a woman with no children of her own. A woman with a huge heart. Touring the ravaged countryside, she would take pity on the homeless, family-less boy. He would return with her to Saudi Arabia. There, he would live a fairytale life of wealth and privilege. Although never formally adopted, as this is prohibited in Islam, or even a *real* prince, his new mother loved him with all her heart. But her love was not enough to erase his pain."

Omar's eyes glistened in the artificial light.

"Yes, Sam. I'm here for revenge."

* * *

"Ballistic missiles are visible to intelligence agencies," I said. "Their flight paths can be predicted, and warnings can be provided to their intended targets. You will lose the element of surprise, emir. Not to mention defensive systems that can come on line for missile interception."

"All true, Mr. Ward. But I will take my chances. Even with proper warning, it is difficult to evacuate three million people."

Faye stepped forward, fists clenched, breath steaming before her in a bullish sort of way. "Then why keep my father prisoner? Why use him and his student to search for the ark?"

Omar flicked his dark gaze to Faye. "I would have disposed of the old fool and his student long ago but Al Sayid found a use for them."

"Who the hell is Al Sayid?"

The portly little man I had first seen outside ambled forward. He pushed his glasses up with a stubby middle finger and blinked rapidly behind them. "That would be me, my dear." He spoke in flawless English.

"Who are you?"

"I'm Professor Al Sayid from the university in Riyadh."

Omar said, "The professor is an avid ark researcher like your father. In fact, Al Sayid added the necessary validity to convince the Turks to close the mountain."

Al Sayid's metal framed glasses slipped to the end of his nose. He promptly pushed them back up. "Your father is onto something. That cave of his is most unusual, and may prove invaluable. But I'm afraid we are down to our final days. Time is short."

"Frankly," said the emir, lip curling with disdain, "I could care less about this blasted ark. Once the missile is launched, I will be happy to go and leave this wretched mountain behind." He paused a beat. "Then I can die happy."

"You and three million people," I said.

He stared at me for a long moment. "For now, Mr. Ward, you will help the others clear the tunnel, which will give me some time to decide your fate."

I sucked in air. "And what of Miss Roberts?"

"She will stay here, with me, of course. The cave is no place for a lady. Farid, take her away." He paused. "And this time do not let this one escape."

The words should have been meaningless, and perhaps they were. But I stopped breathing, and even my heart seemed to pause. But it was Farid's expression, the look of pained regret that showed in the deep furrows of his brow that made me realize my reaction was valid. Farid inhaled deeply, let it out in a steady stream that fogged before him.

I turned to Omar. "*Who* escaped, emir?"

Omar flipped his hand casually. "It is of no concern to you."

I heard the blood pounding in my ears, felt the throb of it behind my temples. *"Who?"*

"Guards," said Omar, raising his voice and looking down at his fingernails. "Take him away. He has much work to do."

A hand reached for me and I knocked it away. Rifles swung in my direction. I ignored them. I took a step toward the emir, and this time a much bigger hand held me back. Farid's hand.

He looked at me with a pained expression, and for the first time I saw real emotion behind those lifeless eyes. "I am sorry, Sam. It was an accident."

"What do you mean, Farid?" I asked, but I knew what he meant. I had intuitively known all along, I suppose.

Omar looked up, alarm on his face. "Farid, I command you to be silent."

The big Arab ignored his master, perhaps for the first time in his career. "It happened three years ago during our first visit to the mountain. The girl had wandered too close to camp, and so our guards picked her up for routine questioning."

"Silence, Farid!"

"She was questioned repeatedly. Had she overheard our plans? She said she had not, but we could not know for sure. I, for one, was certain that she had harmlessly blundered near our camp."

"*Farid!*"

"But then she escaped from her tent, and I was ordered to track her down and bring her back."

My throat constricted, as if seized by a hand.

Farid's gaze was penetrating and unwavering. His voice was surprisingly gentle. "But when I found her hours later at the bottom of a ravine, she was already dead. A rockslide, I believe. Sam, I'm sorry." The big man looked mortified. But I didn't fault him. He was only doing the emir's bidding.

I collapsed to my knees, tried unsuccessfully to breathe. The cold of Ararat seeped up through the fabric of the tent, up through the material of my pants, numbing my kneecap. Finally, I looked up at Omar, and when I spoke my voice shook and did not sound my own. "You are responsible for her death."

Omar shrugged and looked away. "She should not have been on her own. As far as I see it, Mr. Ward, *she* was the cause of her own death. And perhaps you, too."

I shot to my feet in one explosive movement and pounced on the emir, hands going straight to his throat. Behind me came the bolt actions of automatic rifles, armed and leveled at me. Faye screamed. The emir gurgled. I forced him up against the steel frame of the launcher, eyes bulging pleasantly from his wicked face. I concentrated all my strength into my hands and fingers in an effort to snap his neck.

Until I sensed a shadow rise behind me. And from the corner of my eyes, Farid raised his fist high and struck down like the Hammer of God.

Lights out.

CHAPTER THIRTY-FOUR

I awoke slowly from the land of the dead, head pounding. Professor Caesar Roberts was holding a wet rag to my head, a bemused grin on his face. I was beginning to think he *always* had a bemused grin on his face.

"How long," I said, struggling to regain use of my tongue. "How long have I been out?"

"Two or three hours," said Caesar, a sparkle in his eyes. "At least since they dragged you in here and deposited you like a sack of potatoes."

When I finally stood, a wave of nausea swept over me, and I almost disgorged what little food I had eaten during the past few days. Wally sat cross-legged next to the fire, rocking gently, staring down into the lapping flames as if they held the secret to his escape. He didn't look at me, and seemed lost in his own fear. I could see that his

Mickey Mantle baseball card, once sheathed in plastic, was now melted and blackened in the fire pit. I pointed to the remains of the card and asked Caesar what had happened.

"A soldier threw it in the fire," said the professor. "He said it was punishment for the beating you gave him in the tunnel."

"Dammit."

A cold draft worked its way over my skin. Faint morning light issued from the tunnel behind, pushing my shadow before me. In the muted half-light, Caesar and Wally looked ghoulish and pale, like two creatures from a Jules Verne novel. I wondered how long since they had seen the light of the sun.

"Pardon me if I seem insensitive to your pain," said Caesar, the smile on his face wavering, "but where the hell is my daughter?"

My head pounded from the inside out. There seemed to be a faint ringing in my skull. It had been a hell of a punch by Farid. "She's with Omar." I thought of Liz Cayman, inadvertently dead at the hands of Omar. I did not blame Farid. But I would hold the emir responsible. He would pay for stealing my fiancé's life. My life. *Our life together.*

Caesar said, "You okay, Sam?"

"No."

The professor exhaled, looking miserable. "Join the club. I should have known she would try something like this. With her, nothing surprises me. She's quite capable of anything. So what do we do now?"

"I'm still working on that one, professor. First I need to stop the ringing in my head. Either that, or someone get the damn phone."

While I sat there with my head in my hands, Caesar caught me up to date. "We used a map I had created from the journal of Jans Struys. By coming up from the north, we had inadvertently skirted Omar's camp." The map had indicated that this was the legendary cave, but there was no marker, as proclaimed by Struys in his memoir. Frustrated but undaunted, Caesar began hacking away at the ice until he'd uncovered the fabled finger of rock. The marker. Elated, they had found their cave, only to discover that a massive cave-in had blocked further access into the tunnel. Omar and his men appeared shortly thereafter. In summary, Caesar said, "I can see clearly now what I failed to see for the past month. By offering ourselves as workers, I had managed to spare our lives. That was my one good decision in a long series of very bad ones. Now the bastard has my daughter."

"Your daughter is safe for now," said a voice behind us.

We turned. Omar stood in the cave opening, out-of-breath, hanging by the arm of his bodyguard. The light from the fire cast the emir's eyes into twin pools of bottomless pits. "But it is your own well-being that should concern you. Mr. Ward, will you please accompany me?"

* * *

We stood together in the passageway, with Farid off to the side. As always, the bodyguard stared blankly into the near distance, managing somehow to see everything and nothing at once. The stock of his pistol jutted from the inside of his robe. Either that or he was happy to see me. He stood between me and the emir, and it was obvious that I would not get another chance at the emir's neck.

I waited silently as Omar studied his perfectly manicured fingernails. He looked ghastly in the muted light: deep shadows in the hollows of his cheeks and temples. Finally, he said, "I'm prepared to make you an offer, Mr. Ward."

It took all my effort to keep my voice steady. "What offer?"

"You were a photojournalist, Sam. A very good one, from what I hear. I want you to write my story before I die, which I imagine will be soon." He paused, and his dark eyes stared into my own. "I want the world to know why I have done what I am about to do. I do not want the world to think I'm an animal."

"But you *are* an animal, emir. The worse kind: *you kill the innocent*."

Anger flared briefly on his face. His mustache twitched. Farid glanced his way, then back to staring at the wall. "I kill for a higher purpose, Sam. I kill to end the war on Kurds. Much like the bombs dropped on Hiroshima and Nagasaki ended World War Two. Yet the genocide on the Kurds continues. The world refuses to see that. Now they will. I will force them to take notice, to wake up. To acknowledge the problem."

I snorted. "You're doing this out of revenge, plain and simple. An eye for an eye."

The emir's eyes blazed. "You trivialize at your own peril, Sam. My hunger for personal justice, for the brutal murder of my family, takes nothing away from the fact that heinous crimes are enacted on my people on a daily basis."

Omar leaned against the tunnel wall. If Farid was interested in our conversation he showed it by appearing completely uninterested. Omar folded his arms over his chest and stared at me with tired eyes.

"And what's in it for me?" I asked.

"I will leave you a fortune, Mr. Ward. I will give you a portion now, and the rest when the article is published to my satisfaction."

"And what of Faye and the others?" I asked.

Omar shook his head sadly.

I looked him directly in the eye. "I would rather deal with the devil, emir."

He sighed and nodded. "I was afraid you'd say something like that. You give me no choice, Mr. Ward."

I stepped forward. Out of the corner of my eye, Farid shook his head. *Stepping forward was not a good idea.* I stopped and clenched my fists. "What have you done with Faye Roberts?"

"She is safe."

"From your brother?"

"He has been kept at bay. For now."

I glanced at Farid and he nodded reassuringly. *Yes, she was safe.*

I narrowed my eyes. "I will kill you, emir, if any harm comes to her."

"When you are dead, Mr. Ward," said Omar, turning his back on me, "you will hardly be in a position to carry out your threat."

CHAPTER THIRTY-FIVE

We spent the remainder of the day removing rocks and digging with shovels. Most of the rocks were huge, and seemed to be cemented together. We used wheelbarrows to deposit the debris on the south side of the cave. I never mentioned the significance of the small mound on the north side of the cave. And much later, as the long day turned into evening and the evening turned into night, a guard tossed in a leather satchel.

"Dinner," said Caesar.

It was our only meal of the day, scraps of fatty meat and bones and chunks of hard bread. A canteen was included. We ate and drank in silence, although I noticed Wally simply poking at his food, his face long and drawn. He seemed to be retreating into himself, having given up hope for escape. The three of us were filthy enough to make a bar of soap nervous.

While we ate, I pointed to the excavated opening in the cave wall. "Soon, we'll need to support the walls and ceiling with timbers, or risk a cave-in *within* the cave-in."

The professor was nodding. "True, but we haven't gone deep enough yet."

The food was quite good, then again, my standards had dropped considerably over the past few days. A guard came in later, saw that we were done, and ordered us to continue working.

"I don't speak Arabic," said Wally, "but I've come to know what that means." It was the most he had spoken all day.

We continued to remove dirt and rocks far into the night, although I was unable to detect much difference in the wall, which was disheartening. And when it got considerably late, Wally tossed aside his shovel and said, "I'm going to bed."

* * *

While the boy slept, I sat with Caesar off to the side. We spoke in low voices, out of respect to the sleeping Wally. Eventually, the conversation turned to Struys's memoirs.

"I'm unaware that Struys left behind a map," I said. "Only a memoir."

Caesar looked like a politician with a secret. "True, there is no physical map, per se. The map, however, is hidden *within* the pages of the memoir."

"What do you mean?"

"The map exists, Sam. You must read between the lines."

I shook my head. "Other researchers have scoured his memoir from top to bottom, gleaning from it all the known facts of Ararat, applying that book as a guide to find the cave with the marker shaped like a finger. How is it that you were successful where others have failed?"

"I *am* one of those researchers, Sam. I am one of those who scoured Struys's book from top to bottom. I felt that his account had the ring of authenticity as opposed to other, less credible eyewitness accounts. Call it a hunch, but I was convinced that Struys's accurate descriptions of the mountain and its inhabitants proved that not only had he climbed the mountain, but that he had observed it with a journalistic eye for detail. His description of the ark itself is nothing short of breath-taking. The truth, Sam, is in the details."

"Fine," I said, "the guy had an eye for detail. Aside from that, how were you able to discern from his writing an accurate map to this particular cave?"

"Ah, well, even magicians nowadays are telling their secrets. I suppose I can tell mine, too." He paused dramatically. "I began by obtaining the most current satellite photograph of Mount Ararat as provided by the Turkish Department of Interior. Next, I carefully went through Struys's memoir word for word, creating in perfect chronological order each step of Struys's journey over the mountain."

"But that has been done," I noted.

"Yes," said Caesar. "But perhaps not with as much intensity. Next, aided by a friend from Boeing's research and development team, we entered the satellite photograph into their advanced-imaging computer, which brought the mountain to life, in wonderful 3-D." Caesar grinned. "With the touch of a button, I could view the mountain from every angle, panning out wide, or in as close as possible. Like a starship in Star Wars, we sailed through canyons and over rivers."

Faint voices came from down the tunnel, loud and obtrusive. The guards were probably drunk, or halfway there. Wally, however, continued to sleep as if dreaming of sawing logs.

Caesar continued, "The computer assigned coordinates to the mountain, in a sort of grid-like pattern, roughly every square acre. Coordinate AA-123, for instance might be near the southern base of the mountain. Coordinate AA-124, might be the square acre just above it, etc., etc. Next, I entered each step of Struys's journey over the mountain: each trail, each outcropping of rock, each river or stream, each canyon or gully or ravine. When I entered a description of, say, a stream that flowed over a grassy plateau, the computer gave me 52 coordinates that matched that description. Next I entered into the computer the description of a fifty foot granite canyon. The computer gave me seventeen possibilities. I entered every natural landmark as described by Struys along his journey. Each time, the computer gave a list of possible matching coordinates that could likely be found on the mountain.

"And in the end, Sam, the computer provided me one long list of coordinates. Starting from the base of the mountain, it followed a likely trail matching the coordinates for all the landmarks. You cannot begin to know the excitement I felt on that day, Sam, as I stared at that 3-dimensional map of Ararat, as the Dutchman's route came to life before me."

"But surely the emir, or Al Sayid, would have confiscated your map by now, perhaps ensuring that you would not attempt to escape through the rock wall once you broke through the cave in."

His eyes twinkled like distant stars. "They did take it away from me, Sam. However, I would not be foolish enough to ascend Mount Ararat with only one map." From a slit in the rubber sole of his boot, the professor removed a tightly folded and very dirty piece of paper. "I have a copy here, Sam, although the emir has the original, laminated version." He paused and worked the map back into his boot where it was safely hidden. "So you can understand my frustration when I was told that I could not climb the mountain for some obscure political reason."

I thought of the many times I had been to this cave, to be alone with the dead, unaware that this was the cave of legend.

"Yes," I said with certainty. "Yes, I can understand why you had to climb the mountain. But one thing still intrigues me."

"What's that, Sam?"

"*Why?*" I asked. "Why do you search for the ark with all your heart, mind, body and soul?"

* * *

"I am a man of faith, Sam. I am a professor at a very small Bible college in Southern California. I teach Biblical archaeology to prove the validity of the Bible. I believe in the creator and I believe in the afterlife. I believe spirituality is a very personal and individual experience that varies from one person to the next. There's not many like me around, Sam. The growing trend is to scoff at the Bible, but I find it a valuable wealth of information and a treasure trove of future archaeological finds."

I shook my head. "You must be a true man of faith, professor. The story of the ark is too wild for me to accept without some reservation."

He shrugged. "The fact that there are bipedal primates who can build super computers in a universe devoid of other life, could be considered a miracle as well."

"You've got a point," I said.

"Science picks and chooses its miracles," said Caesar. He spoke with enthusiasm, and it was hard not to be drawn to the man. He was probably an excellent lecturer, although I saw him as the type who probably assigned too much homework.

I lay back in the soft sand, and put my hands behind my head. "Your enthusiasm is wearing me out, professor."

He smiled infectiously. "I do have that effect on people."

* * *

The professor was snoring pleasantly. Almost a caricature of the perfect snore. A low nasally rumble, followed by a slight wheeze.

I was wide awake, but it wasn't the snoring that kept me up. I was worried about Faye. I wondered again what

Omar had done with her. I had known him to be driven by a somewhat skewered set of ethics. The sort that said: *I won't rape you now, but I will later when you are officially part of my harem.* Rather loose moral system, but it might just keep her out of some immediate trouble.

I needed to get out of here. I was restless. I was finally beginning to feel like a true prisoner: trapped, without friend or hope. I was crawling out of my skin, itching to do *something*. I moved over to the fire, stretched out my cold fingers for warmth. I glanced around the small cave. To the north was the massive cave-in, which looked impregnable; to the south was the narrow, dark tunnel which led to the guards. I looked up at the ceiling. I couldn't see the ceiling. The smoldering fire was unable to penetrate the darkness, and so it remained hidden behind a black veil. I was trapped.

I chewed on my lower lip, watching the dying embers in the small fire. Caesar and Wally slept noisily, breathing alternately, although Wally seemed to catch up to the old man, and they sometimes snored in unison. My ears wanted to throw up.

I stood up suddenly and moved off toward the dark tunnel, standing just inside the entrance. Beyond I could hear the murmur of the guard's voices; and, although the tunnel was eternally dark, my straining eyes seemed to detect a soft glow coming from beyond a slight bend. Then again, if you strain your eyes hard enough, you can detect almost anything. Even Elvis.

I thought again of Faye. Maybe she had been killed, discarded like a rag doll. I inhaled, feeling the pain of anguish and helplessness and uncertainty. This was all so goddamned *insane*.

I started off down the tunnel, walking carefully, my right hand trailing along the smooth wall for guidance and direction. My fingertips quickly gathered dust and cobwebs. The sand beneath my feet was soft and muffled my footfalls. I breathed easily through my nose. If there was a way out of the tunnel, I was going to find it. And if there was a way of freeing Faye, I was going to find it. If there was a way of getting caught, I would probably find that too.

The voices grew louder and more distinct, although the guards still spoke softly. It was quite late; they had probably drunk themselves into a stupor. One could only hope—

The wind picked up, sprinkling sand over my face. The wind whistled softly over the protrusions in the wall, followed by a gentle moan. Much too peaceful. The voices were mumbling in Arabic, although I could not make out the individual words. Probably talking about the Lakers chances next year. I slowed my pace. The tunnel grew brighter. The brightness steadily increased, and from just around a bend I could hear the crackle of the fire.

He was waiting for me in the shadows of the tunnel. I would learn later from Farid that he had been watching me with Night Vision goggles. First I heard a whisper of moving fabric. Instinctively, I swung wildly into the darkness with a punch that seemed to connect with a shoulder or jaw, either way it was bony. But the guard was already swinging the butt of his rifle around. An explosion of light, as if someone had struck a match inside my skull, flashed behind my eyes. The light flared briefly, and then winked out of existence.

CHAPTER THIRTY-SIX

Throughout that morning, Faye Roberts had been secured to a wooden post within a small workroom, surrounded by what appeared to be explosives. Before noon, she was led to a massive snow-covered rock to relieve herself. The boulder reeked of urine. She covered her nose with the arm of her sleeve and tried to go. But she couldn't, especially with the young soldier casting sidelong glances at her. She gave up.

"Did you get an eyeful, asshole?" she asked, passing him.

She was led to Omar's tent. The emir sat behind his massive oak desk studying what appeared to be aerial photographs of a city. Upon closer inspection she saw that it was Istanbul. The light from his small electric lamp cast deep shadows in the hollows of his sunken cheeks. As usual, the big bodyguard stood silently off to the side, ignoring her completely and staring straight ahead, although Faye knew that that was just an illusion. She sensed the bodyguard was aware of her every movement. Omar looked up from the photographs and forced a smile. "Perhaps you're wondering why I've summoned you to my tent, Professor Roberts?"

"To apologize and release us."

He grinned. "Your spirit is admirable. However, Professor Al Sayid has requested your assistance."

She shook her head. "And why should I help him?"

"If you are uncooperative, he has been given orders to have you killed. Or, perhaps, given to my brother."

"You're an animal."

The Arab leaned back a little and studied Faye. He crossed his arms in an apparent attempt to keep himself warm. "To aid Al Sayid, we had employed another archaeologist from Riyadh." Omar paused. "That archaeologist is dead. Or, more accurately, I had him killed."

"Why?"

"I suspected he was less than trustworthy. However, his work is now incomplete. And that's where you come in, professor Roberts. You will complete his project. I will expect to see results shortly, as the report shall coincide with the destruction of Istanbul, which shall be in a matter of days."

"And then what?"

"You will return to Riyadh with me, to join my harem. There, you will be forgotten. Or at least as good as dead."

"I would rather die."

"That can be arranged, too, although that would be such a waste."

The emir motioned and Farid opened the tent flap and a guard stepped in. The guard reached for Faye. She shrugged him off. "What about my father and Sam?" she demanded.

The emir sighed. "Perhaps you should be more concerned with your own welfare," he said simply.

"What will happen to them?"

Omar's eyes were expressionless, like slivers of coal, the eyes of a predator. "They will be killed, of course."

* * *

She was led from the emir's tent to a much smaller tent in the center of camp, designed to sleep one on either wing. Instead of bunks there were two metal fold-out tables piled with folders, notebooks, and printouts. Even a laptop computer. In short, it looked like her small office at USC. Minus the clean, private bathroom.

Al Sayid was there. The little Arabic professor was comparing two latex samples through a jeweler's eyepiece. The professor stood and reached for her hand. Despite herself, she let him take it. He led her around the fold-out table and to a wooden stool. He eased her down and spread the samples before her.

"I hope you are being treated well."

"I'm in no mood for formalities," she said, then added, "other than formally kicking Omar's royal ass."

"He's a bit insane, admittedly. Rather single-minded in his obsession. I keep my distance from him, and he allows me to search for the ark." He changed the subject, pointing to the latex samples before her. "I'm well aware of your work in the field of paleo-linguistics, professor. Your father himself was highly regarded. Unfortunately, these glyphs are beyond even his expertise." He paused. "I'm no expert. I need your help. I have a fair idea what's being discussed here, but not the specifics."

"What is it that you want?"

The little professor's eyes narrowed. His pupils shrank to tiny black pinholes. "You will interpret these glyphs, Miss Roberts. And quickly. We are rapidly losing time." He checked his watch. "As much as I would like to nose around and watch you work, I have other tasks to oversee. I am surrounded by fools."

"What about food?"

"I will have some delivered." He paused and stared at her coldly. "I have been given full liberty to do with you as I wish. Do not test me." With that he went outside, leaving her alone.

* * *

A Kurdish soldier named Razu returned with food. Bread, cheese and water. Faye decided that Razu was entirely too serious. And he gripped his weapon too tightly for her comfort. Difficult working conditions at best.

Throughout the day, she thought often of Sam and her father. Were they okay? Was Wally frightened out of his skin yet?

She worked far into the night. As the hours passed, the wind slapped against the tent with more regularity. Faye didn't notice the wind, or the cold, or even that she was starving. As always, she was absorbed completely in her work—even when it wasn't *her* work. Ultimately, an exhausted Razu left Faye alone with another guard sitting just inside the tent's entrance.

On the laptop, she worked on her report. The sound of her typing could be heard throughout camp until the early hours of morning.

CHAPTER THIRTY-SEVEN

I had been sleeping fitfully when I detected another presence in the cave: the whisper of boots, the sound of easy breathing, the swish of clothing. I opened my eyes and turned my head, but I could see little. The fire, however, had dwindled to little more than a tired smoldering.

I could smell the intruder: a mixture of sweat and dirt, both in moderate portions. I had just begun to sit up when a hand fell heavily across my shoulder. If I wasn't so tough, I might have yelped like a puppy.

"Come," said the voice of Farid Bastian.

Dusting sand from my face, I followed the big man across the cave and into the black tunnel. The Arab wore a dark robe and a matching headcloth, held tight by a black cord. He swept the powerful flashlight methodically from side to side as we moved through the tunnel. When Farid finally stopped and faced me I saw that he was weaponless. However, Farid himself was weapon enough.

He held out a cigarette, which I quickly accepted. He lit a match and I leaned into it, puffing my cigarette to life. He lit his own, and we could have been two high school seniors sneaking a smoke in the boy's room.

"How's the girl?" I asked in Arabic.

"She is fine," he answered calmly. "The emir will not touch her. That part of him has died. And his brother keeps his distance, for now."

"Does the emir know you are here?"

"He knows only that I'm checking on the prisoners." He grinned and caught my eyes. "That would be you."

"Thanks, I almost forgot."

We smoked contentedly. After a short while, Farid said, "The girl has proven herself invaluable to the professor, at least for the time being."

"Why are you here, Farid?" I asked pointedly.

"Because I am going to kill you in the morning."

I sucked in air around the cigarette. "How? A gunshot to the head? A shove over a cliff?"

"Come daylight, I will methodically shoot the three of you, claiming that you attempted to kill the emir. The soldiers will not question it. Your bodies will be dumped into the Ahora Gorge."

"And we'll be gone forever. Problem solved, and his secret is preserved." I inhaled deeply, and looked at the big man.

We were silent. The light of Farid's flashlight splashed on the far wall. I finished my cigarette and dropped it into the sand and watched it smolder until it died.

"And what of Faye?" I asked.

Farid shrugged. "She will return with us to Riyadh, to join the rest of his harem. There are ways of making women, especially American women, disappear. She will never escape, and she will be as good as dead."

"And a play thing for the Saudi royal princes," I said.

Farid shrugged.

"And why are you telling me this?" I asked.

"I do not wish to kill you," he said.

"But you will if you have to?"

"Yes."

"Do you enjoy killing?" I asked.

I knew Farid Bastian was an ex-Saudi soldier, trained in their special forces. Killing was no stranger to the big man. He said, "I receive little pleasure in killing another man."

I sighed and scratched the stubble at my jaw. "Thanks for the hot tip, big guy, but what am I to do about it?"

"I come to give you fair warning," he said, "And I come to give you this."

He removed an automatic pistol from within the folds of his robe. Then he handed me a fistful of bullets. I stuck the pistol and the bullets into the pockets of my jacket.

"Outside are three of the emir's most trusted guards," said Farid.

"One for each of us?" I said.

"No. Three for you." Farid inhaled and his chest expanded out like a great sail catching the wind. "I trust, my friend, that you will be gone when I come to kill you in the morning."

"I'd hate to spoil your day."

Farid led the way back to the cave, then I watched him disappear into the tunnel, his shoulders impossibly wide, sweeping his flashlight before him.

Darkness descended around me once again.

* * *

I sat alone before the small mound on the east side of the cave and held the cold pistol in my hands.

I had buried Liz Cayman with my own hands, with my own snow shovel. I had dug with manic intensity, sweat pouring from my body. And when the grave was six feet deep, I had eased Liz's lifeless body down into the pit. The blood had been washed from her face and her crushed skull was hidden behind a tangle of black hair. Lying at the bottom of her grave, she looked beautiful and peaceful. I folded her hands across her chest because it had seemed the thing to do. It was hardest watching her disappear under each shovelful of dirt. Mountain climbers have a tradition of burying their dead on the mountains responsible for their deaths. Ararat is no different.

I thought of Omar and his madness and gripped the pistol reassuringly in my hand. Somewhere the wind blew and ruffled my hair and I closed my eyes and leaned forward and pressed my forehead into the cold dirt mound that was Liz's grave.

CHAPTER THIRTY-EIGHT

I woke the others and told them the bad news. Wally gaped at his watch, which was a testament to its manufacturers that it still worked. "My God, that's in five hours! What are we going to do?"

"Figure a way out of here," I said.

"And the big fellow gave you a gun?" said the professor calmly, rubbing his jaw and nodding. I wondered if anything ruffled the old man's feathers. "Rather sporting of him."

"Rather," I said.

"Do you intend to kill the guards?" Caesar asked matter-of-factly, as if the idea intrigued him.

"A shoot-out would be my last resort. Not only are we out-numbered, their guns are bigger. I think Farid provided the gun as an edge, nothing more."

"But maybe we can shoot all three," said Wally quickly, looking from Caesar to myself as if he had just expounded the greatest idea in the history of ideas. The kid was losing it. But who could blame him. Execution wasn't in his course prerequisite. "I'm a pretty good shot, you know, hunting with my .22 rifle."

"Actually," I said. "I have another idea."

* * *

I studied the cave-in. The wall was less dense further up, but the climb up was a treacherous one, which is why the others had not attempted it before. As I studied the wall, looking for a likely route up, Wally paced and ran both his hands through his unruly hair, muttering to himself. Apparently, he was from the shoot 'em up school, raised on Rambo and Commando movies. Caesar, however, was intrigued and watched me with an arched eyebrow.

I hooked the adze of the ice ax onto my belt and gripped a protruding rock above me, and stepped up onto the wall. I searched for another handhold, found one, and took another step up. I did this again and again, as smaller rocks broke free and showered the others below in a storm of dirt and debris. Soon I was thirty feet above the floor, my head brushing the cobwebbed ceiling.

I removed the titanium ax from my belt. Using my free hand, I shoved the ax's sharp-pointed shaft between two smaller rocks. As I pounded the shaft deep, my right foot suddenly slipped and I swung briefly out into space, dangling by one hand like a black gibbon in the rainforests of Borneo. I grunted and reached out with my toes until I found secure footing. A fall from here wouldn't kill me, but two broken legs would make for a difficult escape.

I gripped the adze and began applying pressure. The rock shifted reluctantly. When it did, I shoved the shaft deeper into the wedge and reapplied my efforts.

I looked at my watch. *Four hours until dawn.*

Pausing for breath, I looked down. The kid was pacing in a small circle, leaving behind Sasquatchian footprints in the soft sand. Caesar gave me the two thumbs-up sign, grinning. You'd think the old guy was having the time of his life.

I brought my knees up and kicked the shaft. The rock tilted. Dust sifted down. I shouted for the others to stand aside. I kicked again and again, until finally the rock popped out and tumbled down the wall with enough noise to wake the dead and landed with a thud in the sand, creating a small dirt mushroom cloud.

I re-positioned myself and shoved the adze between the next two rocks. Again, I swung my legs up and kicked the shaft with the heels of my boots. Almost immediately the rock broke loose and plummeted to the cave floor below. I was just beginning to think that maybe the pendulum of luck was swinging our way when I heard a noise coming from the tunnel.

* * *

Two guards stood at the entrance to the cave, one of them holding a flashlight steady on me, while the other swept his around the cave. Both were carrying their semi-automatic weapons at their hips, ready for immediate use.

The one holding the light on me said in Arabic, "What are you doing?"

I climbed down the wall. "I was advised by the emir's bodyguard that we needed immediate results, and so we are working well into the night."

The guard stepped closer, moving with a limp. As he walked, he kept his beam in my eyes, perhaps to disorient me, perhaps to be an asshole. Perhaps both. After a lot of limping, he finally stood before me.

"Are you sure that is all he told you?" he asked, flashing the light from one eye to the next.

"I'm sure," I said.

Bum leg and all, he punched me in the stomach, a swift movement that gave me only a fraction of a second to tighten my abdominal muscles. I sank to my knees, sucking air. He stood over me and I expected the stock of his rifle to come crashing down between my shoulders. Instead, his scuffed boots turned away in the soft sand.

"Just make sure that is all you're doing, *merkep*," he said over his shoulder.

I could have shot them both in the back. But, then, that wouldn't have been very sporting of me. With the guards gone, and my breathing back to normal, I resumed work thirty feet above the cave floor.

And just before dawn, with Wally keeping me posted on the time, I pulled free a final basketball-sized rock and was greeted with something truly wonderful: a cool draft of air.

CHAPTER THIRTY-NINE

I thrust the torch through the opening; beyond, the darkness retreated reluctantly. I was greeted by a refreshing wind that smelled faintly of mildew and dirt and something very old and crypt-like. This side of the cave-in was empty save for a dozen or so large rocks scattered across the sandy floor. The far wall was solid and forbidding, and one thing was painfully clear: there was no way out.

But then where was the source of the cool air?

I slithered through the small opening and, with the torch between my teeth like Fido playing a burning game of fetch, I climbed down the far wall. Once on firm ground, I followed the source of wind. I moved slowly over the sandy floor, boots whispering over the sand, eyes alert for anything.

The far wall came to flickering life as I approached, each fissure and crack emerging from the shadows. The flame danced crazily in my hand, awakened by a breeze whose source was still frustratingly unknown.

I swept the torch near the base of the wall, searching the shadows that crawled to life. The flame whipped crazily in my hand. The tunnel had to be here—

There! Near the floor, was a small, dark tunnel. I hurried back.

* * *

I guided the professor up the rock wall. The few times he faltered, I gripped the fabric of his jacket and hauled him up. All in all, he was a fit man, needing little help.

Wally Krispin was a different story. The kid had the coordination of a newborn. I helped him each step of the way. His bony knees and elbows stuck out every which way, like a human pin cushion. After twenty long minutes, the kid made it up and slithered on his belly through the opening.

Voices suddenly erupted from within the tunnel. Many voices, speaking excitedly.

Dawn.

"They're coming for us."

I plunged through the small opening.

* * *

Thirty feet above the floor, Wally was waiting for me, eyes wide with fear. "I-I don't know how to get down, Sam."

But when angry voices erupted in the cave behind us, Wally Krispin suddenly bolted, scrabbling down the side of the wall like a spider with an extra leg. Halfway down, he jumped without reservation, hitting the soft sand hard, skidding on his face. He got up, spitting out sand and raking his hair with his fingers. Luckily, nothing seemed broken.

I tossed the torch down to the waiting professor. Caesar caught it neatly by the wooden shaft. I knew we couldn't have done that again if we tried. Before climbing down, I kicked rocks back into the small opening, plugging our escape route. It wasn't much, but at least it would slow them down.

I climbed quickly, jumping the remaining half, as did Wally. I hit the sand in a tight roll, coming up to my feet, before stumbling to my knees. In the Olympics, I would have been penalized for a poor landing, but in aeronautics I would have been lauded for a safe set down.

Torch in hand, I led the others to the small opening at the base of the far wall.

Caesar bent down and examined the hole. "Rather small," he concluded.

"I'll go first," I said.

"By all means," he said, grinning, slapping me heartily on the back.

And as the wind thundered through the small opening, whistling like something from the soundtrack of a cheesy horror flick, I dropped to my knees and thrust the torch before me, and crawled into the small tunnel.

* * *

Before daybreak, with only a couple of hours of sleep behind her, a sudden noise brought Faye instantly awake. She looked up from the table, up from her folded arms which had served as bed and pillow and watched as Kazeem strode confidently into the tent, motioning away the solitary guard. The big prince ducked under a low-hanging lantern and stood before her, hands on hips. He watched her silently, breathing noisily through his flared nostrils. His deep-set eyes glowed with wild anticipation, and Faye instinctively glanced around for a weapon. All she could find was her laptop computer. Where was a bottle of beer when you needed one—

"Your father and the others have escaped," said Kazeem in clipped English. "For now."

Faye's eyes widened with pleasure. A faint glimmering of hope surfaced from far, far below. But she said nothing, just watched the big prince.

Kazeem continued, "They have escaped into the mountain. Escape, however, may be too loose of a term as I suspect they have not gone far." Kazeem slid a hand inside his robe and produced a laminated map—her father's laminated map. "Your assistance may be necessary. Come."

CHAPTER FORTY

The tunnel was similar to the size and shape of a heating/air conditioning duct, and as the others were less agile and a lot slower, I stopped routinely to allow them to catch up. Rather sporting of me.

I was waiting for them now, idly sweeping the torch from side to side, illuminating dark stone walls and a filthy dirt floor. Gloomy. Not the place to be if one were claustrophobic.

Wally approached from behind. Breathing hard and fast. I might have spoken too soon.

"You okay, Wally?"

He swallowed hard. "I feel as if the weight of an entire mountain is precariously balanced above me."

"I don't know how precarious, but there is an entire mountain above you."

"That's not helping. Is it me or is this tunnel getting smaller?"

"Try not to think about it," I said sagely.

Indeed, as we continued forward, the tunnel *was* getting smaller: the walls closing in, the ceiling descending. Almost like a mathematical formula: the more the walls closed in around us, the harder and faster Wally's breathing became.

Soon, we were forced to slither on our sides, to reach out with our hands and pull forward with our arms. It was a hell of a way to make progress. It was also hell on your fingertips and fingernails. Sweat dripped steadily from my brow and nose, to be absorbed by the fine dust scattered over the stone floor, making tiny mud pies. Behind me, I could hear the desperate clawing of fingernails, and I was reminded of a crocodile pulling itself out of a lagoon, its dinosaur-like claws scrabbling over the sun-baked shore. That had been long ago on assignment for the *National Geographic*, in a far better place, with a whole lot more sunshine.

Shortly, mercifully, the narrow tunnel ended, dropping down to a smooth stone floor ten feet below. One after another, we slipped out of the narrow crawlspace. Here, the tunnel was more pre-disposed towards bipedal primates. It was glorious to stand erect again, to feel the weight of your body on the soles of your feet, as opposed to your elbows and knees.

The tunnel was narrow, the ceiling non-existent, as shadows disappeared into the gloom above. We walked single file, which would have made our first grade teachers proud. By my estimates, the passage led deeper into the mountain, but then again it didn't take an advanced degree in geology to come up with that one. Lichen clung to the walls, glowing softly in the torchlight. The floor itself was a mixture of uneven rock protrusions and beach-like sand. As usual, our breathing reverberated around us, and we sounded like six, not three. Somewhere water dripped. The air was musty and stagnant, almost tangible, like the basement of an abandoned mansion. Haunted, of course.

"We need to get out of here, and go back for Faye. She's alone with those animals," I said. "Where's the map, professor?"

He removed it from his boot. "Finding a way out may prove more difficult than you think. Remember, Sam, the computer program only showed the way *to* the cave." Caesar peered at the map through his bifocals as I held the torch over him. "Obviously, now that we're in the cave, we're on our own."

"Obviously."

"However, I've spent some time pouring over the pages of Struys's account, and believe I have gleaned a rather accurate map of the tunnel systems within Ararat." Caesar turned the map over. "I've carefully noted each turn, each direction, each choice of tunnel that was made. Now, whether or not Struys neglected to mention a fork in the passage, or a particular left or right decision, is beyond my control."

"Good enough," I said. "We'll follow you, professor. And if we get lost, we eat you first."

Caesar moved forward, and I followed; Wally took up the rear. For the time being, the tunnel led in only one direction, which eliminated the decision-making process.

* * *

Ten minutes later, we came to our first decision: a fork in the tunnel. One tunnel led off to the left, and the other continued to the right. After consulting the map, Caesar confidently pointed to the right and Wally and I followed without question like lambs to the slaughter.

Perhaps an hour later, we came to yet another fork in the road, but to my dismay, Caesar frowned at the map, shaking his head.

I said, "You're shaking your head, professor, because you can't believe how remarkably easy this is to decide which tunnel to take."

Caesar turned the map over and upside down, which I took as a bad sign. He rubbed his jaw. "I'm beginning to think," he said, "that I don't know how to read this."

"We can save time and eat you now," I said. "After all, we haven't had breakfast."

Caesar ignored me. "There's supposed to be three choices here, not two."

I handed the torch to Wally, who held it out for Caesar, as I stepped forward to examine the two tunnel entrances. Both stretched as far as the light would reach. I knelt down and studied the floor.

"What are you looking for?" asked Wally.

"I'm looking for some indication as to which tunnel to choose. Perhaps an ancient scuffmark from an ancient pair of leather boots. Something, anything."

I didn't find a scuffmark, but I did come across something unusual. What first appeared to be a shadow from a rock protrusion, was actually something entirely—

Caesar suddenly yelled, "Wally, the map!"

I closed my eyes, praying Caesar hadn't just said: *"Wally, the map!"*

I turned, my worst fears realized. The flame had burned a hole in the map. Caesar blew gently as ashes drifted down in the torchlight. The map looked as if a fiery cannonball had been shot through it from a pirate ship.

Wally dropped the torch and stammered, "I-I'm sorry."

I moved quickly, retrieving the torch before the flame winked out. Caesar closed his eyes. The older man seemed to be fighting an urge to cry. Instead, he said simply, "The map is quite useless."

"I'm sorry," said Wally again. "I was just trying to help."

The professor took a deep breath, face crimson with anger, contrasting with his silver beard. But then, in a heartbeat, the anger was gone and the familiar old grin returned. His eyes sparkled as if lit by torches of their own. He reached up on tip-toes and mussed the kid's hair. "You've always had two left feet, Wally. Now, I suppose, you have two left hands."

Wally grinned, perhaps relieved that the professor hadn't given him a noogie instead.

I studied what was left of the map. The hole was nine inches across, spanning the interior route within the mountain, from the entrance to the final picture of a little ark that Caesar had drawn. The drawing looked more like a row boat than the vessel that had preserved life as we know it.

"Well," I said and walked over to the shadow along the wall and pushed aside a cobwebbed veil. "The good news is that I've found the third tunnel."

* * *

"The bad news," I said, "is that we don't know which tunnel to take." I waved the torch at all three. "The left, middle, or right?"

The professor said quickly, "The middle tunnel."

"Are you sure?" I asked. "Sure enough to risk our lives?"

He started to nod, but then paused in mid-nod. His thick eyebrows scrunched together in a hairy shelf above his orbital ridges. He dropped his hands to his sides. "Suddenly, I'm not so sure, Sam."

Wally stepped forward, speaking confidently. "I propose we go right."

"Why?"

"Because the main tunnel seems to naturally progress to the right."

"A valid point," said Caesar. "But the wind seems to be coming from the left tunnel, which might indicate a way out."

"But, professor, you just said the middle tunnel," I pointed out, exasperated.

THE LOST ARK

"I was caught-up in the heat of the moment, Sam. Plus, I've been known to frequently change my mind. It's a character flaw. To be honest, I wouldn't bet a wooden nickel on the middle tunnel."

I chewed my lip thoughtfully, or maybe hungrily. Finally, I said, "We will each follow a tunnel, and report back here in ten minutes. Do we all have watches?"

They nodded.

"Good," I said. "Wally, you go right. Professor, you check the left. And I'll follow the middle. Remember, spend five minutes moving into the tunnel, and five minutes coming back. No one gets lost. We meet back here in ten minutes and report on our findings."

"But what do we do for torches?" asked Wally, wetting his lips nervously with his tongue. I decided that Wally *always* looked nervous. Hell, he was making me feel nervous.

I removed the pistol from behind my back and the pocketknife from my hip. I placed the handle of the torch against a suitable rock, then used the butt of the pistol to hammer the pocketknife into the wood. A half dozen whacks later and I had split the torch into three torchettes. I handed one each to Caesar and Wally, keeping the third for myself.

"Ten minutes," I said, and stepped into the middle tunnel.

* * *

In the middle tunnel, as I contorted my body like a belly dancer on steroids around protrusions and limestone

214

stalagmites (once I was even forced to limbo), I was beginning to think that I had gotten the short end of the proverbial stick. The tunnel was difficult to traverse at best.

But shortly, as the light from the torchette crawled over the wall like liquid fire, I came upon a small pile of neatly stacked stones in the shape of a finger. Or a phallic. Either way, I was sure it was another marker (and one that would intrigue any Freudian psychologist). I grinned and looked at my watch. Time to go back.

And that's when Wally's high-pitched scream echoed down the undulating tunnel.

CHAPTER FORTY-ONE

I backtracked through the convoluted tunnel system, banging my head and shins more times than I cared to admit, meeting the professor in the main tributary. The professor was huffing and puffing and holding his chest.

I need to sharpen my CPR skills, I thought.

"Wally," he gasped, pointing to the right tunnel.

When the professor had caught his breath, we stepped into the right tunnel, which was wide enough to drive a Volkswagen Beetle through. So what had happened to the kid? Had he stubbed his toe and fallen?

Holding the torches before us, as shadows scuttled over the uneven floor like fleeing mice, I noticed the tunnel was noticeably cooler than the others, as a small wind meandered over our skin, groping us with phantom hands.

The wind blew louder, howling and I instinctively slowed the pace. It was a good thing, because the stone floor suddenly disappeared into total blackness. One moment it was there, the next it was gone, a straight drop to an unknown depth. I was able to stop in time, teetering on the ledge. A small pebble, kicked by my boot, plummeted over the edge, and I never heard it drop. Maybe it was still falling. The professor, however, bumped into me. I grabbed hold of the old man, and held on. When we untangled ourselves, Caesar moved cautiously forward and held his light near the edge of the pit. "My, God. It's almost invisible. As if it's man-made."

"No time for conspiracy theories, professor."

I leaned out over the pit, careful of the loose rock around the lip—and breathed a sigh of relief. The kid was down there, sprawled on a narrow rock shelf, which had saved him from falling farther into the pit. His torch lay next to him, extinguished. Although I couldn't tell if Wally was breathing or not, at least his neck didn't appear broken.

"He's down there," I said, "but it doesn't look good."

Caesar called down to the boy, a note of hysteria in his voice, but there was no response. I quickly removed my jacket and flannel shirt, tying the sleeves together. I told Caesar to do the same. The nylon jackets were thin, designed exclusively to repel wind and rain. Still, the material should be strong enough to hold a man. And the flannel shirts were well-made and thick, and time would only tell if they would hold up.

I glanced down into the pit. We needed another five feet of material, at least. I removed my boots, then pants. Working in my long underwear, I put the boots back on, knowing I looked ridiculous as hell, but also knowing that I would need the boots for traction.

There was an amused sparkle in the professor's eyes. "Cute," he said.

"You're next, professor. Come on, hand them over."

With our pants tied together, we had enough material. I studied the great hole in the floor, which stretched from wall to wall. There was no way around the pit, from one side to the other, unless there was a vine hanging from above and I was Tarzan of the Apes. Near the side wall, however, there was an upthrust of rock that could be used for leverage.

"How are you with heights, professor?" I asked.

"Better, if I wasn't half naked."

* * *

Braced against the rock, the tow of clothing wrapped around my back in a classic single rope belay, I eased Caesar over the lip and down into the pit. The material was tied between his legs and around his waist, in a sort of harness.

"All you have to do is sit there and hold the torch," I said. "And pray."

The edge of the pit was worn smooth, preventing any friction. I eased the professor down a foot or so at a time, grunting with the effort as my quads burned like hell, for they were in fact doing most of the work. I did this until Caesar hollered up that he was down. Indeed, the weight suddenly slackened, and I stopped myself from shooting back into the wall behind me.

I caught my breath, stretched my aching fingers. Silence surrounded me. Occasionally I could hear Caesar grunting in the pit as he worked to secure the limp form of Wally. I wondered how long until the silence behind me turned into insane Kurds with machine guns.

The line of clothing jerked in my hands, Caesar's way of telling me the kid was ready.

The knots, interspersed from sleeve to sleeve and pant leg to pant leg, provided perfect handholds. Like catching a marlin, I leaned forward, gripped the material, and leaned back as far as I could. I repeated the process until my legs quivered, as if made of rubber. Clenching my jaw, I wondered if my teeth would shatter in my mouth.

And then I saw Wally's inert form appear above the pit. I leaned forward and gripped the kid under an armpit and pulled. He spilled over the rim in a heap of elbows and knees and other sharp body parts.

I spent a minute catching my breath, alternately slapping Wally in the face. I wasn't sure how effective slapping Wally in the face was, but it sure seemed to make me feel a hell of a lot better. The kid didn't respond, but he appeared to be breathing fine. Finally, I dragged him off to the side, away from the pit, giving me room to haul up the professor.

My only solace was that the professor wasn't dead weight. He would help when he could, although the walls were sheer and smooth, like a frozen waterfall, and impossible to climb solo.

I tossed the clothing down to the professor, who had been waiting patiently in the pit. He caught hold of the material and spent some time tying it between his legs and around his waist, holding his torch in his mouth, the flames inches from his gray beard. Finally, he gave me the thumbs up sign.

I grabbed the first knot and pulled hard. My arms shook like powerlines in a storm. I had the sensation that I was reliving the same nightmare. Nevertheless, I pulled with relentless doggedness, pausing only to catch my breath. The chain of clothing piled slowly around me. Too slowly.

I paused again, but it was a long pause, my chin resting against my chest as the weight of one man hung from my fingertips. Sweat poured from my brow, burning my eyes, wetting my lips.

Just a few more pulls—

And then Wally appeared behind me, shaking his head as if kick-starting his brain. He gripped the line of clothing. He braced his huge feet against an out-cropping of rock, and leaned back. He could have been pulling an oar for his college row team. Together, we worked until Caesar's pale hand appeared over the ledge. And when the old man scrambled over the side, I lay back exhausted in a pool of my own sweat.

CHAPTER FORTY-TWO

We untied the clothing and got dressed. Wally had a purple goose egg on his forehead, rising rapidly, ready to hatch. When the kid finally stood, he swayed on his feet as if he were on board a sinking ship.

To see if he was still playing with a full deck, I asked him his name, and he said *Waldorf Krispin*. The kid didn't look like a Waldorf, although *Wally* seemed to fit nicely. I asked for his mother's maiden name. *Richmond*.

I turned to the professor. "Is this true?" I asked him.

Caesar shrugged. "I suggest you stick with answers you can verify."

"Good point." I turned to Wally. "What color are your eyes?"

"Hazel."

I thought they were green, and told him so. Wally became indignant and said he should know the color of his own eyes. I suggested that he had hit his head harder than he thought. Caesar stepped forward and arbitrated. "Wally's eyes could appear hazel when wearing green or blue, but other than that, they're green. So you're both right."

Next, I told the others about the erect pile of stones found in the center tunnel. They agreed the stones could be a clue; either that, or evidence of primitive man's obsession with his own penis.

* * *

As Caesar had had the foresight to bring up Wally's torch, the three of us each carried a light as I led the way back through the middle tunnel, once again contorting my body around the many rock protrusions. Unfortunately, as the professor's body hadn't contorted in many decades, he needed a helping hand. Wally, however, was a natural at picking his way through the tunnel, knees and elbows casting sharp shadows along the walls and ceiling. He looked like a preying mantis.

Shortly, we passed the pile of stones. It hadn't changed since the last time I'd seen it.

We moved deeper into the heart of the mountain. The rock walls were cold to the touch, as if made of ice. Sand covered the floor, and the ceiling arched high above. With each step into the tunnel, Faye seemed further and further away.

The tunnel climbed and narrowed, and our breaths came quicker and harder, echoing off the surrounding stone. We made a sharp left and the professor immediately groaned.

"This can't be good," he said.

The tunnel had become nothing more than a ledge, narrow as a breadboard. The ledge wound along the side of sheer granite wall. A swirling, icy wind billowed up from below, and the torches danced in our hands as if to silent music.

"What do we do, Sam?" Caesar asked.

"We continue forward. There's no turning back."

"I was afraid you'd say that."

The torchlight did little to penetrate the darkness. It was hard to conceive that such a massive cavity existed *within* the mountain. I concluded it either had to be a massive cavern, or a bottomless pit to Hades.

I led the way forward, inching along the narrow rock shelf. The wind was cold as ice, thundering over our ears. Now I knew what an airport runway felt like. As if a cruel practical joke had gotten crueler, the ledge narrowed further yet, and I hugged the wall like a lost lover.

A blast of icy wind suddenly pried me loose from the wall. My heart slammed in my chest as I clawed wildly at the smooth surface until my fingertips found a tiny fissure and pulled myself forward and pressed my face against the cold stone of the wall, sucking in great gulps of air.

As I waited for my hammering heart to slow down, the wind came again, and suddenly all three torches winked out of existence. We were instantly plunged into total darkness. The cruelest joke of all.

"Oh God," said Wally.

* * *

I fought to control my own panic, taking deep breaths, trying my best to visualize how the narrow ledge continued along the granite wall. Then again, I tried to visualize myself on a beach in Cabo, but that didn't seem to work. In as calm a voice as possible, I said, "The way before us angles to the left. Keep that in mind. Move very slowly, do not place your full weight on your front foot until you're sure there's secure footing."

The darkness was complete. The silence overwhelming.

The wind came again, howling like a malicious demon. I leaned into the wall, hand splayed over the smooth rock surface. I closed my eyes, not daring to move. After an unknown amount of time, the wind subsided; however, it continued to moan, which was a bit unsettling.

"Maybe we should hold hands," Wally suggested, voice trembling. "You know, in case one of us slips, or something."

"Sounds like a good idea, for safety reasons, of course," concurred Caesar immediately.

I understood the others' need for human contact, and so I gripped the professor's shaking hand, which was cold and callused. I could smell the sharpness of his sweat, mingled with the stench of my own.

Soon we were inching along in complete darkness, holding hands, the wind tugging us with invisible fingers. We continued like this for either minutes or hours, as time seemed lost to us completely.

Suddenly, the toe of my boot found nothing but empty space.

"Hold on, guys," I said.

I reached down with the tip of the dead torch and discovered that three or four feet of the ledge was missing. I told the others.

"So what do we do?" asked Wally.

I took a breath, wondering if things could possibly get any worse. "We jump."

"And how are we to land in pitch darkness on a shelf that's no wider than my ass?" said Wally. "What kind of plan is that?"

"Granted, it's not the world's safest plan, but it will have to do. I'll go first."

And I did, flying through the inky blackness. I landed safely, stumbling slightly. Luckily, the ledge was a bit wider than Wally's ass.

Caesar was next. He jumped without reservation, like the first jump of Spring into a freezing swimming pool, and landed next to me. I caught hold of his groping hands and kept him safely on his feet

Wally needed some coaxing, and if I listened closely, I could probably hear his bony knees knocking together. Finally, Caesar commanded the boy to jump, or risk suffering a *B* for the course.

Wally jumped—

And landed well short. He screamed, and in a feat of luck, I caught hold of one of his windmilling hands. I pulled him forward, and he spilled across the narrow ledge. The smacking sound I heard was Wally kissing the rock shelf.

We waited a few minutes for Wally to regain his composure, if that was possible, then moved on.

Thankfully, the ledge widened, and shortly we slipped around a tight corner and stepped into what I assumed was the confines of a narrow tunnel, as our breathing once again echoed off surrounding stone walls and the wind mercifully subsided.

"Thank God," Caesar said.

I removed my flannel shirt, and tore free a small section of sleeve. I next searched in the darkness with my hands and found a suitable hand-sized rock. With the steel blade of my pocketknife, I soon produced a blazing drop of liquid sun, which caught in the flannel. I fanned the spark into an orange flame.

The narrow tunnel exploded to life. Surrounding us were dark walls and a low ceiling. I wrapped the burning cloth around the end of my torch, lit the others, and we moved on.

CHAPTER FORTY-THREE

They moved quietly through the complex of narrow tunnels. Ten men and one woman. Beams of light played across the rough stone walls, boots muffled in the thick carpet of sand.

Faye marched silently behind the massive form of Farid Bastian. Hungry, thirsty and cold, she wondered if she had ever felt worse in her life. She didn't think so. Earlier, they had all slid on their bellies through a narrow opening in the cave wall, breaking most of her nails in the process. She had also managed to scrape her chin. Sweat from her brow stung the abrasion, attracted to the wound like iron filings to a magnet.

Farid checked on her often, his concern enough to calm her nerves. She suspected that Farid was the only thing separating her from the animal Kazeem—who was directly behind her—and for that she was eternally grateful.

They were marching quietly down a long and twisting rock corridor when the lead soldier suddenly raised his hand, halting the search party. Faye soon saw why. A rock wall blocked their path. Two small tunnels opened before them. Neither looked particularly inviting to Faye.

The soldier consulted the laminated map, and spoke rapidly to Omar. Finally, the prince summoned Faye.

"We appear to have a problem," he said when she stepped before him. He spoke in short gasps through his open mouth. Sweat dripped from his pale face. "According to your father's map, there should be three tunnel choices." He motioned with a skeletal hand. "As you can see, there are only two."

"What do you want me to do?" she asked. "The map could be wrong."

Omar removed a pistol from his hip and leveled it at her face. "Make it right, or I will shoot you between the eyes."

She stared down the dark barrel. She couldn't breathe, was unable to move. Farid moved forward quickly, gently eased the emir's arms down.

"She does not need to be threatened, emir. She will comply." Farid looked at her and said gently, "I suggest you agree to his terms."

Faye nodded dumbly, still unable to find her voice. Omar exhaled through clenched teeth and re-holstered the weapon.

Faye thought: *Christ, he was going to shoot me!*

"Good," said the emir, voice quivering with adrenaline. "Now, I expect immediate results."

"I-I'll need the map," she heard herself say. Her voice echoed weakly off the dank stone walls.

Omar spoke rapidly and Al Sayid, eyes wide with anticipation, handed her the laminated map. The little professor also gave her his flashlight. A soldier suddenly trained his automatic weapon on her as if the flashlight made her more dangerous.

Farid eased back into the shadows, silent as a shade.

Faye breathed deeply, amazed at what had just transpired. Then again, she knew Omar Ali was a desperate man and would do anything to save his project. She tried to focus her thoughts and control her shaking hands.

She looked down at the map and almost grinned. Her father's child-like renditions of the ark and tunnel entrances were hilarious. The man may have a brilliant mind, but he drew like a chimp.

She felt herself relax and was beginning to think clearly again.

Had her father erred in his research? She didn't think so. The man approached the research of Noah's ark the same way a demolitionist wired a building: *very carefully.*

Then where was the third tunnel?

Faye stepped toward the two tunnel entrances and scanned the corrugated wall, which looked like a frozen waterfall, with many vertical shadows. It was difficult to distinguish the shadows from the cave openings. She moved closer.

Then she thought she saw something—

A faint stirring of cobwebs from within a particularly deep shadow, followed by a cool wind. She was confidant this was in fact the mysterious third opening, obscured by a vertical outcropping of rock that gave it the illusion of deep shadows.

Closer.

The cobwebs appeared to have been recently parted, now hanging to the side like discarded clothing. She was certain this was the route her father had taken. Faye was also certain she had little choice other than to cooperate fully. Or be killed.

"I believe this is the third tunnel entrance, emir," she announced.

Omar was suddenly behind her, peering carefully into the opening. A tiny grin touched the corners of his small mouth. He had manipulated the truth out of her, and he was obviously pleased.

"You've just extended your life, my dear" he breathed. He motioned for the others to follow, and the procession eased through the narrow rock opening.

CHAPTER FORTY-FOUR

We came upon another fork in the tunnel.

Unfortunately, there was no erect pile of stones to point the way. No pun intended. However, Caesar's rowboat depiction of Noah's ark was off to the *right* of the map. Whether or not we were supposed to make a left now, and then a quick right later was impossible to tell with the cannon-ball sized hole in the map. I proposed we go right, and the others concurred.

The right tunnel was wide enough to walk side by side, although the ceiling hung too low for Wally to stand erect. The kid was forced to walk with his head down, Neanderthal-like. In that hunched position, Wally suggested that we never let out publicly that we had all held hands. I told him there wasn't much public in Dogubayazit, and that he should be more comfortable with his sexuality.

Our breaths fogged as the temperature dropped. The tunnel stretched into complete oblivion, and the light from the torches had a terrible time penetrating the heavy blackness. Devoid of any dirt, the floor seemed to have been recently swept clean. Wally began whistling the score to the *Star Wars* movies, although he botched it. How do you botch the *Star Wars* score? Kids nowadays....

It was some time later when two massive shapes materialized out of the shadows, the light from our torches bringing them slowly to life. Twin stone pillars, wide as redwoods, carved roughly from the tunnel itself, loomed high into the darkness and disappeared into the gloom. The pillars sat opposite each other, like hulking minotaurs, guarding their secret labyrinth. Their bases were covered in inscriptions.

Professor Caesar Roberts removed his glasses, cleaned them hastily with his filthy shirt, then pushed them back over his nose. Holding the torch before him, he moved quickly forward and examined the base of the left pillar.

Standing behind him, I saw that the carvings resembled the cuneiform writing found in caves along the foothills around Mount Ararat. Grinning, the professor ran his thick forefinger over the etchings. He could have been a kid in a candy store.

He said to himself: "Strong Sumerian influence, although this may predate the Sumerians, which would be a fabulous find, indeed. Of course, I will need to run a potassium-argon test and take latex samples back to my colleagues at the university. And if there's any pottery or potsherds around we can use archaeomagnetic dating—"

"It looks fresh," said Wally. "As if it had been carved yesterday."

"The coolness of the tunnel and the absence of any weathering would preserve it perfectly. In the desert, these relief carvings would have been sand-blasted into nothing."

"But what does it say, professor?" I asked impatiently.

The professor bent down, knees promptly cracking. Must be hell getting old. He said, "Offhand, I would say this appears to be some sort of narrative. The writing itself is pictographic, the simplest form of Mesopotamian writing. The Sumerians would later formalize writing with the use of symbols to identify ideas—"

I broke in. "And you can read all this?" It looked like ancient graffiti to me.

Caesar nodded. "At one point in my career, Sam, I was highly regarded in the field of cryptology, or paleo-linguistics. Now my daughter has taken up the mantle, so to speak." Caesar paused at the thought of Faye. The old man was a mix of emotions: guilt, pride and exhilaration. Finally, he motioned to the ancient inscriptions. "Although I have been out of the field for some time, this is all very basic stuff. Anyway, I shall do my best."

We stood there quietly while the older man mumbled to himself and held his torch close to the stone, blowing away dust from the inscriptions. I looked at my watch because I had nothing better to do. The watch face was covered in dust and cracked at the bottom and seemed to be permanently stuck on the stopwatch feature. I leaned against the pillar, folded my arms across my chest, closed my tired eyes and waited.

Finally, Caesar cleared his throat and began reading, pausing often and skipping unknown characters: *"The Heavens opened and the earth burst forth, and every living creature was swept away. But the creator granted mercy on my small family. And here, upon this holy mountain, lies the salvation of the world, and only those worthy and blessed shall witness the savior of man. Behold, the Ark of life."*

* * *

Wally whistled. I felt a pleasure of goosebumps crop across my forearms.

"I think," I said, "this is a clue."

"Do you think Noah himself actually wrote this?" Wally asked.

Caesar, face red from bending over and reading the ancient text, stood and wiped the sweat from his brow. "Hard to say for sure. Most scholars, myself included, suspect that Noah's ark was built in southern Mesopotamia, near the city of Shuruppak, which is identified in the *Gilgamesh Epic*. There's plenty of reason to believe that Noah was a wealthy man, capable of hiring and organizing the construction of his ship. In Mesopotamia, writing had become a skill for every aspiring man to acquire. Noah could have acquired such skills himself. If so, then, yes, he could have written this."

"Then who carved these pillars, and why?" asked Wally.

"Obviously they signify something of importance," said the professor. "And my guess is that Noah and his sons did the carving."

"Seems like a lot of work in such a gloomy place," said the kid.

"Building the ark would have been a bigger task, lad. Perhaps they wanted to commensurate such a sacred vessel."

Wally shrugged. "Fine; then where's the ark?"

I studied the pillars, frowning. The twin stone columns were not only immense, but somehow familiar. I removed the folded map from my jacket. And there, above the burned hole, were two symbols that could easily be the two pillars. And, according to the map, Noah's ark was directly behind the left symbol. Could the left symbol be, in fact, the left pillar?

I showed the map to the others. Caesar gasped and grabbed it out of my hands. "My God, you're right Sam."

"How could anything be behind the pillar?" asked Wally. "It's solid stone."

I thought about that as I ran my hand over the smooth surface. And that's when I found it. A seam. Along with cool air. Very cool air. I smiled.

"These pillars are not hiding anything," I said.

"What do you mean, Sam?" asked Caesar, turning to me.

"Sure, they're here to mark something historic and sacred within, but mostly...." and now I pushed hard with my hand. The pillar didn't move at first, but then something rather miraculous happened. The pillar rotated, spinning slowly inward. As the outer section of the pillar turned in, the section behind it appeared. And what appeared...was nothing. "But mostly, it's just a fancy doorway," I said, finishing.

CHAPTER FORTY-FIVE

We stepped into a narrow hallway, with smooth granite walls. The walls pulsed with the eerie white light. The ground vibrated again, and behind us the ramp rose like a drawbridge and slammed shut, sealing us in.

Our breaths fogged before us. The torches were unnecessary. I put mine out, and shoved it inside my jacket. The tunnel was very silent, and reminded me of a strange portal in some alien mother ship. The only noises were our breathing and the scrape of our boots. Wally was doing most of the scraping, following behind reluctantly. With each cautious step, the light became increasingly brighter, pouring into the tunnel as if through a rent in heaven. Before us, framed in the light, was another archway. This was our stop.

I looked out through the archway: the brilliance beyond was overwhelming. It took a moment for my eyes to adjust, but when they did, my breath caught in my trachea as if a hand had seized my throat.

"The ice cavern," whispered Caesar.

And spanning the entire length of the canyon, enshrouded within a veil of ice, was the ghostly image of a massive wooden ship.

* * *

The ship looked sea-worthy to this day, as if caught in a frozen tidal wave, reminiscent of the frozen mastodons found whole and intact in the ice of Siberia, with the undigested food of their last meal still in their bellies.

Professor Caesar Roberts pressed his hands to his chest, lips moving silently, attempting to form words. Wally Krispin caught his breath and said, "Sweet mother of God."

The cavern was oddly devoid of any sound. A frozen crypt. I sensed that I had stepped into something that was meant to be sealed forever, or found by someone more worthy than I. As if I were trespassing into the Holy of Holies.

There was no reluctance on the part of the professor. He stepped boldly onto the rock shelf, boots crunching on a thick layer of ice that coated the stone like a donut's glaze. His footfalls echoed within the massive cavern. In fact, everything echoed. Every breath, every swish of clothing. The professor moved determinedly forward, like a thirsty desert horse with the smell of water in its nostrils, heedless of its master.

"Well," said Wally, moving next to me. "I suppose we should go check it out."

I nodded absently.

Wally and I stepped out onto the ice. "Where are we?" he asked me.

"This is a rock ledge *outside* the mountain. Surrounding us is the Abich II glacier, which somehow neglected to fill-in the entire ledge, leaving this cavernous air pocket. Thus the illusion of the ice cavern. A true oddity in nature."

The sun refracted through the dome of ice. The source of the white light. It was beautiful, pure light.

"I would never have believed it," he said. "It's so unreal. I feel like I'm dreaming, or died and gone to Heaven's Museum."

I wondered absently how much time we had until our pursuers reached us—if they would reach us, although that dilemma now seemed irrelevant. The fact that Omar could use the very same map that we did was reason enough to error on the side of caution.

Our boots crunched over the ice. It was a very real sound in an unreal setting. The sun was high, but there was no warmth within the cavern. We followed behind the professor, who moved forward quickly and recklessly. Once his foot flew out from under him as if slipping on an invisible banana peal planted by Groucho Marx.

"Where are we?" asked Wally.

"We're on the north face of Ararat," I said, and noticed a slight quavering in my voice. I was not used to my voice quavering. "The ice above us is an extension of the Abich

Glacier, flowing down the mountain, although neglecting to completely fill-in this rock shelf."

With each step the structure seemed to grow in size, until it spanned our entire field of vision. Light-headed, I found breathing difficult. Also, I felt a sort of odd detachment, as if I were not truly part of events unfolding before me. As if I were in a dream, to awaken at any moment.

But it's really here.

The ark rose before us like a Celtic megalith, eternally solid, built for the ages. Built to carry the weight of the world. A thick layer of mostly clear ice, perhaps five or six feet thick, enshrouded the ark. The wooden craft seemed to undulate beneath the ice, like an image in a massive funhouse mirror.

The closer we got, the more detail I could make out. The ark appeared composed of massive hand-worked beams spanning hundreds of feet. The professor stood beneath the prow, looking up. With an unsteady hand, he caressed the ice just outside the hull. "Have you ever seen anything more beautiful in your life?"

"I sense that it's sleeping," said Wally. "Like a hibernating dragon, and if we're not careful, it will awaken."

I wondered what he meant by that, and had not realized how prophetic his words would be.

* * *

"I think I'm going to have a heart attack," said the professor grinning, holding a hand to his chest. "But at least I will die happy!"

"How long is it?" asked Wally, rubbing the ice with the flat of his hand. Our three images stared at us from the ice. I could see that we were a motley crew, dirty and torn. But we were all grinning.

Caesar answered, as if speaking a rehearsed verse, "The length was to be 300 cubits, the breadth 50 cubits, and the height 30 cubits; or, roughly, 450 feet long, 75 feet wide, and 45 feet high." Caesar paused. "If only Faye were here to see this. This would have put an end to her skepticism."

My thoughts were on Faye as well. "We'll find her, professor, as soon as we get out of here. I promise you that."

CHAPTER FORTY-SIX

Faye and the others were waiting in a narrow tunnel while the lead soldier once again consulted the map. Faye had grown accustomed to the hunger that gnawed at her insides like a slow-moving worm, as normal now as breathing. Faye stood next to Farid, which happened to be as far away from Kazeem as possible.

"How are you faring, Miss Roberts?" Farid asked in a whisper.

She looked up into broad, handsome face. "I would rather be home with a good book and a glass of Chablis."

He grunted and removed his canteen and opened the lid for her. "It's not wine," he said. "But it will have to do."

She was grateful beyond words. The cool water tasted both wonderful and awful, as if the canteen had never been cleaned. Water streamed down her neck and into her open shirt. Eventually gentle hands pried the canteen away from her. She heard herself thanking him over and over....

* * *

Boots creaked; metal jangled; clothing swished. The stench of old sweat was inescapable. Apparently, the soldiers had neglected to bathe for the occasion. Earlier, Faye had wanted to gag. Now she accepted the stench as an unavoidable part of her immediate future. Omar's ragged breathing filled the entire tunnel. She secretly hoped he would keel over soon. The emir, however, kept plugging along, keeping pace with the group.

The temperature dropped. Faye's breath fogged before her. Her legs felt heavy and tired. She rubbed her arms through her jacket, which was torn now in several places. Her mind drifted. She thought of her post at USC, her many students. One of whom she had had coffee with on many occasions. The thought brought a smile to her lips.

She was studying Farid's massive shoulders and idly wondering if the kingdom of Arabia had any Big and Tall stores, when the bodyguard suddenly stopped. Faye bumped into him. She felt as if she had walked into a parked Volkswagen. "Sorry," she said sheepishly

But Farid didn't seem to notice. Instead, he was staring silently at the two immense objects that had materialized in the tunnel before them. Two stone columns, one on either side of the tunnel. Dust, churned by their many boots, rose up to obscure the columns. To Faye, the artifacts were surprisingly comforting. A touch of humanity in a dismal world of endless tunnels.

The lead soldier quickly consulted the map. Omar stood over him. Kazeem brushed roughly around her and stalked over to the other men, throwing his own beam of light across the map. Kazeem was almost as big as Farid.

"They grow them big in the desert," she whispered to herself.

Faye moved closer to Farid. The big man sensed her presence and shifted his weight uncomfortably. Using the beam of light, he made slow circles in the dirt before him, illuminating the rounded toes of his massive boots.

"Why are you here, Farid?" she asked in a low voice. She found herself studying his face. Each feature was perfect, she decided. Just on a much larger scale than she was accustomed to. He looked like a warrior from the future. She felt incalculably safe in his presence.

"I do not understand your question," he said simply, lips unmoving.

"Why do you associate with the emir?"

He was silent. Finally, he said simply, "I am paid to be here. It is an honor to be here."

"Is it an honor to hunt down three innocent men?" she asked, gazing up into his face. He quickly averted his eyes and swallowed loudly. She continued, lowering her voice and touching his thick forearm with her fingertips. "Is it an honor to hold me captive?"

The circle of light increased in tempo, darting across his scarred boots. Sweat dotted his massive brow. "I do not wish to hold you captive, Miss Roberts."

"Call me Faye."

He looked down into her eyes. "It is not my will to hold you captive…Faye."

"Then help me, Farid."

"I am but one man."

"You are quite a man."

Faye was almost certain he was blushing. The flashlight fell silent, illuminating a small patch of dirt. "I will see what I can do," he said.

* * *

Once again Faye found herself studying her father's map with Omar hovering over her like a bird of prey. His breath was hot and wreaked of medicine. Farid stood off to the side, hidden in shadows, although she felt his protective gaze.

Omar said, "You will decipher these words and tell us how to proceed. I expect nothing less than immediate results. You are useless to me otherwise."

"It's nice to be needed," she said, stepping over to the right column. Almost immediately she determined that the inscriptions here predated much of the known written languages. The usual excitement of discovery coursed through her, but she reminded herself of her predicament.

She turned and faced Omar Ali. "Do I have your assurance, emir, that my father and the others will not be harmed?"

Omar almost laughed. "Why, of course, madam."

She didn't believe him, but she had little other choice. "Then I shall do my best."

CHAPTER FORTY-SEVEN

Wally leaned in close to the ship, his big schnauzer just inches from the protective ice. "What kind of wood is this? Doesn't look familiar."

Caesar said, "The original Hebrew of the Old Testament refers to it as *gopherwood*; however, no one really knows what gopherwood is. Most scholars believe it to be in reference to cypress wood; or, less probable, oak, cedar or larch—all of which were used by various ancient civilizations for shipbuilding. Rather than a species of wood, gopherwood is also sometimes thought to be a process, one in which tree sap is used to make a plywood, generally considered superior than single lengths of wood. Genesis also states pitch was applied to the wood, both inside and out. It's often thought to be a bituminous substance, a mixture of tar and petroleum, mixed with straw or reeds to make ships water-tight."

"Look," Wally said, pointing to something I had missed: a dark hole in her starboard side. Wally suddenly pressed his face up against the ice. "Do you see that?"

"Not with you in the way," said Caesar.

Wally stepped away. "There seems to be a glow coming from within. It's barely perceptible, sort of greenish."

"A glow?" said the professor incredulously. "What the devil are you talking about, lad?"

Caesar and I stepped forward. We both saw it. A muted glow, the color of new grass, seemed to pulse from within. The pulsing could have been my imagination, but the light was there, nonetheless.

The professor said simply, waving his hand dismissively, "I think we're seeing light from the upper portholes diffused throughout the ship, perhaps the reflection of moss or lichen."

The hull of the ship angled gently down to the keel in the shape of a shoe box. Professor Roberts said, "Those who have studied the ark say it's unsinkable."

"That's good," said Wally. "Because it sure wasn't designed for looks."

Caesar ignored him. "You can see the slats for windows on the third deck. Biblical scholars propose that the top two decks were for the animals, and the lower deck was undoubtedly for waste and garbage. The eight crew members, which consists, of course, of Noah and his family, probably had living quarters on the top floor."

"I see it before me," said Wally. "But I don't get it. Where did the animals come from and how did eight people care for them for…how long? Over a year?"

"Those are heated questions among scholars and critics alike; but, as you can see, we have the ultimate answer: we have the ark. Obviously, then, we can discover answers to your questions. Whether or not it's the biblical ark, and whether or not it was used for the purposes as laid out in many of the world's great religions, remains to be seen. Further study of the ark will no doubt reveal those ans—"

"Sam! Father!"

I spun around. Faye was at the entrance, struggling with a Kurdish soldier. She had run partially out onto the rock shelf, but now he was bringing her in, kicking and fighting.

"Sam, I'm so sorry!"

"Faye!" I ran forward, but then pulled up, sliding. Omar had appeared, followed by Farid and Kazeem and a half dozen soldiers, all blinking and shielding their eyes from the awesome glare of the white light.

CHAPTER FORTY-EIGHT

Emir Omar Ali looked ready for the grave. The fact that he had endured the long hike through the tunnel systems said much about the man's constitution—and madness. To his left was Farid Bastian who stood like a huge granite statue, expressionless. He could have been staring at a cottage picture on a bathroom wall, rather than a timeless miracle. To Omar's right was Kazeem, scowling. Behind, the soldiers had forgotten their military training, breaking ranks, standing on tip toes, trying to get a glimpse of the ark.

Faye was removed from view, although I could hear her struggling in the background—and hear the occasional grunt from a well-placed knee to the groin.

"Congratulations," said Omar. "The three of you have stumbled across one of the greatest archaeological discoveries of all time. Enjoy it while you can."

Omar closed his eyes and took a deep, ragged breath, as if restraining his soul from escaping through his mouth. And when he opened his eyes, he said casually, "Kill them, Farid."

* * *

The big man leveled his weapon at us. We waited. Farid's eyebrows knitted together in indecision. He took an impossibly long breath, filling those massive lungs, then lowered the gun. "I will not."

I exhaled through clenched teeth. I hadn't realized I was holding my breath.

Omar did not immediately respond. The fact that his faithful bodyguard had defied him was unimaginable. "You will kill them, Farid," he said again.

In response, the bodyguard stared silently forward, the weapon pointed down.

Omar Ali moved quickly, snatching the weapon from Farid's grasp. "Then I will do the job for you, you ungrateful pig."

"I saw that one coming," whispered Wally from the corner of his mouth.

Omar brought the gun up. The automatic weapon wobbled in his narrow arms, too heavy for him to control.

"Sam…," whispered the professor.

"Be still," I said, "The chances of him hitting us are slim."

"That's hardly reassuring."

From here, I could see the emir's finger tighten around the trigger. I stepped back, regardless, pressed against the ancient hull. As the emir's finger tightened, curling around the trigger, I saw with some dismay that he *did* have control over the weapon.

We were sitting ducks.

Omar's finger tightened around the trigger. He squeezed. But just as he did so, Farid reached out and knocked the weapon *up*. Flame spat from the barrel of the weapon. Bullets sprayed the ceiling, puncturing the ice. Cracks appeared overhead, zigzagging like bolts of lightening. The ceiling shattered with the sound of a thousand bones cracking in unison.

Ice slashed down from above, cutting through the air like a torrent of steel-bladed daggers, one of which knocked me forward, opening a wound in my shoulder. Another chunk fell beside me, crashing through the floor, which began to crumble away, disappearing into the black unknown.

I scrambled to my feet and moved quickly along the length of the great ship, holding my damaged shoulder. A shock of blue sky appeared in the growing hole above. The afternoon sun angled sharply into my face.

The ark suddenly lurched, its ancient timbers wrenching with the strain of movement, groaning with the sound of an ancient whalesong. The ship had awakened, breaking loose from its frozen moors.

And from the confusion, I heard my name shouted. I looked to my left, and saw the professor hunched over Wally. A sliver of ice, as long as an ice pick, protruded from the boy's chest, pinning him to the floor.

* * *

Blood bubbled from Wally's lips. His eyes were wide and wild, like a trapped animal. He threw his head from side to side, screaming. Caesar, at a loss, raised his horrified face up to me for help.

"I can't move him," he cried out. "He's pinned to the floor."

I did the only thing that I could. As Wally screamed, I pulled the shaft from his chest and blood gushed up like a geyser, quickly spreading over the ice floor, steaming. I put my hand to his chest to staunch the bleeding. Blood oozed between my fingers. Wally's eyes rolled up into his head. He instantly passed out.

I picked him up. We moved aft down the length of the ark, dodging the humming shards of ice. Caesar followed the trail of blood. And there, just ahead, was the same small hole in the ship that Wally had found earlier.

"The hole is filled with ice," shouted Caesar.

I removed the handgun from my waist, and fired into the hole. Three shots later I had blasted through the ice. Caesar scrambled in first, and I hoisted Wally up to him.

The ship shuddered violently, separating completely from the ice wall. Howling wind blew in through the massive opening in the ice wall once occupied by the ark. I jumped up and caught hold of the opening just as the ship spilled over the ledge and headed down the steep incline to the narrow canyon nine hundred feet below.

CHAPTER FORTY-NINE

Wind thundered over me. Bleak canyon walls swept past as the ship plummeted. I lay flat against the hull. I could have been riding the back of a killer whale, without the benefit of a dorsal fin. The vessel bucked—perhaps hitting an upthrust of rock—and I was tossed briefly into the air, only to land hard on my elbows and face.

I rapidly slid down the hull.

My fingernails raked the moss-covered wood, clawing desperately at the finely hued beams. But the fossilized wood was impossibly smooth, the ancient ship-builders remarkably precise in their construction. If I fell, I would by sucked under the ship and crushed into a bloody swath along the steep incline.

And then I saw the small dark hole, the only blemish on her smooth starboard side.

I reached desperately with my left hand—

And my fingers hooked into the jagged opening. My momentum swung me around like a compass needle. For the moment I was safe, and I hung by one hand and caught my breath as the canyon walls sped by with increasing speed. In that position, I had a brief glimpse of a lone mountain goat watching me curiously in mid-chew, grass hanging from its furry muzzle.

I pulled myself up into the hole and slipped down inside.

* * *

I fell through complete blackness until I slammed into something unmovable. A flash of light erupted in my head. I groaned, wondering if that piercing in my chest was a cracked rib or two.

As we continued to slide, the ancient timbers groaning in protest, we hit another bump, flipping me like a penny into the air again. I landed on my tail, and bounced like a pinball off unknown objects, until I hit my head on something very hard.

The explosion of light within my skull was very brief and bright, and I felt no pain, only the peaceful bliss of unconsciousness.

Tilt.

* * *

Like tiny, cold pin-pricks, I awoke to the stinging sensation of snow falling on my face. I opened my eyes and blinked. The world around me was blurred and amorphous. My head pulsed like a metronome.

I took inventory. Although breathing was difficult, my ribs didn't appear cracked. My wrist hurt like hell, but I could still move my fingers enough to know it wasn't broken—just a very bad sprain. Nothing else appeared damaged or missing. But then again, this was just a preliminary report.

I lifted my head (thus increasing the tempo of the metronome), and saw that I was partially covered in a thin blanket of snow, which continued to fall around me through a fresh rent in the ark's roof. Above, purple storm clouds hung low in the sky.

As I sat up, a number of sharp pains shot through me, most notably my injured shoulder. I grunted like a very old man emerging from a day in his recliner. Instantly, a wave of dizziness swept over me. Nauseous, I turned my head to throw up what little food I had eaten, but nothing emerged. When the queasiness passed, I stood on wobbly legs.

Before me, as seen through the sifting snow, was a broad, and heavily damaged staircase made of wood so dark it appeared black. The staircase was pushed up through the floor, pulverized. The damage looked fresh and complete, the stairs useless.

I stood in a hallway on the upper deck. The professor had said the smaller animals would have been here. The rodents, smaller mammals, reptiles and probably even birds.

Unbelievable.

Lined on either side of the hallway were what appeared to be narrow compartments. I shook my head and grinned. "Stables," I whispered.

I stepped carefully over the loose snow, and moved toward the small compartments. They were narrow, perhaps four feet by six feet, and some were slightly larger than others. Cramped quarters indeed, and if there had been doors on the stalls they were long gone by now. The walls of the stables rose fifteen feet, stopping three or four feet below the arched ceiling, which was crisscrossed with massive rafters.

I shook my head. *Unbelievable.*

An icy wind moved down the hallway, stirring the snow like silt along an ocean floor. I suddenly cocked my head, listening. There was more than just snow on the wind. Shortly, it came again: a long, wavering moan, muffled and faint, and distinctively human.

I moved in the direction of the sound.

* * *

I found Caesar Roberts holding Wally Krispin in his arms. Frozen tears beaded his cheeks and icicles hung from his gray beard. Wally's face was the color of the pallid sky above. Blood caked his jacket. The kid had bled to death.

I touched Caesar's shoulder. He didn't respond, as if my touch lacked substance, like a ghost returning to haunt the ship. Snowflakes swirled around us. I watched the flakes and listened to the sobs and didn't know who to blame more for the kid's death. Omar, for his madness.

Caesar, for his obsession. Myself, for allowing it to happen. A kid shouldn't be dead. It was wrong, and I felt a part of it.

I stood for a while behind the old man, who held the lanky body in his arms. The snow continued to swirl in an ancient dance and I closed my eyes and thought of the irony: a ship to save mankind, when mankind can't save itself.

* * *

We laid Wally's stiffening body in one of the narrow stables. A fine, wooden tomb.

I needed a cigarette.

Caesar's nose was broken and would need to be set, although the cold of Ararat should keep the swelling down. Still, it looked like a red water balloon, forcing him to breathe loudly through his mouth. Together, we stood quietly a few stalls down from Wally's tomb. Through the damaged roof above, the sky was darkening, and the snow was coming down with more determination.

I said, "We need to get out of here and get your daughter, professor."

He said nothing. The only indication that he even heard me was that fresh tears appeared in the corners of his eyes. He made no attempt to wipe them away, and stood motionless, arms hanging down at his sides. I leaned against a stable wall. The wall was sturdy, even after all these years. Above, the wind whistled over the damaged roof. Some of the wind found my exposed skin, freezing me to the bone. My foul weather gear, ripped in numerous places, did little to keep the foul weather out. Purple clouds the size of small Balkan countries accumulated above. The clouds looked ready for business. The ark shifted its weight, settling deeper into the canyon.

Finally, the professor said, "Yes, Sam, let's go get my daughter."

I couldn't have agreed more.

* * *

"Where's the front door, professor?" I asked.

"The boarding ramp, or, as you put it, front door, would be on the bottom deck. But as you can see the stairs have been destroyed."

"Any other ideas?"

Caesar frowned, and touched his broken nose. He winced immediately, realizing too late that it wasn't a good idea to touch his broken nose. "How about the roof?"

"The roof's inaccessible," I said looking up. "And I don't see a ladder."

To the left, the hallway disappeared into total blackness. To the right, thirty feet away, the tunnel dead-ended into a shadowy wall.

"I propose we go left," I said.

He raked his thick beard with his fingernails. Probably had a hell of an inch. "You're the guide, Sam. And if we get lost, we eat you first."

CHAPTER FIFTY

We moved past dozens of stables of varying sizes. Most were too small for anything larger than a medium-sized pooch. And even they would have been miserable. I pointed this out.

"The ark was built for survival," he said weakly. "Not for pleasure."

"Any reason why there's no doors on the stalls, professor?" I asked, more to draw Caesar out of the oppressive silence that had engulfed him. The old man seemed to have retreated within himself.

We moved silently forward. Our boots whispered over the smooth floor. Finally, he answered, his voice quiet and withdrawn. "Perhaps the ancient shipbuilders used thick reeds or a bamboo-like material to compose the doors. It would have reduced the ship's weight and would have saved time and money." As he spoke, as his mind shifted away from Wally's death, I saw a flicker of his old self. "The lighter material would have rotted away by now. Of course, the stables on the lower decks, housing the bigger creatures, would have utilized wooden doors."

I grinned. "Of course."

The ship continued to make settling noises, the mighty timbers moaning in a sort of death song, as if we were trapped inside the belly of a dying whale.

We moved deeper into the ark, quickly losing what little light we had, the dark wood blended with the deepening shadows. There were no sounds other than our footfalls, which seemed to echo forever. If I wasn't such a fearless explorer, I'd be nervous.

Finally, I stopped and removed the burned-out torch from inside my jacket and removed the 9mm Luger from my waistband and checked the clip. Three bullets left. I removed one and studied it, a brass 9mm 124 grain, jacket bullet.

"Don't try this at home," I said.

I used my pocket knife and *carefully* removed the bullet's casing, somehow managing to keep my fingers from getting blown off. I tapped out a small pile of gunpowder.

"You must have driven your mother crazy," said Caesar, standing a safe distance away as if I were a carrier of the Plague, "with stunts like this."

"Who do you think taught me this one?" I positioned the Luger above the gunpowder and aimed it back down the hallway. "Stand back."

"Trust me, I'm back."

I pulled the trigger. The muzzle flashed and the powder burst into a small ball of fire. I held the torch over the flame until it was lit, then stamped the fire out.

"Do you always go around defacing priceless artifacts?" asked Caesar.

"This is my first," I said, and shoved the Luger under my waistband. It was warm against the small of my back.

My ears still ringing from the gunshot, I held the torch before us and led the way forward. "Let's get out of here, professor. I would guess that Omar will make a run for it, perhaps back home to Riyadh to re-access the situation here."

"And taking my daughter with him."

I grabbed his jacket sleeve. "C'mon, old man."

* * *

The hallway with the stables ended in a low, wooden archway. Through the archway were a series of small rooms, three in total, all connected. The professor proclaimed these to be the sleeping quarters for the ancient mariners. The rooms were ten feet by ten feet. Or, in the spirit of things, about six cubits by six cubits. Caesar and I moved from room to room, ducking through the low archways.

"The ancients were a small race," said the professor. "In all likelihood, Noah stood no taller than five feet."

"Cute," I said.

"I suppose so."

I pointed to the interconnecting doorways. "Doesn't leave much room for privacy."

"They were too busy for any privacy, Sam. From sick and injured animals, to battling the volatile rising waters. Indeed, they would have needed quick access to all crew members."

The fourth room, however, was massive. According to the professor, it was the captain's cabin. Like the others, it was empty, save for an ornately carved pole in the center of the room. Rounded and domed at the top, it could have been a phallic symbol. Perhaps, I mused, to express their suppressed sexuality over the long stay on the ship. I kept the theory to myself.

The pole was covered in intricate carvings of entertwined serpents, culminating in a single massive head. Caesar walked around the pole. "Eight bodies and one head," he reported

"Perhaps symbolic of the eight crew members and their ship," I suggested.

"Perhaps."

The serpent's eyes gleamed black. The head was unusually worn and polished, like the newel of a staircase. The base disappeared straight down into the floorboards. I had an idea.

I touched the serpent's head. It was cold and smooth. I pulled it toward me, like shifting a gear into second, minus the clutch. Caesar gasped. Immediately, a door swung silently open in the far corner of the room, a door that had been concealed until now. Faint green light issued out.

"Appears Noah had a secret room," I said.

CHAPTER FIFTY-ONE

It wasn't quite a room.

Instead, we stared silently down a long, breath-taking hallway. We could have been two Viking warriors standing at the threshold to Valhalla. An arched cove ceiling gave the corridor visual and physical height. Dark wooden columns, spaced evenly along either side of the hallway like rows of alert sentries, were capped with saucer-shaped capitals, reminiscent of the Greek Doric pilasters. Between the columns were massive floor-to-ceiling murals that emitted a green, phantasmagoric luminance. The soft light cast our shadows behind us, and for the moment, the torch was unnecessary, although I was reluctant to extinguish it.

"What do you think, Sam?" said Caesar. I could hear his tongue scrape over his dry lips.

"I think this is some weird shit."

"Shall we go in?"

I was reluctant. The flickering torch seemed to lap the air with renewed enthusiasm, like an eager puppy. "How did Noah feel about trespassers?" I asked.

Caesar looked at me, arching an eyebrow. "You think it might be booby-trapped?"

I shrugged. The walls continued to glow, as they had done for a long, long time. The torch whipped crazily in my hand, although I didn't feel much of a draft. Black smoke billowed up from the flame, smelling vaguely of burnt hamburgers at a Fourth of July picnic. I think I was hungry.

"It may be our only way out," urged Caesar.

"A valid point."

"And soon the snow will cover the ark entirely, including us, just as Omar had hoped."

I thought again of Liz Cayman. I thought of my life here in Turkey, the years wasted in mourning. Omar had stolen much from me. I gripped the torch until it shook in my hand, knuckles white. It was time to end his madness.

"C'mon, professor," I said, stepping into the glowing hallway.

"What about booby-traps?"

"We'll take our chances."

* * *

There were no poison darts or trap doors. At least not yet.

Our footsteps stirred the ancient dust into billowing clouds, ghosts awakening from a deep slumber. The green light refracted off the dust motes and exploded into something surreal and dreamlike, shifting and churning, surrounding us in a sort of green aurora borealis. The color touched everything, bathing us completely, transforming our clothing and skin. We looked like two giant tree frogs. Even the professor's teeth glowed green. I'm sure mine were no different.

As the dust settled, we stood before the first mural, which rose from floor to ceiling, perhaps ten feet tall. It depicted a lush landscape. Rolling green hills. Long green grass blowing in the wind. Even the sky had a blue-green glow. On the hills were scrawny cattle, vastly different from our scientifically bred and genetically enhanced beasts. Some of the paint had flaked away, revealing the dark wood beneath. To my untrained eye, the painting seemed to have been done simply, although expertly contrasting light and shadow. A sort of harbinger to the late Nineteenth Century impressionists. The brush strokes were short, quick and bold. I sensed it had been created in a burst of inspiration, with little forethought.

I rubbed my grizzled jaw. "What do you think, old man?"

"Rather well done," he said.

"Rather," I said.

"The artist was before his time," said Caesar. "It belongs in a museum, or at least on my living room wall."

"I think Noah would have something to say about that."

The columns were spaced evenly, framing each mural, and sculpted in bas relief by a master craftsman. The scene on the first column was one of a mighty river surging over boulders, wending its way through the countryside. Large trees, perhaps cypress trees, crowded the banks. Birds sat on the branches of the trees. Gargantuan ferns hung out over the water, as predators, such as wolves and jackals, patrolled the undergrowth. A boy stood knee deep in the river and washed what appeared to be earthen pots. Another fished along the river bank, pole held loosely in his hands; he could have been asleep.

"Somebody had a lot of spare time on his hands," I said.

"Good point," said Caesar. "Taking the biblical story of the Flood at face value, the crew was on board the ark for over a year. With that said, I would suggest these masterworks were created while *on* the sea voyage, as I note a sense of longing for what was lost."

I sensed it too. The painting on the opposite wall was of an old woman amidst a flower garden, wearing a patchwork collection of tattered clothing. She was hunched over a row of purple chrysanthemums. Rather than rendering the old lady in minute detail, her chubby form was merely implied; the artist chose instead to concentrate on the effects of light and shadow, contrasting the primary colors of red, yellow, and blue, with the complements of green, purple and orange. The brush strokes were side by side, rather than overlapping. The result was pure, verdant energy—the colors exploding across the wall in a visual orgasm.

"I'm sensing a pattern here," said the professor. "Other than being a masterwork of impressionistic painting—five thousand years before the impressionist movement began in France—these paintings appear to be a sort of homage to earth and nature."

"Or eulogy," I said.

Caesar shrugged. "Also, the murals and carvings could have been therapeutic. Talk about your rainy day blues."

The next pillar depicted jagged mountains. Again, the craftsmanship was unrivaled. Grass swayed in the wind. Near the base of a mountain, a farmer moved behind his mule, plowing deep furrows into the earth. Birds soared overhead, out-stretched wings catching the light of the setting sun. Deer, ibex, antelope and something that looked amazingly like a unicorn bounded along the many animal trails. There were no predators, and again life seemed to be celebrated.

Caesar said, "There is more going on here than just a spontaneous, undetailed rendering of simple life. There is a love for life. A love for the simple act of living. Perhaps even a tribute to life." He paused. "But there is one thing I don't get: how is the paint glowing?"

I thought about that. "The base for the paint may be pigments extracted from phosphorescent lichen, combined with linseed oil for added adherence. Of course the cold of Ararat would preserve it perfectly, perhaps even glowing to this day."

"But why use glowing lichen as a base for the paint?" Caesar asked.

I shrugged. "What better way to enhance your requiem for Mother Earth?"

Caesar inhaled. He seemed to want to reach out and touch the painting. He managed to control himself. "Truly a miracle," he said.

"At this point, professor, I've lost sight of what is a miracle and what isn't."

Next was a portrait of a striking woman. Hair hidden behind a shawl, she was robed in many colorful layers of heavy material. The bones of her face seemed both fragile and strong. Lips full and unpainted. Her eyes were not just green but *Earth* green. The color of new grass. Budding leaves. Moss on a tree.

"Naamah, I presume," I said.

"I certainly hope so," said the professor. "Otherwise Noah has some explaining to do."

We were silent, staring at the woman who stared back at us. I said, "Do you think Noah was the artist?"

Caesar inhaled. "Isn't it pretty to think so?"

There were more paintings. More columns. We saw scenes of family life, community life, workers plying their trades. But as we neared the end of the hall, we sensed an ominous change, from the innocent to the carnal. Drunken brawls. A public stoning of two children...then we came upon the next mural.

It was a massive public orgy. And detailed at that. Caesar leaned forward, hastily wiping his glasses. His face turned a shade redder than a turnip. "Rather imaginative," he mumbled.

Hundreds of bodies were contorted and writhing and gleaming with sweat, men and women sprawled across the furs of bears and oxen, men vastly outnumbering the women. No orifice was left unviolated, no man or woman left wanting. As a whole, they could have been one endless, undulating serpent of flesh. They appeared to be in a palace, or perhaps a temple. Gleaming fixtures surrounded the room, and golden human-like statues stood regally off to the side, impassively watching the heaving masses, perhaps the only items left unmolested in the room.

I took a deep breath and let it out slowly through my nose. The painting was disturbing. Most involved in the orgy seemed unwilling participants. Indeed, some were even bound, although not gagged.

"I can't say the women are exhibiting the same looks of sexual glee as the men," I said.

"And even some of the men seem a bit repulsed," added the professor. He tilted his head and raked his beard with a single index finger. I think his glasses were fogging up. "Limber bunch."

"So what do you make of it, professor?"

"Makes Sodom and Gomorrah look like a carnival ride."

At the end of the hall we came to the final mural. It showed a starry night above a field of green meadows. It could have been "Starry Night" by Van Gogh. The grass was bent as if blown by gale-force winds. And yet there was something quite ominous about the painting.

"Do you see it?" asked the professor.

"Yes."

A blazing fireball streaked across the sky, followed by a long, burning tail. The fireball seemed to be on a direct course with Earth. We were silent, digesting the information portrayed in the painting.

"An asteroid," Caesar finally said, nodding to himself as if to confirm his own suspicions. "It would have impacted the earth with the force of ten thousand nuclear explosions. Earthquakes, volcanoes and tidal waves would have swept throughout the land...perhaps global, perhaps not. Great cities, small towns, and villages would have been equally drowned in an instant. Nothing would have been spared."

CHAPTER FIFTY-TWO

From the hallway we moved into a small, domed room. The room was vaguely reminiscent of a tabernacle, complete with lectern and altar.

"A place of worship," I said.

"Yes," said Caesar. "Which in hindsight seems obvious, especially for one as deeply devoted as Noah."

Sconces made of gold hung in pairs on the curved walls, distributed liberally throughout the circular room. Stretched before us were eight rectangular wooden mats. They appeared to be designations for kneeling. If so, they looked uncomfortable at best; then again, perhaps sore knees inspired humility. Beyond was a limestone altar carved in the shape of a box, that must have been hell loading onto the ark. And at the back of the temple, sitting side by side on the raised semi-circular platform of the lectern, were two massive alabaster sarcophagi. The alabaster glowed ivory-white in the flickering torch.

The temple was very silent, and a little spooky. The only noise was Caesar's labored breathing through his damaged nose, and the crackle of the torch, which continued to whip in my hand as if from a draft, although I was fairly certain there was no draft. The air itself was heavy and difficult to breathe. I found it difficult to relax in the presence of the two stone coffins.

Caesar was game, moving between the wooden mats, rubbing his thick beard. "Many fertility cults arose with the advent of farming," he said. "Later, in Mesopotamia, nature gods were worshipped. The gods were organized as a democratic council, reflecting the political relations among the various city-states of Mesopotamia. Although Noah is believed to have lived near Mesopotamia, it is interesting to note that he worshipped a single godhead. Also, it is thought that he was an adherent to an ancient tradition called the Sethites, named for one of the sons of Adam."

I followed Caesar to the altar. Built from a single massive block of limestone, it was surprisingly archaic, edges roughly hued. It seemed to pre-date much of the artistic splendor within the ark.

Caesar said, "Noah brought seven pairs of clean animals into the ark to be sacrificed. Early in biblical tradition, God demanded blood sacrifices to appease his wrath and atone for man's sin."

"Just as long as it wasn't virgin maidens."

I had an extreme sense that precious time was slipping by. We needed to find an exit. And soon. Even now, Faye might be on her way to the Kingdom of Saudi, via the emir's private Lear jet.

We moved beyond the altar, up two or three stairs to the lectern. The torchlight crawled over the two sarcophagi. Both had sliding panels on one end. The panels appeared to slide down into grooves, locked in place with stone pins on either side. Removal of the pins would doubtless open the sarcophagi. The flickering light revealed a simple form of writing etched deeply into the crown of each coffin.

"Two very old vampires?" I suggested.

Caesar ignored me and leaned over the first sarcophagus, blowing away dust, revealing more of the writing. "Some speculate that Noah was entombed within his ark, coming full circle, if you will. Although according to a Lebanese tradition, he was buried in the mountains near the ancient city of Damascus." Caesar paused. "However, found in the Apocrypha, those books not included in the Protestant Bible today, is the legend that Adam's body was preserved on the ark as protection from the Flood."

"Adam and Eve." I grinned, then waved the torch toward the inscriptions. "Maybe these engravings will shed some light on the identity of our friends."

Caesar breathed loudly through his mouth, ruffling the whiskers around his lips. His nose had taken on a deeper shade of red. Magenta, perhaps. It seemed ready to explode. He shook his head with great regret. "Unfortunately, these pictographs or ideograms pre-date anything I'm familiar with, although they do appear to be calendrical." Caesar paused, a wicked twinkle his eye. "Of course, we could open them and see what's inside."

I shook my head and stepped back. "And risk the wrath of God?"

"Wrong ark, Sam."

"Still, that sounds like a very bad idea."

He sighed, "Yeah, you're probably right. Let's wait for the experts."

I gladly moved away from the sarcophagi. The wavering torchlight crawled over the curved walls. Sconces gleamed, shadows fled. The platform, however, was empty. I sighed, frustrated. We had reached a dead end.

I stopped in mid-step. No, not entirely empty.

At the far end of the curved wall was a small opening, perhaps five feet high and no wider than a man's shoulders —a very short man's shoulders. Just inside the opening was the beginnings of a wooden staircase that led straight up into the darkness.

* * *

We left the temple with its creepy stone coffins. The stairs were spaced far apart, each riser more than ten inches high. The five foot tall Noah would have taken two steps for every one of ours. There were no balustrades to guide our hands, just smooth walls to either side, cold to the touch. With each step, the temperature dropped until our breaths frosted before us. The increased cold would keep Caesar's nose from exploding.

The stairs ended in a short landing and a blank wall, like the Winchester mansion with its stairs to nowhere. "Was Noah insane?" I asked.

Caesar brushed past me, feeling the wall with the tips of his fingers. "No, Sam, although many claimed he was."

I leaned a shoulder against the fossilized wood and watched him quietly, wishing I had a cigarette. Even something that resembled a cigarette. The professor's fingers began tracing a wide, rectangular outline. He nodded, grinning through his nest of whiskers.

"It's a window," he said.

"Doesn't look like much of a window, professor."

He ignored me, pushing with his hands. The veins on his neck stood out like frayed rope. "You could help, you know," he said, grunting.

"Sure," I said. "Looks like fun."

I moved over and applied my own weight to the wall. Suddenly two massive shutters swung out to either side. A shaft of murky light slanted through the opening, falling across Caesar's triumphant face. The shutter itself was held in place by hidden joints that creaked horribly, but worked perfectly.

"They probably used a rope to haul the shutters back in," said Caesar. He leaned out the window, grinning like a fool. The wind whipped his hair into a gray cyclone. Snow fell across his shoulders and stuck to his beard like Velcro. Watching Caesar, I could almost imagine another old man leaning out this same window at the end of a very long journey. Perhaps even releasing a dove....

* * *

The ark's hull was wedged tightly against a steep ice cliff. We climbed through the square window and shimmied our way down between the hull and the cliff to the canyon floor below.

We moved past the ship's prow, which rose majestically up into the swirling snow. A short while later, I stopped and looked back. Already the ark was barely distinguishable under a thick blanket of snow, and soon it would be buried entirely. Perhaps forever.

CHAPTER FIFTY-THREE

Snow blew directly into our faces, funneled through the granite cliffs that rose steeply to either side. The weather was merciless and foul, and seemed intent to kick us when we were already down. But we persisted doggedly, often moving blindly through the storm.

We emerged onto the Abich glacier, far above Omar's camp. Alert for crevasses, knowing we would have been incalculably safer roped together, I led the way across the ice field. Caesar, subdued since leaving the ark, followed silently. Together, we moved cautiously down the glacier, toward camp, keeping to the safety of boulders which thrust up through the ice like the bony plates of a stegosaurus.

* * *

I spotted a solitary guard, smoking a cigarette, an AK-47 hanging casually from a strap around his neck, trudging slowly through the snow on the north side of camp. Probably at the tail-end of a graveyard shift.

The guard stopped and propped his weapon against a boulder and sat on a rock ledge that could have been carved naturally from the mountain. He appeared to be speaking with someone. Or talking to himself.

I motioned for the professor to wait. But the stubborn bastard shook his head and continued to follow me. Like father, like daughter.

We descended from above, and when we were ten feet away I slowed the pace. The howling wind masked our crunching feet. I removed the gun from my waist, and took a deep breath—

* * *

Sheltered in a small cul-de-sac, safe from the wind, two guards were playing hooky from their rounds, hidden from view. When they saw us, their cigarettes dropped from their opened mouths, and if they saw my gun pointed at their faces, they didn't care. Immediately, both swung their weapons in our direction. Caesar lunged into view, flying through the air, tackling one of the soldiers like a linebacker sacking a quarterback.

"Ah, hell," I said, and threw myself into the next soldier.

We tumbled together in the snow. His hand gripped my throat. When I found leverage, my face no doubt purple from lack of oxygen, I knocked his hand away and leveled a clean blow to his jaw. The force of my punch shoved the back of his skull into the ice and his eyes rolled up into his head.

I shook my hand, which hurt like hell. I turned to see how Caesar was faring—

Caesar stood over his man like a predator guarding his prey. The guard lay on his side holding his stomach as if his intestines would spill out. Caesar smiled wolfishly. "Damn, that felt good."

* * *

The cul-de-sac was a nice place to have a smoke. So I did, snagging one from the breast pocket of the older soldier, along with a lighter. As I puffed contentedly, I stared at our two prisoners. Black-eyed and cut, both looked as if they had seen better days.

In Arabic, I said, "When does the emir plan on launching the warhead?"

The older one, still holding his stomach and having difficulty breathing, was heavy-set and sported a thick beard. He looked much too soft to be a soldier. Despite his pain, he grinned. "It's your lucky day, my friend."

"I'm short on luck and patience," I said. "What do you mean?"

He stood proudly. "I'm the ballistic technician hired to arm the weapon."

"Why are you here and not with the others?"

"I needed a smoke, worked all day. Also, I skipped the unveiling ceremonies."

"Unveiling? What do you mean?"

"The tent has been removed in preparation for tonight's launch."

"The missile has been armed?"

The man beamed proudly. "By none other than me."

"What's your name?" I asked.

"I'm Jabbar, from Ankara."

"Do you realize that you've just set in motion a process that could kill hundreds of thousands?"

He shrugged. "If not me, then it would have been someone else. The pay was good."

I wanted to punch him in the mouth, break every tooth in his scrappy little face. "How long until it's launched?"

He glanced at his watch. "Thirty-two minutes."

"How long will it take to disarm the missile?" I asked

"It's been a while since I've disarmed a launching sequence." He shrugged and looked up, doing the calculations in his head as if the fate of millions were not at stake. "I would need at least two hours."

I pointed my gun at his head. "I will give you twenty minutes."

"Twenty minutes should be fine."

I suddenly turned and hit the other soldier, who had only recently awakened, across his forehead with the stock of his own rifle. It was too late in the game to worry about him, as my level of human compassion was approaching zero. I tied him up with his own jacket, and pushed Jabbar before me.

"C'mon," I said. "We have a bomb to dismantle."

CHAPTER FIFTY-FOUR

We hid behind a snow-covered boulder just outside of camp. Soldiers were loading boxes and personal belongings into the chopper. The prince was packing it in. No doubt returning home to his capitol in Riyadh. And Faye would join his harem, hidden forever from Western eyes, with no means to escape. Until she was too old and ugly to please young princes. And then perhaps she would take a long walk into the empty desert.

Off to one side, Farid was supervising the whole operation. The big man had saved our lives, risking much in return. The price would almost certainly be termination and the loss of face, and to the Arab that is priceless.

Jabbar sat quietly between us. There was a spark in his wild eyes. I found it interesting that Jabbar put up little protest. Indeed, he seemed almost eager to cooperate.

I turned to the professor and motioned to his automatic weapon. "Do you know how to use that thing?"

Caesar grinned. "I imagine you press the trigger and point."

"I see you're no slouch. But remember: aim low. These things shoot high."

"So what's the plan?" asked Caesar.

"We need a diversion," I said.

"But I thought blowing up the launcher was the diversion."

I thought about that. "Okay, we need a diversion for the diversion."

"What do you intend to do?" he asked.

"I'm not sure yet. Any ideas?" I asked.

"I thought that was your department," said Caesar.

"And what's your department?" I asked.

"I'm the extra muscle," he said.

"Okay, now I'm worried."

* * *

A Kurdish soldier stepped away from the others and headed our way. As he walked, he unbuckled his belt. It was then that I noticed something wafting up around us. Something foul. *Perfume de toilette*. In our haste to find shelter close to camp, we had not stopped to consider the convenience of such a large boulder in close proximity to camp.

Latrine. He was coming to relieve himself.

"Why didn't you mention this was the community latrine, Jabbar," I hissed quietly.

"You didn't ask, my friend."

I scowled.

"Sam, he's heading straight for us," said the professor, his voice rising with alarm. "What do we do?"

"Start by being quiet. And sit tight," I said.

The soldier removed his gloves, and continued toward us. I waited quietly, holding my breath. The crunch of boots grew louder. The soldier was humming a Kurdish folk song.

I extended my fingers, waiting. A boot appeared from around the boulder—

I reached up and grabbed the coat lapels of the startled soldier, yanked him to the ground, and punched him in the face, splitting my knuckle on his cheekbone. The blow dazed him, but still he managed to shout for help. The second punch knocked him out cold. His head lolled to the side, tongue hanging out like a happy dog.

"Hell of a punch," said Caesar. "Someday you'll have to show me how to do that."

I put my finger to my lips, *shushing* him. But the guard's shout of alarm had already alerted the others. From camp I heard the sudden running of feet and the shout of orders.

I peered around the boulder. The soldiers had scattered for cover, keeping to the tents and even the chopper. All leveled their weapons at us.

"Okay, Sam," said Caesar, peering around his side of the boulder. "I think it's time for a really good idea."

I removed a grenade from the belt of the soldier. I hefted it like a baseball. It just *felt* destructive. I wondered how far I could throw it.

The first shot *zinged* off the top of the boulder. Followed by another, and another.

Caesar looked at me, amusement in his eyes. The man was infallible. "I think they're onto us, Sam."

"Uh huh."

He motioned to the grenade. "You going to use that thing or just admire it?"

More bullets smacked the boulder, whistled overhead like mosquitoes on speed. Each report deafening, echoing off the distant granite cliffs. In a less stable part of the mountain, the reports would have attracted the attention of an avalanche. As it was, Omar had selected a good site for the launcher, with little chance of catastrophe.

To keep them on their toes, I swung my rifle around the boulder and pulled the trigger. The AK-47 bucked wildly, akin to holding a mongoose by the scruff of the neck. Sudden shouts of alarm. I had surprised the hell out of them, temporarily stopping the deluge of bullets.

I said to the professor, "You follow my lead."

"What are you going to do?" he asked.

"Just watch," I said.

The bullets picked up again, almost tentatively so, smacking against the rock, zipping by overhead. I took a deep breath and pulled the spring from the grenade, arming it.

CHAPTER FIFTY-FIVE

My mental timer ticked off the seconds: *Five one hundred*.

I heard the muted hiss of the grenade's fuse as I gripped it the same way I threw my fastball back in college.

Four one hundred.

I stood. Muzzles flashed from around tents and equipment—where the soldiers had sought refuge.

Three one hundred.

Bullets whipped by overhead, a little too close for comfort. I briefly took aim—

Two one hundred.

And threw the grenade as far as I could. It arced slightly in the air, like a throw from right field to home plate. The soldiers stopped firing and turned to observe the small oblong object that had just landed among them. As recognition set in, a shout of alarm erupted in unison. Soldiers scattered in all directions.

The grenade rolled to a stop near one of the two helicopters, and I ducked behind the boulder, waiting. Almost in succession, two distinct explosions ripped through the cool air. The first was from the grenade itself, and the second was the fuel tank from the closest chopper. The ground jolted as a fountain of fire gushed into the sky, a geyser from hell. Burning pieces of metal and wreckage flipped through the air.

Such a fragment hit the snow in front of us just a few feet away, a burning section of the helicopter's cockpit, hissing in the snow. The plastic and glass had melted and fused together.

"Mother of God," whispered Caesar. "That's a hell of a distraction."

Men were screaming, howling. Some seriously injured. It was unfortunate that they were between me and Faye. I grabbed Caesar by the sleeve. "C'mon. Let's get out of this stink hole."

* * *

We kept low to the ground. To our right, the helicopter was a smoldering fire of unrecognizable wreckage. Meltwater flowed from under the burning mass, as the chopper sank into the melting glacier.

Most of the action, however, was centered around Omar's tent. And then I saw why. A section of the Arab's tent had burned away, leaving a gaping hole.

Had Faye been hurt? Something inside me wanted to die. *Christ, what if she got hurt?*

There was no time to think about it because a soldier, tending to an injured comrade, spotted us and swung his weapon around, firing a volley that went high overhead. He adjusted his sites and a trail of mini explosions followed at our heals. Running, I returned his fire. Turns out my aim was pretty good. The fabric of his coat shredded as I nearly cut him in half.

There were no other challengers. And soon we came upon the launcher. It sat like a black insect against the darkening sky. A disconcerting hum emanated it. I knew the sound well. *It was armed.*

* * *

Jabbar led the way to a series of wooden shacks off to the side, explaining that this is where the computerized launch direction console was located. For the time being we had gone unnoticed.

He pushed his way through a heavy door and we stepped out of the wind. He flicked on a track of halogen lighting.

The shack was a pyromaniac's dirty dream. Coils of black powder wires. Detonator caps. Many things marked: *Dangerous, Highly Flammable And/Or Explosive!* Skulls and crossbones abounded.

Jabbar went immediately over to the launch box in one corner of the room and punched a sequence of numbers on a rubber pad. The black box clicked open. Tangled wires spilled out. The wires looked more like a spaghetti dinner gone amok. Jabbar lifted the plastic coils and frowned. He scratched his head and mumbled something about the wires in Turkish. He mumbled that they looked like a spaghetti dinner gone amok. I glanced inside the box and saw an electronic counter. There was ten minutes left before launching.

"Get to work," I told Jabbar.

There were three entrances into the workroom/shack. I moved back and forth between the west and south entrance, while Caesar covered the north entrance. The hallways were empty. I could hear muted shouts from outside, mixed with machine gun fire. I wondered just who the hell they were shooting at.

Caesar's gray eyes were distorted behind his broken glasses. He took them off and rubbed them. I asked how things were going on his end, and he said fine. I saw that his clothing was torn. His hair disheveled. Cut and battered, he looked little like the distinguished professor I knew him to be.

I glanced inside the control box. *Six minutes*.

"Hurry, Jabbar!"

He waved me off with a flick of his wrist. He was punching in sequence after sequence of numbers. Also, he appeared to be re-routing the cables. Finally, Jabbar stepped back and held his arms out dramatically like a Broadway singer. "It is done," he proclaimed.

"Then why is the counter still counting?" I asked.

Jabbar frowned. "Hmm." He tapped a fingernail on his small front teeth. He reached inside the black box and poked around a bit more.

More shouts from outside. The machine gun fire had trailed off to a few scattered pops, perhaps as the soldiers realized we were not out there. I moved from doorway to doorway. I could feel the sweat on my brow. We were rapidly running out of time. Caesar continued to peer down the hallway, squinting through his damaged glasses.

"Hurry, Jabbar!" I said.

"Believe me, my friend, you don't want to rush me. I am the last person in the world you want to rush. And, quite frankly, you're making me nervous."

"Point taken. Now hurry!"

Three minutes....

We waited another minute, Jabbar mumbling incoherently, fingers working frantically. He emerged from the box again, perspiration dotting his brow. "I think she's ready."

"Then why is it still counting?"

"This is getting to be bothersome," he said. "I am most embarrassed, my friend," said Jabbar. He scratched his head and seemed to turn a shade red.

We were down to the last minute. Jabbar hummed to himself, impervious to the fate of thousands. I stuck the gun behind his ear. "That missile goes off, then your head goes off with it."

Thirty seconds...

"Ah, yes, this should be it!" His fingers danced crazily. "There!"

The clock, inevitably, was still counting down.

"Why does it keep *doing that*?" he moaned, frustrated.

Ten seconds. I pressed the gun against the back of his head. My hand shook. Sweat stung my eyes. *Five seconds.*

He squealed with delight, like a pig at the sight of a trough of muck. He seized two wires, one red, one black. He held each in a hand.

And pulled them apart.

The counter stopped at 2 seconds.

I lowered the gun and exhaled. Jabbar turned and grinned, and then his eyes widened in horror.

* * *

Caesar gasped and I heard his weapon clatter to the wooden floor. I swung my AK-47 around just as Caesar was raising his hands high into the air, the barrel of a Luger pressed into his swollen nose, forcing his broken glasses up over his forehead. The man grinning behind the gun was Kazeem. His dark gaze flicked my way. "Put your weapon down, Mr. Ward."

I did as I was told.

Caesar glanced in my direction. "I'm sorry, Sam. He came from the left. Hell, I thought there was a wall to the left. I think I need a new pair of glasses."

"Shut up, fool." Kazeem's eyes were wide and wild, completely unstable. He pushed Caesar away and pointed the weapon at Jabbar. "Step away from the black box." He spoke in English, perhaps for the benefit of us all.

And when Jabbar stepped away, Kazeem promptly shot him in the neck, a small red flower instantly appearing above his collar, blossoming rapidly. The concussion echoed loudly in the small room. Jabbar fell forward to his knees, and then flat on his stomach. He was dead before he hit the ground. Kazeem's eyes glowed with pleasure, my candidate for Sociopath of the Year.

I had deliberately set the stock of my rifle on the toe of my boot. The idea was to kick the rifle up, catch it and shoot our way out of this mess. At least, that was the *idea*.

But before I could attempt the impossible, a massive shadow materialized behind Kazeem. Farid stepped into the light. He pressed a curved scimitar, or *jambiya*, between the shoulder blades of the Arab prince. "Put down your weapon, emir, and kick it away."

Kazeem stood motionless, perhaps in disbelief, until prompted by the point of Farid's *jambiya*. He set the weapon down, kicked it away. "You're making a deadly mistake, nomad," said the prince to Farid.

Farid ignored him and cast his glance my way. "The emir is boarding the helicopter as we speak, my friend, and he has the girl. I suggest you hurry."

"What about you?" I asked.

"I'm here for some unfinished business."

CHAPTER FIFTY-SIX

Once, long ago, Farid had been in love. Bhutan had worked in the palace in Riyadh. She had been a concubine, flesh for the insatiable young princes. She had risked much to meet with Farid in stolen moonlit rendezvous. Until they were caught by Emir Kazeem Ali. She had been seized, and Farid had been briefly imprisoned. He would learn later that Bhutan had been publicly beheaded. A lesson for those who fall in love in the Kingdom.

Now, in that small wooden room, with the Americans gone, Farid ordered Kazeem to turn and face him.

Both men filled the small room almost to capacity. Sweat stood on Kazeem's brow, chest rising and falling rapidly. Farid, in contrast, breathed easily, a glimmer of pleasure in his eyes. He said, "Now, emir, we end this once and for all."

"Surely you will not strike an unarmed man."

"No, emir. I do not play by your rules. Withdraw your *jambiya* and prepare for battle."

Kazeem laughed and stepped back. In a practiced motion, his own jewel-encrusted *jambiya* appeared in his hand as if by magic. The *jambiya's* hilt was decorated with emeralds, as was the handguard; it looked more like a museum piece than an efficient weapon. But Farid knew better. The young prince was well-trained in the use of the scimitar, as were most of the Arab royalty. The bodyguard's own *jambiya*, in contrast, was fashioned from simple hand-worked steel.

The two warriors circled each other, swords raised in the on guard position. The scene could have been extracted from the *Arabian Nights*. Outside, beyond the walls of the cramped workroom, came shouts and machine gun fire. The sounds went unnoticed within the room, neither taking their eyes off the other. Farid's heart beat calmly in his cavernous chest. He took long, even breaths. His widely-set nostrils flared. He was unaware that he was grinning, although he knew that he was taking considerable pleasure from this moment. Perhaps too much pleasure.

Maybe I'm no better than the prince, who takes such enjoyment in the destruction of things, thought Farid. But Farid knew that he had never enjoyed killing. Until now.

Kazeem's thin lips curled into a wolfish grin. He projected confidence, but Farid detected an undercurrent of concern in the way the emir's eyes shifted unsteadily, in the way his chest rose quickly with each shallow breath.

Yes, thought Farid, *you should be concerned.*

Kazeem lunged forward, thrusting the point of his gilded blade at the bodyguard's chest. With the flick of the wrist, Farid parried. Sparks exploded. The clang of steel reverberated loudly in the small room. Kazeem stepped back, panting through his open mouth.

"She was just a whore," said Kazeem.

"I loved her, emir."

"You defiled her, you pig! I was supremely pleased to watch her die. In fact, she called out your name until the moment the ax dropped. Apparently she was under the false impression that you would save her."

Bright flashes of hate seared Farid's brain. But he forced himself to stay calm, breathing deeply through his nostrils, controlling his anger. The anger, he knew, could come later, but not now. No, not now.

Kazeem attacked, attempting a classic feint-and-lunge maneuver. Farid parried it easily and punched the prince in the face as hard as he could. Kazeem's head snapped back, blood jetting from both nostrils. It had been a hell of a punch. Farid's hand ached pleasantly. The prince looked at the blood on his robe, and then at Farid.

Hell hath no fury like a spoiled prince scorned—

Kazeem pushed himself off the wall, and lunged recklessly. Farid parried and riposted, his blade opening a slashing wound across the emir's chest. The prince cried out and looked down, and in that instant, Farid swung his steel blade in a deadly arch. Kazeem's eyes opened in horror. The whistling blade swept through the air and through the emir's neck. As swiftly as if through butter. Blood poured free from the ghastly wound like a macabre necklace. The emir's eyelids fluttered crazily.

"It is supremely pleasant watching you die, emir."

Farid stepped back as the large head, at least twenty-five pounds worth, toppled over the still-standing body and thudded on the wooden floor, coming to rest near Farid's blood-spattered boots. With the tip of his sword, Farid sent the headless body crashing backwards.

CHAPTER FIFTY-SEVEN

Unchallenged, Caesar and I moved along the rear of the launcher. We peered cautiously into camp through the gently falling snow. Soldiers were everywhere, moving quickly from tent to tent, searching. Between us and the helicopters (one of which was still in smoldering ruins) was a vast, empty stretch of ice. It might as well have been Siberia.

"Cover me, professor," I said.

"Cover you with what?"

"With your gun, professor. Keep the soldiers at bay while I make a break for the chopper."

He nodded, but looked puzzled. The chopper was fifty yards away. Even from here, I could see the pilot going through his pre-flight checks, face hidden behind a helmet shield.

Inhaling, I darted out into the open glacier.

* * *

I went unchallenged for the first twenty yards, running low to the ground, until several small explosions erupted at my feet, sending up showers of icy particles.

Who was shooting at me?

I looked over my shoulder—and stopped running. The professor was taking dead aim at me again, looking down the sights of his weapon. "Don't shoot at me!" I pointed up the slope. "Shoot at them, goddamn it!"

The professor lowered his weapon, cheeks turning bright red. He cupped a hand around his mouth to direct his voice. "Sorry, Sam. Now that you mention it, shooting at you does seem a little dangerous."

Bullets suddenly ripped through the ice to my right, moving rapidly to cut me down. I jumped to the side, rolled, and returned fire. Behind me, I could hear Caesar's own weapon rattling away; at least he wasn't shooting at me. Farther up the slope, two soldiers scrambled for cover behind a snow-dusted boulder.

I ran hard for the black chopper. As I did so, a bullet tore through the armpit of my jacket, but missed me. I kept my head down and alternately fired in the direction of the soldiers above.

Thirty yards from the chopper...

As it prepared for lift-off, the combined sounds of the twin turbines and rotor blades was almost deafening. I picked up my speed.

Twenty yards...

The chopper lifted slowly in the air, scattering snow in all directions. It hung briefly above the slope. Then turned to port, on its way down the mountain.

"Ah, hell," I said, and tossed aside my weapon and angled across the hard-packed ice to cut-off the rising aircraft.

* * *

The big cabin door opened. Omar appeared holding a small revolver. The muzzle flashed. Bullets impacted the ice in a random pattern around me. Luckily, the emir was a horrible shot. I considered varying my course, until I realized a varied course might match the emir's own erratic shooting pattern.

I saw one of Omar's shooting problems: Faye was beating his exposed back with her fists, forcing him to hold her off while he methodically snapped off shots at me. Maybe Omar was thinking twice about Faye joining his harem.

I ducked as a bullet whistled past my right temporal lobe. He was getting closer.

Omar finally backhanded Faye, sending her reeling into the cabin, where she disappeared from view.

The son of a bitch.

I was ten feet from the helicopter.

Point blank range.

The Arab grinned and nodded, as if confirming once and for all that he would be victorious in the end. His destiny and all that shit. I watched his finger tighten around the trigger—

But he was out of bullets. He blinked uncomprehendingly at first; then, in anger, hurled the revolver at me, which promptly bounced off my shoulder, and hurt like hell. Lucky throw. And as the helicopter gained altitude, I jumped and extended my fingers…and grabbed hold of the starboard landing skid.

* * *

The ASW attack helicopter lifted quickly to five hundred feet. Straight up into the swirling snow. I dangled like an autumn maple leaf at the end of a bare branch. I adjusted my grip, knotting my arms around both the horizontal skid and forward vertical skid. The chopper continued to gain altitude. Snow fluttered crazily, stirred by the downblast generated by both of the main rotor blades and the four-bladed tail rotors. Below, the camp was barely discernible through the storm. The missile launcher looked like a dark cancer on the pristine landscape.

I swung my right leg up and over the horizontal skid, taking the weight off my arms. I caught my breath and tried to think clearly. My left leg hung out into open space. My face was pressed against the metal skid. Wind pounded me. A few moments later I realized it was impossible to think clearly. But I knew I had to get on board the chopper. Somehow.

* * *

The chopper swept low over the mountain. The wind hammered me into immobility. I feared that I would be torn away by the thundering wind. I tried reminding myself that I was a fearless explorer, but that didn't work. I told myself to think of something positive. But the best I could come up with was that I hadn't fallen yet.

Below, the Ahora Gorge appeared majestically, cutting deeply into the heart of Ararat. Meltwater from the Abich glacier fell hundreds of feet down a steep cliff into a churning whirlpool. The pool fed a frothing river that marched down the center of the gorge.

Omar appeared again in the cabin door, this time with an AK-47. I kicked away from the horizontal skid and shimmied up the forward vertical, which arched underneath the belly of the chopper. Sparks ricocheted behind me. I was safe for the moment, away from his angle of fire.

The chopper banked to port and gained altitude until we were hidden within the eye of the storm, surrounded by the roiling gray mist. Here, the beat of the rotor blades was amplified, unbearably loud. The mist had a way of dampening the skids, which may or may not have been intentional.

The chopper hovered like a UFO seeking its next bovine victim. I swung my feet around the arched vertical skid. Time passed slowly. The helicopter pulsated with life. The cloud continued to billow and fold in on itself, stirred awake by the spinning rotor blades. I had a sickening feeling about what was to come next. And I wasn't disappointed.

The chopper tilted forward, then dove down through the cloud cover, its mighty turbines drowned by the thundering wind. The clouds opened; the mountain appeared through the slashing snow.

The chopper suddenly leveled, turbines grinding, stabilizers shuddering. The tremendous gravitational forces tore my hands loose and I swung upside down, held in place only by my crossed legs. Blood rushed to my head. I reached up and gripped the metal landing skid just as the chopper banked to starboard, throwing me hard into the vertical skid. The shock caused my breath to burst from my lungs.

Omar appeared once again like a bad dream, squeezing off a few more shots, but I was already moving hand over hand up the vertical skid and away from his line of fire. I dangled under the craft like a South American spider monkey, minus the prehensile tail. And certainly not as cute.

Next, I endured a series of aerial maneuvers that were not only insane, but would fill any number of barf bags. The chopper wove and looped and plunged and twisted, the pilot challenging the craft's capabilities to the limit.

But I was too stubborn, or stupid, to fall.

* * *

We were now deep within the Ahora Gorge, the helicopter's tiny shadow weaving in and out of the corrugated face of the granite cliff. Compared to the enormity of the canyon, we were nothing more than a flyspeck. Before us rose the north wall. As we approached, I wondered if the emir was crazy enough to kill us all.

Then the chopper abruptly angled up.

I took advantage of the minor reprieve in aerial acrobatics, and swung my feet onto the horizontal skid. There I squatted, facing the open hatch. The cabin could seat up to five soldiers, although the ASW was designed for a three-man crew, including both a pilot and co-pilot. Omar, standing just inside the cabin doorway, saw me and swung his assault rifle in my direction.

In the same instant, I lunged forward into the cabin.

CHAPTER FIFTY-EIGHT

The first shot impacted my shoulder like a blow from a mallet, the 7.62 mm bullet spinning me in the air, knocking the breath out of me. I collided with the emir before he could fire again, hurling the prince to his back.

The bullet had entered my shoulder between the pectoral and deltoid muscles, exiting violently through my back. That would leave a mark. Warm blood spread instantly from both the entrance and exit wounds. For now my arm was merely numb; the pain would set in shortly. Faye was slouched behind the co-pilot seat, hanging on to the craft's fire extinguisher, lip bleeding. She scrambled to her feet when she saw me. I could see the pilot trying to look over his shoulder, his face obscured behind the faceplate. Probably wishing he had a rearview mirror.

Hunched forward in the small cabin, Omar stood and withdrew his ceremonial *jambiya* from his hip scabbard. "I assume," he said, his voice coming to my ears as if from far away, "that if you are here, than my brother is dead."

I thought of Farid. I did not yet know what had happened in that small control room, but I was relatively confident of the outcome. From the corner of my eye, I saw that Faye was carefully removing the fire extinguisher from the wall. I had to keep the emir talking, despite the pain that was setting in, despite the blood pooling beneath me. "Yes, emir, your brother is dead."

Omar shook his head sadly, although he displayed little regret. "Am I to assume that Farid had something to do with his death?"

"You assume correctly, emir."

A pained expression crossed Omar's haggard face. It was brief and fleeting, more of a subliminal display of pain. "It was inevitable, I suppose. Kazeem was always jealous and perhaps intimidated by Farid's skill and size. Indeed, Farid was a good bodyguard, perhaps the best, but he had gotten soft of late, and that is unacceptable."

"He was tired of the senseless killing. You have killed many in your quest for revenge."

"And I will kill more," he said, leveling the *jambiya* at my chest. "At least one more."

He lunged forward, but a sudden burst of carbon-dioxide enriched foam pummeled him, knocking him off balance. Omar screeched in frustration and swung his blade wildly in reposte, knocking the canister out of Faye's hand. Covered in foam, dripping from his nose and chin, the emir looked like the victim of a college fraternity prank. Faye searched desperately for something to defend herself with, and grabbed a shiny pair of pliers that was wedged behind the co-pilot chair and the floor. Sloppy maintenance. She looked at the pliers and blinked, but held them out bravely, as if she intended to ply the emir to death.

"Sam," she said, not daring to take her eyes off the emir, "now it's *your* turn to save *me*."

Waves of pain rocked me. Blackness encroached along the edges of my vision. I needed to stop the flow of precious blood from my wounds, but now was not the time. I stood on jelly legs. Attached to the wall was a white metal box. A first aid kit. I ripped the box free from its mounts and swung it into the back of the emir's head, knocking him forward. The *jambiya* plunged harmlessly into the black fabric of the co-pilot seat cushion.

Shockwaves of pain erupted in my shoulder.

I gasped.

Stars flashed in my head like Vegas neon.

The emir shook his head and pulled the weapon free from the seat. He turned and faced me and tried a quick over-the-top jab at my wounded shoulder. I parried it with a swipe of the box, which rattled in my hand from the impact.

The emir lunged wildly again and I side-stepped the sword and swung my good arm around his neck and held on, squeezing with all my remaining strength.

"Shoot him," he gasped.

Who the hell was he talking to?

I looked up to see the pilot aiming down the sights of his Browning 9mm pistol. He removed his helmet to get a better aim. "But I don't have a clear shot, my lord," he said.

"I'll take my chances, godammit!"

I didn't like the direction this was going, but then Faye suddenly appeared from behind the co-pilot's seat and swung the fire extinguisher down as hard as she could. The metal clanged off his thick skull.

Good girl.

The unconscious pilot slumped forward over the control column, bleeding profusely from a serious head injury, and promptly threw the helicopter into a stomach-turning dive.

CHAPTER FIFTY-NINE

I fell forward through the cabin, spilling over the complex dashboard. Faye ended up in the co-pilot seat. Wind thundered through the cabin. I pulled the unconscious pilot off the control stick. Churning water rapidly filled the windshield. Faye screamed—

I yanked hard on the column. The stabilizers kicked in and the craft swung out of its steep dive. I adjusted the cyclic and we flew low over the water.

Faye looked at me, face ashen. "A Disneyland ride from hell," she said, holding a hand to her chest. "I think I'll be sick for a week." Suddenly her eyes widened and she pointed and I dodged to the left just as the emir's *jambiya* lodged deep into the control panel, cracking glass and severing control knobs. The chopper slewed to the side, on a collision course with the canyon wall. I reached for the throttle, but the emir was clawing at my shoulder, digging his fingers deep into my wound. Pain registered in my brain as bright white flashes. I struggled to retain consciousness.

The cliff rapidly approached.

I grabbed the emir's hand, slick with my own blood, and twisted his fingers until they broke. He screamed. I adjusted the column, and we immediately banked to port, safe.

"Hold the column steady, Faye," I said, gasping.

"How?" Panic in her voice.

I grabbed her hand, placed it on the control stick. "Like this, Faye, and keep it steady." I turned and faced the emir.

Who was now holding the pilot's 9mm Browning, aimed at my chest.

* * *

Wind blasted through the open cabin door. I could see the corrugated canyon wall sliding slowly by as if in slow motion. The wall was composed of layers of glittering quartz. Faye managed to keep the craft steady. Maybe too steady. Omar held the Browning in his right hand. The pinkie and ring finger to his left hand were swelling fast. He was bleeding from a cut lip. "Goodbye, Sam Ward."

"If you kill me," I said quickly. "Who will fly your craft?"

He paused, and looked at the pilot. So did I. The pilot could have been dead, although snot appeared to bubble in and out of his left nostril. Blood trickled down through his thick hairline and across the bridge of his nose. He looked like he'd gone a round or two with Tyson.

"Your pilot is in bad shape, emir."

Omar shrugged. "I'll take my chances with the girl."

I snorted. Faye was in the cockpit behind me. I turned my head slightly in her direction. "The girl?" I snorted. I raised my voice. "She just might be the *worst* pilot in the world."

Did she understand? Or was she insulted?

I should have known better.

Faye threw the stick forward, and the craft pitched violently, and the emir fell into me. We grappled with each other. Although he lost the gun, he ended up more or less on top of me. Immediately he leveled two punches into my damaged shoulder. Yellow starbursts erupted in my head. Each punch like another gunshot. I wanted to pass out. *Needed* to pass out.

"Sam!" cried Faye. "I'm losing control!"

The helicopter swerved hard to starboard. The emir and I rapidly slid toward the cabin door. I reached out and hooked my good arm around the doorframe. My legs swung out into open space. The emir slid into me, clinging to the material of my jacket. The wind pummeled us. The chopper continued to swerve to starboard, and Omar lost his grip, screaming, sliding down to my waist. He looked down, then looked up at me with panic-sticken eyes. His face was white.

"Help me...Sam," he said, and tried to claw his way up my dangling body.

"Quit...moving...asshole," I said through clenched teeth.

I tried to pull both of us up, but there was no strength left in my arm. So we hung there, and the wind thundered over us. Faye had somehow managed to level the chopper. Good for us. I heard her shouting my name, but I was too weak to answer. I rested my forehead against the cool cabin frame. The coolness felt nice. I think I was running on hot. Perhaps, I mused silently, we would hang from the doorway until the chopper ran out of fuel.

Omar spoke from below, his voice rising up as if from a deep well. It had an odd strength to it, as if he had tapped into some previous unknown reserve. "She was beautiful, wasn't she, Sam?"

"Noah's ship was the most beautiful thing I ever saw."

He slid a little further down. "You won, Sam."

I shook my head. "No. You simply lost."

And then he was gone. I looked down and watched him hit the landing skid, flipping briefly, his screams lost in the thundering wind. The rocks below were unforgiving, which echoed my sentiments exactly.

CHAPTER SIXTY

Faye tied the pilot's bomber jacket around my damaged shoulder, stanching the bleeding. A very bad tourniquet, but it would have to do. I needed a doctor. I needed pain killers. Instead, I pushed the pilot aside, and sat in the pilot's seat.

"I hope you know how to fly this thing," she said.

I scanned the controls. I knew my way around a cockpit. "We'll be fine," I said, and eased the control stick forward, increasing the power to the two 1,500-horsepower turbines. I kicked down hard on the rudder pedals and turned the cyclic over to the side, and snapped the tail around, banking sharply to port. I twisted the throttle all the way against the stop, and we streaked hard and low over the steep mountainside.

Faye grinned, and rested her head on my good shoulder. "I take it you *do* know how to fly this thing."

* * *

Hovering at five hundred feet above camp, I was wary of return fire, although I knew that light-caliber machine gun rounds would be ineffective against the ASW's armored cabin. And as of yet, the Kurdish soldiers did not suspect who was flying the craft.

The snowstorm had almost cleared, now just a light sprinkling. The launcher sat like a giant wart on the snowy landscape. Near the rear of the launcher I could see Caesar firing his weapon like a true terrorist. Farid was with him. Farid was holding something shaped vaguely like a baby.

I checked the instruments, easing the collective downward, holding the grip of the cyclic gently between the fingers of my right hand, controlling the balance of the aircraft, the throb of the rotor blades diminishing considerably until the landing skids touched down.

Caesar looked our way, eyes widening in shock. His red nose could probably be seen from outer space, along with the Great Wall of China. Faye waved from the co-pilot seat.

Farid looked at me and grinned, shaking his big head. Promptly, the bodyguard squeezed off a few more shots in the direction of the soldiers, then grabbed Caesar by the shoulder. Soon, both were running toward the craft.

* * *

Once Farid and Caesar were aboard, we deposited the pilot in the snow. As I lifted the craft into the air, my feet finessing the rudder pedals, the dull throb from the propellers deepened. I'd missed that sound. Bullets ricocheted harmlessly off the ASW's armor. We rose to a height of four hundred feet.

"I was getting a little worried," said Caesar. He noticed the make-shift bandage around my shoulder for the first time. "Appears you've had a tough time of it."

"He's been hurt, father," said Faye. She reached out and caressed my right hand, the same hand that was gently maneuvering the cyclic. "He was hurt saving our asses, I might add."

Caesar patted my shoulder. Although it was my good shoulder, a shockwave of pain pulsed through me. "Anyone have any painkillers?" I asked hopefully.

Caesar picked up the first aid kit and frowned at the head-sized dent in it. He opened the box and produced a bottle of aspirin. I ate four raw. Anything to dull the pain.

"Where to now?" asked Caesar.

Before I answered, I looked over my shoulder at Farid. The big bodyguard was hunched behind the co-pilot seat, the cabin too small for him to stand erect. He was staring down through the cockpit window. I saw now what was in his arm. The warhead.

"What do you think, big guy?" I asked him, arching an eyebrow. "Give them something to remember us by?"

Farid was covered in blood that did not appear to be his own. "Do it," he said grimly.

I flicked on the arming switches to the two Hellfire missiles, both equipped with the newly-developed blast/fragmentation warheads, and hung from pylons under the fuselage. I took a deep breath, willing the aspirin to act quickly. Seconds later, the laser seeker locked onto the coded laser energy reflected from the target. The laser-guided Hellfires were ready.

"Hold on," I said.

I flicked a switch and the helicopter shuddered as the first rocket, propelled by a single-stage, single thrust, solid propellant motor, exceeded a thrust of five hundred pounds and left its rail, blazing through the afternoon sky, reaching speeds of upwards near 950 miles per hour.

The missile, capable of leveling tanks and concrete factories, as they had done so well in Desert Storm, entered the Scud launcher. There was a brief pause before a blinding explosion illuminated the mountainside like the dawning of a new sun. I immediately launched the next Hellfire, and the mountainside erupted into a burning pyre, black smoke billowing into the air.

We were silent, watching the burning wreckage. Faye leaned over and kissed me long and hard. When she was done she looked me in the eye. "Boys and their guns."

"It's a big gun."

"I'm sure it is."

I banked to port and rose to 13,000 feet, near the chopper's maximum elevation and pushed the throttle forward. We reached a cruising speed of two hundred miles an hour, leaving the burning ruins of the emir's revenge machine behind us.

I was going to need more aspirin.

SIX MONTHS LATER

Mount Ararat
North Face, 12,000 feet

The three of us were in a familiar cave.

Outside was a crooked finger of rock, pointing accusingly into the morning sky. We sat before a crackling campfire, fueled by dry shrubbery. I removed a bubbling pot of oatmeal from the fire, and poured the steaming contents into three tin bowls. As we ate, Professor Caesar Roberts said, "Today is the day, dear girl, that we finally put this matter to rest."

"Only if you say so, father," said Faye, laughing. "Aside from the pack of ravenous wolves we narrowly escaped, I've found this second trip to be rather relaxing. And it's good to be away from my students."

The small dirt mound was still there, as I hoped it would be forever. This would be my last visit to Liz's grave. When finished with our breakfast, I packed our equipment and helped the others with their backpacks.

Caesar looked at his daughter, running his fingers through his neatly trimmed beard. "Are you sure, dear girl, that you didn't see it? I mean, *it was right there in front of you.*"

As Faye adjusted her backpack, she said, "For the last time, father, no. I was too worried about you two. I ran into the ice cavern with blinders on, seeing only the three of you before I was yanked back into the tunnel."

"And you never saw a massive ship hidden behind the ice?" I asked.

"Refer to my prior comment," she said dryly.

"What do you think, old man?" I asked.

"I think she's telling the truth."

I led them out the cave and onto the Abich glacier.

* * *

I had been left with a nasty scar on my chest and back. Although the scars looked impressive, they never tanned. We had landed the helicopter at a small airstrip outside of Dogubayazit. The Turkish government had officially declared that the deaths of the handful of Kurdish soldiers involved in the Omar Ali affair were, in fact, the result of a Kurdish uprising. We had been confined in Turkish prisons for over two weeks, questioned relentlessly about the activities upon the mountain. In the end, we were set free. Officially, there was no mention of Emir Omar Ali. He had died not only in shame, but in obscurity. And the entire mountain had been picked clean of the missile launcher.

Farid Bastian was back with his own people, living from one oasis to the next, following ancient trade routes, living a simple nomadic life far removed from the court intrigue of the Arab royalties. At least, that's what he said in his last e-mail.

I'm back now with the *National Geographic*, here on this day to finish an article I had begun almost three years ago. Life is like that sometimes.

Now, high above the Abich glacier, we turned into a little-known granite canyon. Above, storm clouds were gathering. We moved deeper into the canyon until I was sure we had come to the spot where the ark had plummeted six months before. I stopped and set down my backpack. The others did the same.

"Why are we stopping?" asked Faye.

"We're here," I said.

She looked around the mostly desolate canyon. Massive ice cliffs rose to either side. "So where's the ark, Mr. Ward?"

"It's here," I said. "Of course, it's been buried under many dozens of snowstorms."

"Of course," she said, humoring me, touching me lightly on the shoulder. The gleam in her eyes was wicked. "Then again, maybe it's right here in front of me and I'm the only one who can't see it, like the emperor and his new clothes."

I handed Caesar an ice shovel. "Are you ready to start digging, old man?"

He grinned. "I'll do anything to shut her up."

As a light snow began to fall, Caesar and I began digging. And, yes, this time I did have my camera.

The End

ABOUT THE AUTHOR

J.R. Rain lives in a small house on a small island with his small dog, Sadie, who has more energy than Robin Williams. Please check out his website at www.jrrain.com.

THE LOST ARK

4499680R00182

Printed in Great Britain
by Amazon.co.uk, Ltd.,
Marston Gate.